Sage and Marshall lay in front of the fireplace, kissing

Desire hovered over the living room, smothering them with its thick, intoxicating perfume. The wine, the music and the gentle breeze gliding through the balcony doors heightened their growing passion.

Marshall swept her hair off her shoulders. His mouth was sweet, soft, pleasing. He pressed his lips against the slope of her neck and she moaned with pleasure. Sage had a strong sense of her own feminine power and sensuality, but Marshall's kisses turned her inside out. Overwhelmed by the intensity of his touch, she pitched her head back, words spilling from her lips between jagged breaths. Tracing his fingers along her back in a loose zigzag pattern, he teased her earlobe with his tongue. "You like that?"

"Love it."

"Want more?"

Books by Pamela Yaye

Kimani Romance

Other People's Business
The Trouble with Luv'
Her Kind of Man
Love T.K.O.
Games of the Heart

PAMELA YAYE

has a bachelor's degree in Christian education and has been writing short stories since elementary school. Her love for African-American fiction and literature prompted her to actively pursue a career in writing romance. When she's not reading or working on her latest novel, she's watching basketball, cooking or planning her next vacation. Pamela lives in Calgary, Canada, with her handsome husband and adorable daughter.

Games
of the
Heart

PAMELA YAYE

KIMANI™
ROMANCE

To the entire Kimani team: I want to thank everyone who was involved in bringing this story to life. A big thanks to the editorial assistants who answer all of my questions; the marketing team for another gorgeous cover and intriguing blurb; and all the people working behind the scenes. Keep doing what you do. You're doing an amazing job!

KIMANI PRESS™

Recycling programs
for this product may
not exist in your area.

ISBN-13: 978-0-373-86125-5

GAMES OF THE HEART

Copyright © 2009 by Pamela Sadadi

www.kimanipress.com

Printed in U.S.A.

Dear Reader,

I'm not a risk taker. Never have been, never will be. I don't speed, I don't do extreme sports and you'll never catch me on one of those bug-eating reality shows (I don't care how much they pay me!). So imagine my surprise when ballsy, gutsy Sage Collins barged into my thoughts, plunked herself down and insisted I write her story. A story about a fiercely driven celebrity manager who'll stop at nothing to advance her career.

The vivacious city chick never imagined a handsome guy with old-fashioned family values would get in her way, but from the moment Sage meets Marshall Grant, she knows her plan is in trouble. Their connection is instantaneous, powerful, consuming. Sage is a strong-minded woman, but beneath the Gucci business suit is a wounded heart that only one man can mend. One *fine,* supertall man who knows a thing or two about seduction!

I can't wait to "hear" what you think, so post your thoughts and opinions about Sage and Marshall's story at www.pamelayaye.com.

With love,

Pamela Yaye

Acknowledgments

Jean-Claude and Aysiah Yaye:

I love you more and more each day. I feel incredibly blessed that I get to share my life with both of you. May the next seven years of our lives be even happier than the first.

Mom and Dad:

You are the picture of happiness and love. I know what a "good" marriage looks like because I saw it growing up each and every day. I haven't forgotten my promise. One day I'll take you guys on that dream vacation. Hawaii, here we come!

Bettey Odidison:

Sister, you are such a blessing. I love you, I'm incredibly proud of you and I miss you! I can't wait to see you again, so hurry up and find Mr. Right so I can help plan the wedding (hee, hee)!

Kenny Odidison:

I have a big brother who looks out for me and who'll hook me up when I need it. What a blessing! Thanks for always having my back, Ken. You have turned out to be a truly wonderful man.

Sha-Shana Crichton *(my supercool agent and friend):*

Because of you, I'm living one of my dreams. You've played a significant role in my career and I feel fortunate to have you. You're a great listener who also gives quality advice. Know that everything you say and do on my behalf is appreciated.

Kelli Martin:

When I see your name in my in-box, I'm so excited I practically jump out of my seat! I look forward to reading your editorial notes and am amazed at how much attention you give each line, each page and each chapter. Thanks for all of your hard work and for taking the time to get to know me better. (But I knew we'd click the second you said you liked Jagged Edge!)

Chapter 1

"Come on, you stupid thing," Sage Collins grumbled, huffing vigorously. "I gave you my change, now give me my damn Kit Kat candy bar!" Forgetting that she was at Indianapolis's illustrious Westchester Academy, and that impressionable young children were milling about, she smacked the vending machine glass powerfully with her right palm. "I want my chocolate bar and I want it now, you good for nothing piece of—"

"What's going on here?" demanded a voice behind her.

Sage didn't bother to turn around. Her eyes were fixed on the chocolate bar, held captive between a jumbo bag of Cheetos cheese puffs and a can of roasted peanuts.

"Do I need to get security?"

Now the man had her attention. Sage tossed a look over her shoulder and quickly regarded the taller-than-average brother. He was a giant of a man. Built like an NFL linebacker, but without the jiggly beer belly and menacing stare, he had extrawide shoulders, ripped forearms and a pair of strong, sturdy legs. Staggered by his height, but not the least bit intimidated by his brisk tone, she expelled a breath. "This machine sucks," she told him, sweeping her bangs off her forehead. "If I had matches, I'd torch it."

"Ever stop to think that maybe it's the *customer* and not the product?"

"No, because it robbed a six-year-old of his allowance five minutes ago."

His furious scowl matched the heat in his eyes. "You're acting like a deranged psycho, and I'm supposed to believe you? Are you on medication or something?"

Sage was a mature, cultured, twenty-eight-year-old woman, but she felt like smacking the man hard upside the head. Hot with anger, she scrutinized the burly stranger with the aggressive wide-legged stance. His plaid shirt should be in a box on its way to Goodwill charity donations and his faded jeans had obviously seen better days. *In Las Vegas, a brother would never be caught dead wearing scuffed shoes,* she thought. They dressed to the nines or not at all. But up here in Indianapolis, dressing casual took on a whole new meaning. The man needed a new pair of Birkenstock shoes, and most importantly, a new attitude.

"Are you from around here?"

"No, and I don't have a name or phone number, either."

Snorting, he shrugged dismissively. "Don't flatter yourself. I'm not interested."

"Sure you aren't. That's what all the rejected guys say."

His face darkened. "Move out of the way so I can take a look at it."

"No thanks." Turning around, she bumped the machine with her hips. The Kit Kat bar fell, along with a jumbo bag of Doritos chips and several packs of gum. Bending down to retrieve her goods, she donned a proud smile. "I told you I didn't need your help."

"You didn't pay for those things! What you're doing verges on theft."

"So what are you going to do, make a citizen's arrest?" she asked, the absurdity of her words mocking him. His cologne, like his shirt, screamed for attention, but Sage wasn't going to give him another second of her time. Turning away, she quipped, "I wish I could stay and continue this riveting verbal exchange, but I have a game to watch."

Grinning, she ripped open the bag of Doritos chips and popped one into her mouth. "Mmm, delicious!" Deaf to his threats, she continued down the hall, and ducked inside the gymnasium. In the ten minutes she'd been gone, the stands had filled up and now a row of spectators stood beside the bleachers. Middle-aged men wore the home team's lively orange jerseys, adoring mothers waved homemade signs and teenage girls stomped their feet to the swish of the cheerleader's pom-poms. The scent of popcorn and nacho cheese mingled with colognes, perfumes and sweat.

Smiling apologetically, Sage inched past a row of overzealous fans with spiky hair and vibrant face paint. Stepping over a wailing toddler, she took her place beside her stout, barrel-chested boss, Leo Varick. At fifty-eight, the former sixties child star had been in the entertainment business since birth and a celebrity manager for decades.

Plunking down on the bench, she reached in her handbag and pulled out a bottle of Perrier water. Shifting uncomfortably, her jean-clad legs colder than blocks of ice, she munched hungrily on the bag of chips. She'd had nothing to eat on the connecting flight from Atlanta. But after partying at the Voodoo Lounge with her girlfriends until dawn, she needed a solid meal, and not the packs of crackers the stewardess had offered.

"What do you think so far?"

"I think a lot of these kids have raw talent."

"Anyone stand out?"

Sage shrugged. "Not really."

"That's because you haven't seen Khari Grant yet."

Stuffing the last Dorito chip into her mouth, she brushed the salt from her hands. "That's the fifth time you've mentioned this kid's name today. He must have some crazy skills on the court, because I've never seen you this excited."

"Khari's the real deal. One day fans will be lining up just to see the kid practice."

"If he's such a big-shot athlete, how come I haven't heard any buzz about him?" Sage sipped her water. "I'm always on the ESPN sports channel message boards, and I haven't heard jack about a high school player named Khari Grant."

"Until last season, Khari was just another point guard, but he went through a major growth spurt and now he's mopping the floor with his opponents."

"But he's still a teenager. How good could he be?"

"Khari Grant is one of those rare athletes who only comes along once. Six years ago LeBron James took the basketball world by storm, and it's just a matter of time before Khari does the same thing. Soon he'll be signing endorsement contracts and…"

Crossing her legs, she inspected the frantic crowd of basketball fans. It was the first week in January, and despite being weighed down with bomber jackets, sweaters and velour sweat suits, spectators cheered relentlessly for the home team. Sage had only been in Indianapolis for twenty-four hours, but she already missed home. Unlike Las Vegas, the city was a dark, gloomy gray, and from what Leo had told her on the plane, it was only going to get colder. *Thank God we're only here for the weekend,* she thought, stuffing her chilled hands into her wool coat.

"Did you see that?"

"No, I missed it. What happened?"

"He hit a three pointer from half court!" Shaking his head in awe, Leo flipped open his folio case and perused the documents inside. "The kid's stats are amazing. Twenty-one-point average, three blocks, a couple steals, and he makes the other team work hard on defense."

Aware of her boss's love of basketball, she decided this was the perfect time to talk to him about the executive position job, and her plans for the future. "Leo, I tagged along on this scouting trip because I was hoping we could talk about my career. I want to know if you've given any more thought about who'll be replacing Ryan."

"Why? You interested?" Chuckling, he turned his attention to his scouting report.

"Yes. In fact, I'm *very* interested."

"No offense, Sage, but you don't have what it takes to be an executive manager." He patted her leg sympathetically. "You're great at what you do. The kids love you."

"But I'm tired of babysitting overpaid pop stars whose only ambition is to be on the cover of *US Weekly.* I need a change. And I know I'd do a kick-ass job as the second in command. I've made so many contacts in the entertainment industry, it'll be a cinch to slide in and take the reins."

"A cinch, huh?" His tone reeked of sarcasm. "Sage, you don't want the job, trust me. You'd have to put in ten or more hours a day, and although there's an enormous salary hike, there'd be a lot more responsibility too."

"Sounds like it's right up my alley," she argued. "I can do it, Leo. I'm capable, I'm qualified and people love me!"

With a deep sigh, he folded his beefy hands in his lap. "All that might be true, but the executive manager job is no joke. You'd have to lead by example and stay on top of things. I'd expect a lot more from you."

"And I'm ready to give you more. All I'm asking for is a chance. A chance to prove myself and take Sapphire Entertainment Agency to the next level." Sage paused to let her words sink in. Ignoring the butterflies ruling her stomach, she faced her boss, convinced that this was the single most important moment of her career. "Leo, I think it's time we branch out and add more pro athletes to our client roster. We only have a couple, and we're not going all out for them. It'd like to be the one to head our athlete's discussion."

His cell phone rang to the sound of the Jay-Z classic, "It's a Hard-Knock Life." Whipping out his iPhone handheld, he checked the number and leaped to his feet like a jack-in-the-box. "Hold that thought. It's Mariah's people. I have to take this call." Phone at his ear, he jogged down the stairs and out of sight.

Around her, fans cheered and a few energized ones started the wave, but Sage was too upset to join in. Leo thought she was joke. Just another pretty face working at the agency. He hadn't come right out and said it, but she caught the underlying message.

Sage considered her options. Bribing Leo with VIP passes to the hottest clubs in Vegas wouldn't work. As a regular in and around town, he had access to everything.

But there had to be something she could do. Something that would demonstrate just how serious she was about the executive manager position. Eight years of controlling arrogant, snotty child stars was eight years too many. At first, Sage had been enamored with the glitz and glam of the business. Concerts. Backstage passes. Private parties. When she'd first attended the Academy Awards and saw all of her favorite actors, she'd become a bumbling fool in a Versace evening dress. Drinking flutes of champagne didn't help, either. And every time Terrence Howard swaggered by, she imagined tripping his wife and shimmying up to the handsome star. But these days, Sage would rather watch paint dry than go to another movie premiere.

The turbulent roar of the crowd yanked Sage from her thoughts. Candy wrappers rained down on her, cola splashed onto her shoes and popcorn fell like yellow balls of snow.

"What the hell?" Feeling around in her purse, she grabbed a handful of Kleenex tissues, and cleaned the stain from her leather Gucci boots. *Have these people lost their damn minds?* she wondered, picking kernels out of her hair and tossing them on the ground.

Sage looked up just in time to see a tall, majestic being suspended in midair. Palming the basketball in one hand, he waved off the bug-eyed defender with the other. He dunked the ball with such power, the backboard shook like a leaf in the wind. Fervent applause echoed around the gym, bouncing off the ceiling, the floor and the walls.

Mesmerized, she leaned forward in her seat. Sage didn't need to look at the back of the kid's jersey to know this man-child, the future heir to Michael Jordan's throne, was Khari Grant. She watched him play. He had the speed of Allen Iverson, the athleticism of Kobe Bryant and the grace of an African gazelle. No awkward moves, no misdirected plays, no jogging back on defense. Nothing but no-look passes, long-range jumpers and three-point shots.

Somewhere between a Khari steal and a Khari dunk, Leo returned. "I told you the kid was something special."

Sage closed her gaping mouth. "I've never seen anything like him," she managed, resurfacing from her trance. "I mean, I've watched hundreds of basketball games, trying to do research for us, but I've never seen a high school player dominate the court the way he does. And he's only seventeen. He'll be invincible in a couple years! Who represents him? In the Know Management? Sports for Life?"

"Neither."

"That's weird. Why would he have chosen a smaller, less-known firm?"

"Wrong again. The kid doesn't have a manager."

Her head snapped back. "Are you kidding me?"

"I wish I was." Leo tucked his phone into his suit pocket. "See the big lug sitting at the end of the home team's bench?"

Sage followed Leo's gaze. It was the angry brother in plaid. "I had the unfortunate pleasure of meeting him outside. What about him?"

"That's Khari's father."

Staring at him with fresh eyes, Sage reexamined the surly guy she'd met in the hall. Without the scowl, he was a different man. He still needed a gift certificate to a Ralph Lauren boutique, but she noted the defined features of his profile. The nose was straight, the mouth sensuously wide and full and his gaze startlingly intense. Marshall Grant had perfect posture, strong male features, and when he cheered his smile revealed slight dimples. "Are you sure, Leo? He doesn't look old enough to have a teenage son."

"He's thirty-seven." Pushing his Armani eyeglasses up the bridge of his nose, he lowered his head and his voice. "Marshall knocked up his girlfriend and they got married just before sophomore year of college. They split up when the kid was around ten. Apparently, Roxanne had a drug and alcohol problem and refused to seek help. When Marshall returned from Kuwait, he chose not to reenlist."

"He served in Kuwait?" she asked, shocked.

"And Bosnia too."

"Hold up. How do you know so much about him?"

Leo held up his folio. "It's all in here. Why do you think I was studying the scouting report on the plane? I've got to bring my A game if I'm going to convince Marshall Grant that I'm qualified to represent his son."

"What reverence. You make it sound like this guy is next in line for the throne!"

His smiled fizzled like an Alka-Seltzer tablet in water. "Grant spent five years in the navy before joining the navy's counterterrorist unit. Since being discharged, he's had a string of community service jobs and now runs a center for teens at risk."

Nodding, she considered their ten-second exchange in the

hallway. "A glorified truant officer, huh? He's definitely in the right field."

"Marshall will be a hard one to crack. He won't let anyone get within a mile of Khari. He thinks someone's going to cheat his son."

Sage laughed. Nudging him playfully with her shoulder, she teased, "You're not scared of him, are you, boss man?"

"You wouldn't be laughing if you knew what Khari's projected net worth will be once he turns pro." Glancing over his shoulder to ensure no one was listening, he dropped his deep baritone to a whisper. "Fifty million."

Sage was glad she was sitting down. If she had been standing, she would have tumbled forward and knocked herself unconscious when she hit the gymnasium floor. "Fifty million dollars," she repeated, her voice rising with excitement. "At your standard twenty-percent fee and agency costs, you stand to make almost three million bucks!"

Licking his lips, he adjusted his crisp marine-blue tie. "You're quick on your feet, Collins. I haven't done the math yet, but that sounds about right."

"Mind if I take a peek at the scouting report?" she asked, swiping the document from his briefcase. While Leo droned on about Khari's baseline jumper, Sage slowly perused the five-page document. This kid was destined for greatness and she wanted a piece of the action. All she needed was an in. Something to endear her to Khari and his family. Something to help her stand out from all the other agents. Soon, Indianapolis would be crawling with slick-talking managers promising cars, cash and favors. It was imperative she do something while they still had a lead.

Sage raised an eyebrow, a mischievous grin tugging at the corner of her lips. There it was in black and white. Her in...

It was something so small, so insignificant, she'd almost missed it. "I can get to Khari," she announced.

"Right, and I can change water into wine."

"I'm serious, Leo."

"What are you going to do? Seduce the kid with your womanly wiles? Forget it, Sage. Leave this to a pro."

"Are you forgetting that I was the one to sign Hailey Hope,

A-Town Boys, and a long list of other up-and-coming teen stars?"

"But that was years ago. You haven't brought any new clients to the agency in months. And from where I'm sitting, that's bad for business."

The sting of his retort cut like a blade. Leo was right. There was a time when she was the celebrity manager to watch. But these days Sage just didn't have it in her to schmooze. Traveling between Vegas and L.A. on a weekly basis was taxing, and although it was only an hour flight, it cut into her workday. Keeping her existing clients happy was difficult enough without the added pressure of having to court other celebrities; but all that was about to change. Signing the next basketball phenom would catapult her into the spotlight, and it wouldn't be long before other superstar athletes were beating down her office door.

"Give me a week."

Leo raised his eyebrows. "You think you can sign Khari Grant in seven days?"

"Maybe less, but I didn't want to sound overconfident—even though I am."

"Sorry, Sage, I can't do it. You mess this up and there goes my million-dollar commission. I'll handle this one myself, but the next case is all yours."

"Please, Leo. I'm begging you. My career needs this. Hell, I need this."

His answer was a firm "no."

"Like I said, I'll see to it that the next client who signs on at the agency belongs to you."

Low-spirited but convinced she could successfully expand into the sports market, Sage searched for the right words. Her sharp mind and boundless creativity had been her springboard to success and would one day help make Sapphire Agency the best in the business. "What if I sweetened the deal? If, I mean, *when,* I sign Khari, I'll split the commission with you."

Wearing a contemplative expression, Leo stroked his pointy jaw. "I don't know. I have a lot riding on this. If you blow it, it'll ruin any chance I have of signing him."

"I know what I'm doing, Leo. Trust me." Sage batted her lashes for good measure and flipped her silky hair over her shoulders. Playing the beauty card was beneath her, but she was desperate. "All I need is seven days."

Several agonizing moments went by. Then, Leo gave her the nod. "Okay, I'll give you a chance to prove you've still got that Collins magic. Don't mess this up," he warned, eyeing her sternly. "There's a ton of money at stake!"

"Don't worry, I won't."

"You have one week and not a second more."

Sage winked. "That's all I need."

Chapter 2

Adjusting her baggy gray cardigan, Sage stared down pitifully at the white blouse underneath. Worried Marshall might recognize her, she'd ditched her designer threads for glasses, polyester pants and penny loafers. Scratching the itch on her forearm, she expelled the bitterness clogging her lungs. Sage didn't need the Fashion Police to spring from the bushes to know she looked awful. No makeup, no jewelry, hair hidden under a thermal cap. If her girlfriends could see her now, they'd fall over laughing. If it wasn't mentioned in *Vogue*, Sage didn't give it a second glance. But this wasn't about winning a fashion contest or getting some guy's attention. She had a job to do, and nothing, not even wearing used clothes and dollar-store perfume, was going to deter her from signing Khari Grant.

According to the scouting report, Marshall Grant was generous with his time and money. In addition to his at-risk youth center, he was the conditioning coach of the Westchester Academy basketball team, did regular talks at inner-city schools and delivered groceries to seniors. Reading about Marshall had sparked her imagination and given her a foolproof plan. All she had to do was deliver her spiel and let him do the rest.

As Sage climbed the steps, she felt her conscience prick her with the pin of truth. Assailed by doubts, she took a moment to rethink what she was about to do. Some might say posing as a volunteer was a cruel, unconscionable scheme. Booting the thought from her mind, she pressed the doorbell. Bringing attention to the plight of needy children could never be a bad thing, even if she did have ulterior motives. Her words breathed confidence. What she was doing was a good thing. A *very* good thing. Commendable even. Pleased that her plan would benefit the less fortunate, she made a mental note to talk to all of her friends and clients about sponsoring a child in Haiti.

While she waited for someone to answer the door, she took in her surroundings. The lawn was edged with shrubs and trimmed bushes. Mature oak trees shielded the windows from intrusive sunlight and, aside from a few scattered leaves, the lush, landscaped yard was litter-free. Sage could hear dogs barking, but the neighborhood was surprisingly quiet.

Sage patted back a yawn. It hadn't been easy finding the place. All of the streets in Meridian Hills looked the same, and she'd wasted an hour driving around searching for Marshall's address. A kindly dog walker had pointed her in the right direction and ten minutes later she pulled her rental car up to 73 Irvington Lane.

Battling a mixture of fear and anxiety, she jabbed the buzzer again. She pulled her finger away, but the bell stuck and continued to chime. "Oh, shoot." Unzipping her tote bag, she groped around for her car keys. She was trying to pry the buzzer loose when the door swung open and Marshall Grant appeared.

"Can I help you?"

Groaning inwardly, she slipped her keys back into her pocket. Things were not off to a promising start. Marshall was supposed to be impressed with her, not growling at her. Standing ruler-straight, Sage fed him her friendliest smile. "I'm sorry about that, but the buzzer got stuck. You should get that fixed."

Marshall looked peeved and Sage sensed that he was about to slam the door in her face. "I was hoping to speak to you for a few minutes, but I can come back if now's not a good time."

To her surprise, he said, "It's all right. Go on."

Sage could tell that he was trying not to be rude. Good, he did have a soft side. That would make her job that much easier.

Moving her clipboard aside, she pointed to the World Mission logo on the pocket of her sweater. "My name is Sage Collins and I'm a volunteer for World Mission International. Might I speak to you for a minute about our life-changing sponsorship program?"

His lips relaxed into a grin. There was that dimple again. Today he didn't seem nearly as intimidating as he had two days ago. Sage didn't drool over brawny-looking men, but there was something about Marshall Grant that made her heart pitter-patter. He had a powerful chest, big man hands and a voice deeper than the Grand Canyon. Dazzled by the warmth of his smile, she stared up at him, utterly captivated.

"Sure, I have a few minutes to spare." Leaning against the door frame, he folded his arms across his chest. "You were saying?"

"I…was…ah," she sputtered like a fish out of water. This was a first. Men didn't leave her flustered. She left them tongue tied fools, not the other way around. But the more she tried to focus, the more delicious Marshall Grant looked. Soulful eyes, and a cleft chin that softened his facial features and detracted from his imposing height, he was as cool as he was fine.

Leo's image flashed in her mind, yanking Sage out of her lustful haze and back to the present. Collecting her thoughts, she glanced down at her clipboard. "Thank you so much for your willingness to make a difference in a child's life. Six thousand children lose a parent to AIDS every day. At World Mission, we believe that we can make a difference." Sage held up a picture of Chibu, a seven-year-old Haitian boy with sad eyes. She didn't know anything about the child, but from what she'd read online, he was an orphan, living in a center with hundreds of other kids. Moved by his story, she had filled out the sponsorship application and committed to paying forty dollars a month to maintain his care. Now Chibu would receive medical care and she would use this real-life story to reach Marshall.

"AIDS ravaged Chibu's family and left him to fend for himself. He's been living at the Center of Hope Orphanage, and though his basic needs are being met, he's unable to attend school. His reading and writing skills are poor, but at World Mission International we believe that with you and the help of others like you, we can bring hope not only to the village of Jacmel, but to the entire country."

"I can tell by listening to you that this organization is near and dear to your heart." Admiration filled his eyes. "You're very passionate about what you do. That's commendable and I wish there were more people like you."

"You do?" Reading Chibu's story had stirred some powerful emotions in her too. She was supposed to learn more about Marshall and Khari, not prattle nonstop about the problems plaguing Haiti, but she couldn't help herself. "As citizens of the world, it's important that we all do our part, don't you think?"

"I do. It's not easy going door-to-door, especially during the winter." His voice was awash with nostalgia. "The first job I had was signing people up for the *Indianapolis Post*. It's a very difficult job, isn't it?"

"You're right. It is." Or at least she imagined it was. After Sage left Marshall's house, she wouldn't be knocking on any more doors. It was back to the Four Seasons to work on the second half of her plan.

"I remember this one elderly woman who lived in Stanford Park. She took one look at me and slammed the door in my face!" Chuckling, he shook his head at the memory. "I had ID, but some homeowners still wouldn't give me the time of day."

Thankful she'd had the foresight to go to the World Mission office, she smiled inwardly. A quick trip downtown had put a small dent in her sign-Khari-Grant fund, but it was money well spent. The supervisor, Ms. Pittney, had beamed as she scooped up T-shirts, pens and other merchandise bearing the World Mission logo.

"I'm glad you stopped by. I've been thinking about doing something like this for a while, but never got around to it."

Her eyes danced over his face. His skin was a rich, creamy shade of brown, and he had a strong, defined chin. Policing her thoughts, she blinked hard, and quickly regained focus. Enough lusting. It was time to make her move. She had done her good deed for the day, now it was time to do something for herself. And nothing would make her happier than signing Khari Grant. "Do you have any children, sir?"

"Sir?" Marshall shook his head in disapproval. "I know I'm old, but I'm not *that* old," he teased, his tone rich with humor. "How old do you think I am?"

"I don't know. Thirty?"

He rewarded her guess with a smile.

"You're not going to tell me?" she asked, liking how quickly he had changed from the snarling homeowner to the grinning neighbor. Attractive in a long-sleeve, collared black sweater and slacks, he looked more relaxed than he had at Westchester Academy. But then again, he wasn't trying to stop her from beating up on the school vending machine. Today, she was a humanitarian. Feeling flirtatious, and enjoying their playful banter, she cocked her head to the right. "If you tell me your age, I'll tell you mine," she promised.

"Only if you come inside for a quick drink."

He didn't have to ask her twice. "I'm right behind you, Mr. Grant."

One look inside Marshall's house and Sage knew he was a momma's boy. Everything from the dainty glass tables, plush, luxurious rugs and frilly cushions was a doting mother's handiwork. From the outside, the house was no showpiece, but the three-story home boasted lofty ceilings, gigantic picture windows and polished floors. The house felt lived-in and had obviously been decorated with tender, loving care.

"Would you like something to drink?"

"A glass of water would be great," she said, holding her clipboard to her chest. "Walking around all day is exhausting."

"I bet," he agreed with a sympathetic nod. "Has there been a lot of interest in the sponsorship program?"

Remembering what Ms. Pittney said about last year's Christmas campaign, Sage shook her head regretfully. "Not as many as we would have liked. More people sign up during the holidays. I guess it pacifies their guilt for buying things they don't need, but by the time the New Year rolls around most sponsors have had a change of heart."

"That's terrible."

The solemn expression on his face squeezed her heart. He

really did care about the orphaned kids in Haiti. And there was no doubt in her mind that she'd be leaving with a financial contribution for World Mission International. An image of Ms. Pittney flashed in her mind, assuaging her guilt and bolstering her spirits. "It's warm and toasty in here." Glancing around, she rubbed her gloved hands together. "I'm from Las Vegas and not used to such cold weather."

"What brought you all the way to Indianapolis?"

Caught off guard by his question, Sage racked her brain for a suitable answer. Snippets of her hour-long conversation with Ms. Pittney resurfaced. "World Mission has its headquarters here, and I felt it was important to make the trip out." Marshall nodded, his eyes kind, and his expression sympathetic. Encouraged by his obvious interest, she went on. "I'm on a multicity tour to drum up more corporate donations. The AIDS treatment center in Haiti is desperately underfunded and on the verge of being closed."

"Well, on behalf of Mayor Ballard and the entire city council, welcome to Indy." Smiling, he motioned to the suede armchair to his left. "Make yourself comfortable. I'll be right back with your drink."

"Thank you," she said, resisting the urge to do the cabbage patch in the middle of the area rug. Sage never imagined it would be this easy getting close to Marshall. Five minutes into the plan, and she was sitting inside the Grant house. By the end of the week, Khari Grant would be her newest client. Confident she'd be thousands of dollars richer, she settled into her seat with the grace of a queen.

The harsh, riveting sound of Marshall's voice knocked the grin off Sage's face. He was warning someone named Dale Williamson to stop calling his house. Occupied with her thoughts, she hadn't even heard the telephone ring. Sage could tell by the hostility in his tone that he was pissed off. It was the same tone he'd unleashed on her when he caught her kicking the vending machine.

Intrigued, she stood and tiptoed across the living-room floor. Holding her breath, she pushed open the kitchen door and peeked inside. Marshall stood beside the stove, his teeth clenched and his fists tight.

"I don't care what agency you're from. My son's future is not for sale. And if you call here again, I'll have you charged with harassment."

Sage gulped. Sweat dripped down her back and the knot in her stomach tightened. Those weren't empty threats. Marshall meant business.

"No, I don't want you to call me back next week. My answer isn't going to change. Khari's going to study medicine and that's all there is to it. The NBA will not take care of my son in the way he needs. He needs an education first, not groupies and more money than he knows what to do with."

Filing that piece of information away, she pushed open the door farther.

"I'd prefer if you left us the hell alone."

Her shoulders sank. So much for a lead! News of Khari's remarkable basketball skills had gotten out and now offers were rolling in. It was just a matter of time before sports agents from In the Know Management and Legends of Tomorrow and a host of other agencies descended on the city.

"Who are you spying on?"

Sage whipped around so fast, the door whacked her on the butt like a wooden paddle. Khari Grant dropped his backpack at his feet and sidled up beside her. Like most basketball players, he was lean, trim and over six feet tall. Imitating her posture, he bent down and pushed open the kitchen door. He listened for a few minutes before turning back to her. Shrugging his shoulders, he said, "That's just Dad being Dad. He gets like that sometimes." His lips expanded into a boyish smile. "What's up? I'm Khari."

"Hi, Khari," she greeted, liking the teenager instantly. "I'm Sage."

"Cool name."

"Thanks. I like it."

Khari chuckled. "So you work for World Mission, huh?"

"No, I'm a—" Sage caught herself before she unwittingly blew her cover. "Yes, I volunteer a few days a month. But I have a regular job there too."

Bending down, he retrieved his backpack from the floor and

slung it over his shoulder. "I gotta hit the books. Got a paper to write about Hamlet and his boy Horatio. Check you later."

"About what you saw when you walked in," she began, feeling the need to explain. "I wasn't eavesdropping. Your dad sounded upset…I was going to go in the kitchen to see what was wrong, but I…I got scared," she lied, praying he believed her.

His smirk told her he didn't. "It's all good, Sage." He winked. "I do it too sometimes."

The kitchen door swung open. When Marshall spotted Khari, his entire face came alive. "Khari, you're home. How was study group?"

"All right, I guess. I'm starting to get the hang of this Shakespeare stuff."

"Did you get back your physics test?"

Wearing a sheepish expression, he scratched the side of his neck. "I got a B minus, but it wasn't my fault. Mr. Diefendorf wouldn't give me extra time."

"Khari, if you're going to get into Harvard, you have to bring your grades way up."

"I don't want to go to Harvard, Dad. I'm going to play in the NBA. Coach says I've got what it takes to make it all the way."

"No, you're going to med school." His voice was firm. "If you get your degree and decide you still want to play professional basketball, that's fine, but at least you will have something to fall back on if things don't work out."

"I don't know about all that. I ain't—"

"Pardon me?" Marshall's words came out in a stern rebuke, not a question.

Khari stared down at his sneakers. "I'm not thinking about medical school right now, Dad. I just want to pass English Lit and graduate with my friends."

Marshall opened his mouth, but when he spotted the woman from World Mission standing by the fireplace, watching them intently, he swallowed his words. "We'll talk about this later. I'll be up in a few minutes to help you with your homework."

Khari continued upstairs.

"I'm sorry about that. I almost forgot you were here," he confessed, handing her a glass of water. "Here you go."

"Thanks." Sage took the drink from his outstretched hand and inadvertently grazed his fingers. Her heart pulsed with desire. Their connection was intense, and when he smiled at her, she knew he had felt it too. Underestimating the power of his touch, she stepped back to create more breathing room. "He seems like a good kid. And tall too!"

Marshall chuckled. "I hear that at least fifty times a day."

"I bet. He must take after you."

Sensing she had ventured into troubled waters, Sage adjusted her cardigan and slipped back into character. Returning to the couch, she picked up her clipboard and retrieved a World Mission brochure. "Now, if you'll just fill out your personal information on this sponsorship form, I can be on my way."

"There's no rush," he told her, with a dismissive wave of his hand. "Can I interest you in something to eat? A muffin, some chocolate chip cookies, maybe? They're homemade."

His endearing half smile and the soft hue of his voice warmed every square inch of her body. *I wonder what it would feel like to have those big, strong hands on my*— Sage shook the thought from her mind. She tried to focus on something anything but his toned arms and that broad chest—but her internal wiring was on the blink. Sage inhaled. There was something in the air. It was profound, crippling, more devastating than a tropical storm, and if she wasn't careful, she'd blow her assignment on the first day. "That's very kind of you, but no thanks."

"It's going to take me a few minutes to fill this out." He uncapped the pen, but she remained the focus of his gaze. "I hope I'm not keeping you from anything."

"Not at all." Pleased that she'd regained control, she stood patiently, determined not to be affected by his scent, his dimples or his calming vibe. For some reason, his buttoned-up persona and commanding presence was a serious turn-on. One she hadn't expected. Overwhelmed by the silence, and wanting to keep the mood light, she said, "It's been a busy day, but as long as I get home in time for *24,* I'm good!"

"That show's amazing. It's in its seventh season, but I've never missed an episode."

"Me too!" she gushed. "The writing is great, the plot is tight and the characters are hot, especially Jack Bauer. Ummm…"

Marshall chuckled. "You're too cute to be with such a rebellious hothead. Not to mention he's almost twice your age."

Sage sequestered a smile. *So he thinks I'm cute.* No doubt, the clean face, casual clothes and curly hair gave her a more youthful look; but just how young did he think she was? His genial, if-only-you-were-older expression told Sage everything she needed to know. Marshall Grant thought she was jailbait.

"All my guy friends go gaga over Elisa Cuthbert, and I bet you do too."

"She's not my type. I prefer a more sophisticated woman."

Their eyes held for a beat too long. Standing there, looking large and in-charge in his black-on-black ensemble, Sage wondered what it would be like to kiss the attractive single father. Her breathing sped up as her body slowly became infected with lust. *I must be really desperate to be fantasizing about kissing this small-town guy.* Unable to reel in her emotions, she stared into his soft, luminous eyes. The last time she'd had sex, platform shoes were still in style, so being in close quarters with a dark, chocolate hunk was more than Sage could stand. Basking in the light of his smile, Sage licked her lips, and settled her nerves with a deep breath.

They studied each other for a long, quiet moment. Marshall had a presence about him, something fierce and compelling that she wouldn't be able to withstand much longer. The man was Denzel Washington in *Training Day*—cool and deliciously sexy. Her mission was in trouble and it was only the day one. *Damn!*

"Stay awhile. At least long enough for me to pick your brain about the season premiere." He hadn't lowered his voice, but she inched closer. "Were you as shocked as I was when Schector was killed?"

Sage had known Marshall all of five minutes, but when he gestured for her to take a seat, she did, and then chatted animatedly about her favorite TV show. Marshall was a deep thinker, who appealed to her on strictly an intellectual level. Or at least, that's what she told herself every time her gaze strayed from his face to his chest.

"Looks like you're almost done," she said, watching him scrawl his signature at the bottom of the form. "World Mission appreciates your generosity, Mr. Grant. You're going to help so many needy children."

"I told you, none of that 'Mr. Grant' stuff. Call me Marshall."

For a moment, she couldn't speak. Had he just given her *the* look, or was it just a figment of her imagination? With her goal front and center in her mind, she stuffed the sponsorship form in her purse and thanked Marshall for his time. "I should get going."

"I know this is going to sound strange, but I just have to ask. Have we met before?" The words shot out of his mouth, pinning her to the couch. "I never forget a face, but for the life of me, I can't seem to place you. Maybe it's the glasses. Do you wear contacts, as well?"

"Um, no, I…" Her voice stalled. Nothing came out but a pathetic squeak. Lowering her eyes, she tugged at her black thermal cap. She'd overstayed her welcome and now Marshall was hot on her trail. "I really have to run." Scrambling to her feet, she snatched up her purse and made a break for it. But Marshall met her in the middle of the living room, looking amused and becoming more handsome by the second.

"I'll show you out." Laying a hand on her back, he gestured toward the short, narrow hallway that led to the foyer. Sage felt like she was walking on a trampoline. Her legs were quivering and she worried she might trip over her feet. It was hard staying calm with Marshall at her side, watching her every move.

"Be safe," he cautioned, unlocking the door. "And next time you're in the neighborhood, be sure to stop by for a drink. We can talk more about trying to save the world."

Frowning, she stopped and glanced up at him. *That's it? No, "I'd love to take you out sometime," or "How about you give me your number?"* Going out with Marshall was risky, but Sage felt oddly disappointed by his lack of interest.

"Again, thank you so much for supporting World Mission." Playing her part to the hilt, she handed him a fridge magnet, and hurried down the steps. When Sage turned and saw Marshall watching, she added more bounce to her walk. A toothy smile on her lips, she waved and hopped into her trusty rental. *I shouldn't have run off,* she thought, throwing the car into drive, *but now I have that fine, ex-military man right where I want him!*

Chapter 3

"He's late," Sage announced, her eyes fixed on the front door of Champions Sports Bar. Aside from the couples playing pool and the heavily pierced server shuffling back and forth between the kitchen and the dining area, the place was empty. "Are you sure he'll be here? It's almost nine. You said he'd be here at eight."

The bartender nodded. "I'm positive. Every Saturday night Marshall and his army buddies swap war stories until closing."

"Where do they sit?"

He motioned with his head. "Corner booth, next to the washrooms."

"How many guys?"

"Usually five, sometimes as many as eight." He added a splash of vodka and a pinch of Cointreau triple sec liquer to the metal shaker, then shook it vigorously. "They crack jokes, play pool and hit on the ladies."

Convinced it would be the same game once he got a look at her sexy outfit, she smoothed her hands down the length of her miniskirt. "Does he have a girlfriend?"

He furrowed his scruffy eyebrows. "Hell if I know. I just fix the guys drinks. Never seen a woman with him though."

"This is for your trouble." Sage slid a twenty-dollar bill toward him.

"Hey, if you need anything else, just ask!" he yelled, his voice suddenly infused with enthusiasm.

"Thanks, kid," she said, though he could only be a few years younger than she.

"The name's Gamble and I'm here 'til closing!"

Feeling restless, and anxious to see Marshall, Sage headed for the row of pool tables. She'd visited the Grant home yesterday, and for the last twenty-four hours she had thought of nothing but Khari and Marshall. Well, mostly Marshall. And the more she thought about him, the more persistent her doubts. He was sharp, clever, discerning. Hell, he'd been a sharpshooter! There was no fooling him. If she wanted to taste the sweet juice of success, she'd have to modify her plan. There was too much at stake for her to mess up.

Taking a sip of her cocktail, she rested the glass on one of the raised wooden tables. Life-size photographs of sports icons covered the walls, flat-screen TV's were mounted in corners, stadium chairs sat on polished floors and fan memorabilia was splashed across the room. Champions Sports Bar had a high-energy atmosphere and Sage knew it was just a matter of time before every seat in the place was filled.

Spotting the dartboard, she went over and retrieved the five missile-shape darts. Playing a round of darts would kill some time and provide the perfect distraction until Marshall showed up. She leaned forward, arching her back and lifting her shoulders, Sage released the first dart. It struck the wall. Shaking her head at the error, she tried again. Same results. The third dart hit the bottom of the target.

"At least it hit the board this time."

Sage cast a sideways glance at the man beside her. He was of average height, had rippling forearms confined to a rock-hard chest and a black muscle shirt.

"Do we know each other?" she asked, wishing he'd disappear.

"We met a few weeks back at Studio 29."

His voice was coarse, but Sage didn't know if that was his natural tone or if he had a case of bronchitis. Either way, he was giving her a headache. Resisting the urge to cover her ears with her hands, she said, "No we didn't. I've only been in Indianapolis for three days, so there's no way we could've met last month."

"Don't try to play me. You were smiling in my face, ordering the priciest drinks on the menu, then slipped me some bogus number at the end of the night."

"We've never met," she repeated, imaging herself shooting him with a dart. Picturing a dart pricking his butt cheek brought a smirk to her lips.

"What's so funny? You laughin' at me?"

"Like I said, I'm not from around here. I'm in town on business."

"For real?" His scowl fell away and was replaced with a hearty grin. "My bad. Sorry 'bout that. I'm Denzel."

Oh, no, you're not, she thought, facing the dartboard.

"What's your name?"

To signal the end of the conversation, Sage narrowed her eyes in precision and shot the dart. It landed on the outer wire.

"Looks like you could use some pointers."

"Bye. Enjoy the rest of your night. Have a nice life."

"Don't be like that, girl. You know you want my help."

"No, I don't," she argued. "I know how to play. I'm just rusty."

"It's no fun playing alone."

"Yes, it is."

"Come on, girl." Denzel took giant steps toward her, his hot vodka breath preceding him. "I promise to take it easy on you."

Sage faced her tormenter. "I don't need your help. Now, if you want to play a game, that's another story. How about a friendly round to start? Is twenty bucks low enough for you? Or should we do ten?"

"Naw—twenty bucks a round is cool."

"No, I meant *per dart.*"

"That's a hundred bucks a game!"

"That's not going to be a problem for you is it, Denzel?" she asked, forcing herself not to laugh in his face. "It's up to you. I don't want you to feel pressured."

He gulped. "That's chump change. I can handle it."

"Good. We'll take turns shooting the darts. The first one to zero wins!"

"Sounds fair to me," he agreed, his eyes flicking anxiously

around the bar. The place was starting to fill up. Massaging the back of his neck, he fed her a shaky smile. "Ten minutes ago this place was empty. Now, it's, uh, full."

She retrieved the darts from the board, then offered them to him.

"I can't." He held up his hands and stepped aside. "What kind of guy would I be if I didn't let you go first? I'm a gentleman, girl. Go on and do your thing."

Sage leaned forward, poised to shoot. "I was hoping you'd say that."

"She's kicking his ass!"

The men sitting in the corner booth howled with laughter.

"Damn! She got another bull's eye!" Roderick Baxter thumped his fist against the table. "And she's making it look easy too."

Marshall tasted his Hennessey cognac. Swallowing proved difficult. His jaw ached from laughing. If Roderick wasn't poking fun at the player-wannabe strutting around the room like a seventies pimp, he was taking cheap shots at Denzel Patterson, the missing member of their three-man group.

"I feel for Patterson, though. There's a crowd around them and everything." Emilio Sanchez shook his head. "He'll never be able to live this one down. Getting spanked by a woman at darts? Twice? Shoot. We might as well look for a new hangout spot, because after tonight, he'll never be able to show his face in here again."

"Serves him right for going over there in the first place." Roderick draped an arm around the booth. "We told him not to, but he wouldn't listen."

Marshall defended his friend. "Can you blame him? We've all been there. How many times have you approached a beautiful woman only to have her shoot you down so bad you're heart plunged to your knees?"

"You're right, Grant," Emilio agreed, his dark brown eyes full of lust. "And that sister over there is hot to death. That chest, those hips, and check out her legs."

"She could wrap them around me twice!" Admiring the woman from afar, but wishing she was only a breath away, Roderick smoothed a hand over his mustache. "I'd do basic training all over again if she was the drill sergeant!"

Chuckles broke out across the table.

Returning his gaze across the room, Marshall watched the crowd dissipate, leaving Denzel and the shapely sister in the denim miniskirt. When she turned around, he got a clear, unrestricted view of her face. As he watched her count her winnings, it suddenly clicked where they had met before. It was the World Mission volunteer. Marshall thought she'd looked familiar, but couldn't immediately place her. Downing the rest of his drink, he slipped out of the booth. "Be right back, fellas."

"Aw, not you too, bro." Roderick gripped his forearm. "You saw what happened to Patterson. Don't be a fool, man. Leave that woman alone before you end up crying in your drink."

"It's not like that, Baxter. I know her."

"That's the same stupid mess Patterson said."

"It'll be okay, man. Hang back."

Releasing his hold, he shrugged a shoulder. "All right. Don't say I didn't warn you when she does the Moon Walk all over your pride."

"She won't. I wouldn't be going over there if I thought she was going to diss me."

Dubious about his friend's chances of success, he said, "Fifty dollars says you won't get her phone number."

"Make it a hundred and you're on."

"There'll be no I-owe-yous, either. I want my money tonight. Hear me, Grant?"

"I hear you."

Roderick pointed north. "There's an ATM machine at the entrance. Make sure you have my dough when you come back!"

Disregarding his friend's warning, he strode purposefully through the dining area. By the time he reached the bar, Denzel had slunk away and the woman was alone.

"What's a girl like you doing in a place like this?" It was an old line, but that didn't stop him from using it. From what he remembered about the World Mission volunteer, she had a quick laugh and a great sense of humor. After filling out the sponsorship forms, they'd sat in the living room talking about movies and sports and music. "I thought you looked familiar."

Sage cast a smoldering look over her shoulder. "Do I know you?"

Deflated, but not defeated, Marshall maintained his smile. "You came by my house a few days ago. We talked about World Mission's sponsorship program." He was rambling, but didn't stop. He'd rather make a fool of himself in her presence than return to the booth a hundred dollars poorer. "I live on Irvington Lane, across the street from the park. Mine's the gray and white house with the basketball hoop out front."

A pensive expression on her face, she slowly spun around on the stool. "Um…Marshall—Marshall Grant, right?"

Nodding, he sighed inwardly. She remembered him. Pleased, he planted himself in the seat beside her. Roderick might crack on him tonight, but it wouldn't be because this gorgeous woman shot him down. "I almost didn't recognize you."

"How come?"

Dressed in a cashmere sweater that plunged boldly between her breasts and an itsy-bitsy skirt that skimmed her thighs, she exuded a raw sexuality that demanded attention. She had smoky eyes, and her light brown hair was swept off her shoulders in a side ponytail. Sage Collins was the sister every woman in the bar wanted to be and for good reason. And her work meant she was trying to make the world a better place too. His dream girl. A vixen—and a shapely one at that—with a heart of gold.

Leaning in to ensure he was heard above the clamor, he said, "No baggy gray sweater and gym shoes. Tonight, you deserve a place in that Victoria's Secret fashion show. Wings and all!"

Sage laughed. "And the other day?"

"Your beauty was concealed to meet the needs of orphaned children."

"Nice save."

"Thanks." In the hopes of eliciting a smile, he said, "I can't imagine what you'd be doing here alone. Your date's a fool for making you wait. Give him hell when he shows up."

Sage smiled, the sheer warmth of it crippling him. "I was supposed to meet a friend for drinks, but…" Straining her eyes toward the door, she sighed. Glancing down at her watch, she said, "It looks like I've been stood up."

Marshall couldn't believe his luck. She was alone? If he bought her drinks and kept making her laugh, maybe she wouldn't mind joining him for dinner. He would get to know her better and impress the guys in the process.

"Well, it was nice seeing you again, Marshall." Sage finished her drink, then placed the empty glass on the bar. "See you around."

Touching her arm gently, he motioned to her vacant stool. "Don't rush off. Let me get you another drink. What are you having?"

"An Orgasm."

Marshall was quick to laugh. "You're joking, right?"

"I couldn't be more serious."

He studied her for a moment. "All right, an Orgasm it is."

"Ah, if it was only that easy," Sage quipped with a dramatic sigh.

"It is. All women need to do is ask and men would gladly give them the world."

"Right. Is that before or after you ask to hold some money until payday?"

"That's cold," he said, slumping in his seat. He couldn't believe a woman this attractive and this intelligent had ever had trouble with the opposite sex. She was fit, free and oh so fine. What more could a guy want? "It sounds like you've been dating the wrong fellas," he told her. "We're not all lazy freeloaders, you know. At least I'm not."

"And what makes you so different?"

"I was raised in an era of strict discipline, butt whuppings and Al Green!"

Her laughter filled the room with its sweet perfume.

Marshall soaked up the sound, giving his ears their fill. There was nothing like flirting with an attractive woman to inflate a man's ego. Sage was the "It Girl" in the bar, and that made *him* the man. His confidence stirred, rose, pushed him to say something he'd never live down if his friends heard him. "All we brothers want to do is please you. But you sisters are harder to crack than a Rubik's Cube puzzle!" Marshall chuckled long and hard. "Women make men into who they are, so don't get mad if we come on too strong."

Sage rolled her eyes.

"Present company excluded, but you sisters are fierce! Dropping it like it's hot at the club, prancing around in your too-short tops, barely-there-skirts and sexy, five-inch stilettos." He shrugged. "It's a woman's game. We men just play along."

"Oh," she crooned, her voice octaves higher, "so that's why you guys dog us out all the time. Because we're smart and sexy and not afraid to show it?"

"You've got it all wrong. That's not what I'm saying." In the hopes of redeeming himself in her eyes, he said, "I heard something on *The Dr. Robin Show* on the radio that challenged my views about male and female relationships."

"Really?" Sage raised her eyebrows. "And what was that?"

"Love is selfless. When you love someone, you're actually loving yourself in the truest, realest way. If you shortchange the people you love, you're doing a disservice not only to them, but to yourself."

"Relationships 101, according to the cynical youth center director. Interesting."

Marshall frowned. "How did you know I run a center? I didn't mention that when you were over the other day."

"Khari told me," she lied, hoping he wouldn't press the issue. "All this talk about honesty makes me want to confess."

"To what?"

"We've met before."

His eyes bulged. "We have?"

"Last week my boss took me to the basketball game at Westchester Academy. I was starving, so I decided to buy myself a snack, but when I put my money in the vending machine…"

Marshall stared at her lips. They were full and moist and looked softer than a Georgia peach. She had a beauty mark above her lips, Bambilike eyes, and her breath smelled sweet.

"I shouldn't have been so bitchy, but I was running on three hours of sleep and one measly cup of coffee. I just wanted to apologize for acting so childish."

The sheer intensity of her smile almost knocked him off his stool. Changing the channel in his mind, he fought to remember what they'd been talking about. Women complained that men didn't listen and here was another shining example. Normally he was focused, attentive, alert. In his line of work he had to be.

Let your guard down and you could lose your life. But something about this woman left his brain scattering like a pack of marbles. "Ah, sure, okay. No problem."

"When I looked over my shoulder and saw you standing there, glowering at me, I had memories of my high school principal, Mr. McCaffery." Shuddering, she closed her eyes as if haunted by his image. "The man was old, mean, and hated kids, especially me."

"We met at my son's basketball game?" Marshall asked, finally gathering himself. "You were the psycho —" he cleared his throat "—I mean, the nuisance beating up the vending machine?"

Her smile fell. "Yeah, it was me."

"You?" His eyes glazed with doubt. "That's impossible."

Pretending to be angry, she accused him of being distracted by one of the young, female servers. "I just finished telling you my side of the story. Weren't you listening?"

"I'm sorry, I don't know where my mind was." He did, but admitting he had been fantasizing about her would scare her off. Unconvinced she was the culprit, he examined her face closely. She didn't look like the woman he had butted heads with, but she could have been. "No way that was you! She had bangs. That much I know for sure. She kept blowing them out of her eyes."

"What can I say? I'm a chameleon," she said, crossing her legs. "I'd go crazy if I had the same hairstyle longer than a month, so I change it whenever the mood strikes."

"Your hair was different when you were at the house yesterday. It was shorter, darker, right?"

"Yeah, I had it done this morning." She touched the nape of her neck. "Like it?"

"Love it."

Their eyes met. Stroking his jaw, he noted the vibrancy of her skin and the sensuous width of her smile. Silky-smooth layers cascaded over her shoulders, softening the bold, eye-catching shade. How come he hadn't noticed her nose ring? Or her striking bone structure? If he had spent less time admiring her luscious backside and more time making eye contact, he wouldn't look like Bozo the Clown now.

"Let me take you out for dinner. Or you could just join me and the guys tonight."

Sage took a sip of her cocktail, mulling over his invitation. One-on-one, Marshall Grant was putty in her hands, but would he be as sincere around his army buddies? One woman sitting at a table with four men did not make for a pleasant evening. They'd be tripping over themselves trying to impress her, while all she wanted was to be alone with Marshall. Not liking her chances at four-to-one, she politely declined. "I already ate," she lied, motioning to the empty plate on the bar. Sage didn't know who it belonged to, but she was glad the prop was there. "Maybe next time."

If Marshall was disappointed, his face didn't show it. "No problem, but we should definitely get together sometime."

"It's twenty below outside," she said, coyly. "Where are you going to take me?"

"Slide me your number and you'll find out."

The bartender produced a ballpoint pen. "There you go," he said cheerfully, resting it on the counter. "Just holler if you need anything else."

Seconds later, Sage handed Marshall a napkin covered in her scrawled handwriting. "Happy now?"

"Very." He took the napkin from her outstretched hand. His touch, though slight, stirred the fire within her. And when he leaned over and whispered a few scintillating words in her ear, her heart bounced up in her throat. "Be sure to call," she said casually, though it sounded like an order.

"It was nice seeing you again, Sage. And I will."

Not ready for him to go, she put a hand on his forearm. "Thanks for the drink. And I'll try to remember what you said about…orgasms."

His mouth stretched into a scrumptious grin. "You do that." A wink, then he stood and strode away.

Chapter 4

"What do you mean he won't set a wedding date?" Sage asked, wedging the cell phone between her ear and shoulder. Needing to exercise, but unfamiliar with the city, she had decided to drive down to Westchester Academy and jog on the outdoor track. The hotel gym was temporarily closed for renovations, and she couldn't afford to miss a third consecutive workout.

"Tangela, you guys have been engaged for two years. How much more time does Warrick need?" Sage put her keys into her pocket and walked briskly toward the field. The wind was fierce, but the sun was strong and bright. A minute into her jog and she'd be nice and warm.

"You're preaching to the choir, Sage. I've had this conversation with Warrick so many times, I'm starting to argue with him in my sleep!"

Sage laughed. Despite the circumstances, her best friend still had jokes. Sage had known Tangela Howard ever since she showed up on their foster mom's doorstep fifteen years ago, clutching a stuffed elephant and a bag of dirty clothes. Exiled to the basement, the girls had regaled themselves by dressing up in Ms. Claxton's nurse uniforms and imitating her thick Trinidadian accent. In a matter of weeks, they had joined forces against the hot-tempered woman, and even after all these years, they were still tighter than a new pair of pumps.

"What's the hold up now? Last year he postponed the wedding because of his father's stroke. That's understandable, but I thought you said his dad's been up and running for months."

"That was then. Now he said he's too busy expanding his company to think about planning some wedding," she explained.

Dumbstruck, Sage closed her gaping mouth. "'Some wedding'?" she choked out. "What does he mean he doesn't have time to plan some wedding? It's *his* wedding—to the woman he loves."

"I know. Can you believe he said that? I cook, clean and even massage his crusty feet, and now he's telling me he doesn't have time to get married!"

Stretching on the track, Sage shook her head. How had her adventurous, free-spirited friend become a kept woman begging a man to marry her? Sage had never considered marrying any of her ex-boyfriends. But then again, no one had ever asked. Waking up to the same man for the next forty years sounded as exciting as an early-morning root canal. No way. Marriage wasn't for everyone, and Sage was smart enough to know it wasn't right for her. All she needed was a foot rub, Usher on blast, and some toe-curling sex. Send her on her way with an orgasm and a smile and she was happier than Pamela Anderson in a bridal boutique. "Tangela, you know what the problem is, don't you? You're spoiling him. You do too much for Warrick and now he doesn't appreciate you. Ever heard the saying, 'be sensible in love or end up getting burned'?"

"But how can you love somebody too much?" she questioned, her voice filled with genuine wonder. "I love taking care of Warrick, and he's a good man. I just want us to make things official. Hell, at this point I'd forgo my dreams of a church wedding and marry him at the justice of the peace. All I want is to become Mrs. Warrick Carver."

Sage couldn't resist saying, "That's what you get for moving in with him. I told you not to do it, but you wouldn't listen to me. Now he's treating you like the hired help because it's *his* house."

"Oh, please! Don't act like a saint because you lived with Jake *and* Adrian," she pointed out. "How can you tell me not to do something you've done twice?"

"That was years ago," Sage explained, bristling at the accusation. "I was young and stupid then and I had nowhere else to go. *You,* on the other hand, make good money as a senior flight attendant. You had your own house, a car and plenty of money before you ever met Warrick. Sure he's bought you a lot of nice stuff over the years, but nothing you couldn't buy for yourself."

"You're right." There was a hitch in her voice. "Sage, you know Warrick. You've seen us together. Why do you really think he won't set a wedding date?"

Sage paused. Her best friend was hurting and the last thing she wanted to do was pour more oil onto the fire. But what kind of friend would she be if she didn't tell Tangela the truth? "Girl, you know I love Warrick like a brother, but I think he's playing you. He's doing just enough to keep you around. After all, he didn't pop the question until you threatened to leave, right? You applied the pressure and he caved. He dangled that Harry Winston diamond in your face and you snatched it up quicker than a rabbit with a big, fat, juicy carrot!"

"It's not like that," she protested. "It's great that he has money, but I'd marry Warrick even if he wasn't a millionaire."

"I know, Tangela. I know." Sage sat down on the cold pavement and tied her shoelaces. "Are you still thinking about moving out?"

The silence was profound.

"I don't know. There's a lot going on right now and...I'm not sure."

Tangela was holding back. Something else was troubling her, but she didn't want to talk about it. Instead of pressing the issue, Sage offered to help. "I'll be back next week, but if you need somewhere to go—"

"I know. Use the spare key, feed the fish and don't eat all of the shredded wheat," she repeated in a lifeless tone of someone who'd heard it many times before.

Sage laughed. Bending her hips like a pretzel, she slowly reached down and touched the tips of her sneakers. Five more minutes of stretching and she'd give her lazy body a good dose of exercise.

"How are things going up there? Made any progress with that Marshall guy?"

Recalling what happened last night at Champions Sports Bar

frustrated Sage afresh, but made Tangela laugh hysterically. "If it wasn't for Denzel, the player from hell, I would've spent the rest of the night hanging out with Marshall."

"Ooh, that sounds intimate," Tangela cooed. "What's this Marshall guy like?"

Sage paused. Good question. What *was* he like? If Tangela had asked her four days ago, she would have said Marshall Grant was a brute of a man with a down-home Michigan attitude and a sexy Brooklyn swagger. But yesterday she'd seen a charming side to him, a protective side, and she liked it.

The sound of Tangela's voice cut into her thoughts. "You're stalling. That must mean he's superfine! Is he light-skinned with good hair?"

"No."

"Is he buff?"

"You know it."

"Does he drive a Hummer truck?"

Sage joked, "The closest Marshall's ever been to a Hummer truck is peering at one through the showcase window."

"He doesn't sound dreamy," Tangela confessed, after a lengthy pause.

"He's supertall and he has the most gorgeous smile, but he doesn't look like Antwan or anything. Honestly, he's the last guy you'd expect to see me with."

"And you're attracted to him?"

"I know, it's crazy, but there's something about him that turns me on. Every time I see him, I break out." Sage giggled. "Tangela, it's disgusting. Brings back memories of when I was thirteen. *Not* good times."

"Girl, you're too much! Thanks, I needed a good laugh."

"I'm glad I could entertain you, but I only have a few more days to sign Khari and things aren't looking good. If I blow this, there goes the executive manager position, and I'll be stuck toting around child stars for the rest of my life."

"Don't be so hard on yourself, Sage. You'll get the job done. You always do."

"I wish I had your faith, but it's been one problem after another. Leo will have my head if I don't come through."

"Remember, success doesn't come to you, you have to go out and get it."

"Oh, so now you're quoting me," Sage teased. "It's good to know my pearls of wisdom aren't being wasted…" Hearing the distant sound of male voices, she turned in the direction of the parking lot. Marshall and Khari were climbing out of a rusted Jeep, equipment bags on their shoulders and water bottles in their hands. *What the hell?*

Her Puma tracksuit, hat and gloves were stylish, but her hair was gathered in a sloppy ponytail and she didn't have a lick of makeup. If she had known Marshall would be here, she would have dressed up. Or at the very least, put on some mascara. Jogging in low-rise jeans and leather boots would kill her ankles and raise suspicion, but at least she'd look good doing it. Now, instead of sauntering over and striking up a conversation, she had to find a way to escape unseen. Damn!

On the line, Tangela called her name, her voice loud and frantic. "Sage? Are you there? Is everything all right? Sage?"

"I gotta go." Sage hung up the phone, slipped it into her pocket and took off back to her car like a lightning bolt.

Sage had one foot inside the rental car when she heard a familiar voice behind her.

"Where are you running off to?"

So much for a clean getaway, she thought, facing Marshall. She could see Khari starting to run in the distance. "Hey, what's up?"

"I thought that was you out on the track," he said, coming over.

"It's a small world, isn't it?" Sage had never been the shy sort, but the way he was looking at her made her wish she was anywhere but there. Lipstick would have brightened her face, and concealer would have minimized the hideous pimple on her chin. His eye contact was intense and admiring, but that didn't mean he didn't notice the unsightly blemish.

"I'm beginning to think you're stalking me." His gaze tore into her, and goose bumps pricked her arms. "Everywhere I go, you just happen to be there. Coincidence? I don't think so. There's something else going on here."

Sage swallowed the lump in her throat. Had she been had already? Mouth dry, hands trembling, she racked her mind for something to say in response. All she had to do was play it cool. Men couldn't resist a charming, attractive woman. Not even occasionally uptight men like Marshall Grant. Armed with a witty comeback, she raised her chin and flashed him a sexy smile. "You've got it all wrong. *You're* the one stalking *me!* Every time I turn around, there *you* are," she told him, poking her index finger in his chest. "Yesterday at Champions, and this morning you just happen to show up in the middle of my workout."

His grin was slow in coming.

"I won't call the police this time, but don't let it happen again."

Marshall tossed his head back, his full-bodied laugh loud and strong. Wearing a smile, and radiating sheer masculinity, he took a step toward her. "You didn't answer my question. Where are you running off to?" He leaned against the driver's-side door, foiling her escape.

"Nowhere. Just back to my hotel."

"I still can't believe you're from Vegas. It never occurred to me that people actually *live* in that city."

Sage shrugged. "I hear that a lot. People who've never been to Vegas assume it's nothing but bright lights, casinos and five-star hotels, but there's more to the city than meets the eye. I've been there for ten years, and I'm there to stay!"

"Really?" His face was wrinkled with skepticism. "I can understand the lure of the Strip, but from what I hear, the city is riddled with crime, poverty and pollution."

"Most residents don't frequent the Strip. That's tourist stuff. And people don't move to Vegas to 'have a good time.' They move there to find jobs, cheaper housing, and better opportunities. I know a lot of entrepreneurs who failed in other cities, but their businesses are now thriving in Vegas. If you have the drive, ambition and the right personality, Vegas is a gold mine." Sage paused, wishing he wasn't looking at her so intently. It was hard to concentrate when Marshall was staring down at her, his lips moist, his smile penetrating. His gaze unsettled her. Made her loose mind run rampant with lustful thoughts. Thoughts she had no business having.

"A week ago, a reporter for the *Indianapolis Chronicle* wrote that Las Vegas is a city consumed by greed, competition, and fueled almost entirely by the sex industry. Are you telling me that's a lie?" he asked, a suspicious look clouding his features.

"Vegas is a sexy city. What can I say?"

Her sly grin incited a chuckle from Marshall.

"As for the pollution, crime and poverty, it's no worse than anywhere else. I've traveled a lot and I've learned to appreciate the good *and* the bad. Poverty is everywhere, even in wealthy countries like Norway, Switzerland and Japan. It's just better hidden."

"I never really looked at it that way," he confessed.

"Most people don't."

"But I should know better. I was stationed in Kuwait for years, and a lot of Kuwaitis have a self-righteous attitude. Prostitution, drugs and crime happen everywhere else but in their own backyard." He stared down at her, the expression on his face one of appreciation. "Thanks for the reality check."

"Anytime," she told him. "Now quit trailing me and we'll be cool."

They laughed together.

"What's so funny?"

Marshall pulled his eyes away from Sage and gave Khari a smile. "Nothing. Stay out of grown folk's business." His tone was light, but there was no mistaking the underlying meaning. "You finished your laps already?"

"I sure am," Khari said, dousing his face with water. His gaze slid to his father's companion. "I remember you. You're the World Mission lady, right?"

"That's me." Sage waved at Khari, suddenly envious of the relationship he had with his dad. As a teen, she'd desperately needed a mentor to help her navigate the treacherous waters of high school. But there had been no one to check her homework, or talk to about her problems, and she had secretly longed for a father's love. She had to settle for her foster mother's.

"Dad, we should go." Khari approached the Jeep truck, opened the passenger door and slid inside. "Coach will bench me for tomorrow's game if I'm late for practice."

Games of the Heart

Marshall wasn't ready to leave. He wanted to continue talking to Sage. "It's times like this that I wish you had your license."

"I could have gotten it last year, but *you* said I wasn't ready," Khari shot back, a smug smile playing on his lips. "If I could drive, you wouldn't have to chauffeur me around and you'd have more time to do other things."

Sage pointed at the school. "Don't you practice here?"

"We did, until scouts and reporters started showing up. The cameras were distracting, so Coach arranged for the team to practice somewhere private."

"Your son's an incredible basketball player. He's bound to attract attention."

Khari poked his head out the window. "You've seen me play?"

"Who isn't a Khari Grant fan in this town?" she replied good-naturedly. "You've captured the heart of the entire city!"

"I'm the man, huh?" he joked with a chuckle. "I'm going to go all the way, World Mission lady. I'm going to make it to the pros!"

Her laughter was cut short by the sharpness of Marshall's tone.

"Basketball's a team sport, Khari. It's not about you. And you're certainly not the man." Khari started to apologize, but Marshall withered him with a look. "How do you think your teammates would feel if they heard you say that? If you want the spotlight to yourself, go play golf."

Lowering his head, Khari sank down into the passenger seat. He tugged at his seat belt, clicked it into place and stared out the windshield.

Marshall turned back to Sage. "Sorry about that."

"I'm sure Khari didn't mean anything by it. He was only—"

"We have to get going," he said, interrupting. "I guess I'll see you around." Face pinched in anger, he strode toward the Jeep SUV and flung open the driver's side door. Seconds later, when the battered SUV disappeared in the thick stream of morning traffic, Sage knew her mission was in serious trouble.

Chapter 5

"**I** need more time." Sage stared at her boss, who was visible on her laptop computer. She would have preferred talking to Leo on the phone, but he had insisted on having a videoconference.

"Did you hear me, Leo? I said I need more time." Climbing Mount Everest would be easier than gauging her boss's mood. She couldn't read the expression on his face and if his eyes weren't open, she'd swear he was sleeping.

"I heard you, and the answer is no."

Her eyes strayed to the window. It was the first time she'd seen the sun since arriving almost a week ago, but Sage wasn't fooled by its splendor. The wind raged against the hotel and icicles dangled from the balcony railing. "I was employee of the month three times last year! Trust me, Leo. I can do this."

"Sure you can."

"Are you forgetting that I lured Devin Skye away from In the Know Management? She had a successful run on that Nickelodeon show."

"That's old news. You signed her how many years ago? In the prophetic words of Janet Jackson, what have you done for me lately?"

Sage could hear snickering in the background and knew their intimate videoconference for two wasn't so private. Nine years as a celebrity manager was ancient by Hollywood standards and although most of her clients were pubescent, law-abiding teens, Sage was ready to take her career to the next level. Starting now. Annoyed that she didn't have her boss's full attention, she said, "If you're too busy to talk, we can do this another time. I just hope someone else doesn't sign Khari while we're sitting back twiddling our thumbs."

The mention of Khari's name brought Leo's gaze into focus.

"I can persuade Marshall to sign with us. I just need another week. Two max."

"I knew you couldn't do it." Leo shook his head, the disappointment in his eyes piercing her soul. "I applaud your efforts, Sage. I really do, but your time is up."

His words mocked her, momentarily weakening her resolve, but she rebounded before frustration set in. "Marshall's warming up to me. I've made a lot of progress in the last six days. In fact, he…" Sage racked her brain for something, anything that would impress her boss. "He's taking me out for dinner tonight."

"It's time for you to step aside and let me take the reins. I'm going to square his debts, buy him a Porsche and see to it that he never has to work again. That'll bring him around."

She shook her head. "Money isn't the right angle, Leo. Marshall Grant can't be bought."

"Everyone has a price, Sage. *Everyone.*"

There was an exception to every rule and Marshall Grant was it. Integrity was at the heart of who he was and he'd rather do without than break the rules. "His place is real nice. It's small, but cozy and he has all new furniture."

"You've been inside their house?"

Detecting awe in her boss's voice, she donned an innocent, wide-eyed look. "Oh, I was there for hours," she lied, hoping he believed the tale she was spinning. "If Marshall didn't have to go to work. I would have closed the deal right then and there." It was an outrageous lie, but it was the only thing she could think of.

"That's the closest anyone's ever got to the family."

"I'm not surprised," Sage said. "Marshall's very protective of his son."

"Khari was there?"

"Yeah. Great kid, and smart too. With his grades and basket-ball skills, he can get a full scholarship to any school of his choosing."

"Good work. I can't believe you pulled that off."

"Does that mean you'll give me an extension?" she asked, her voice hopeful.

"No." His voice was firm, like a steel door slamming shut in her face. "I need you back here pronto. Hailey Hope's up for a Teen Choice Award and I need you to accompany her to the show. It's in Orlando, and the Hope clan has never been to O-Town. Throw out the red carpet. Take them to see the dolphins. You know the drill."

Her eyes tapered. "I'm not going."

"Yes, you are. I'm still your boss and that's an order."

"But I'm making progress with Marshall. You said so yourself!"

"You were lucky."

"Luck is the time when preparation and opportunity meet," she told him matter-of-factly. "Don't give up on me, Leo. I can make this happen."

"Pack up and come home." His tone was brisk, reminding her that he was the one in charge. "I'm tied up here right now, I should be out that way soon. Tell Marshall to expect me when you say goodbye."

Her mind raced, spinning futilely with no end in sight. "I'm taking my holidays," she announced. "I'll be back in three weeks."

"That's not how things are done around here, Sage. You have to apply for time off like everyone else and wait for *my* approval."

"Really?" she challenged, eyes blazing. "I don't remember Jamaar or Whitney putting in notice when they went to the Bermuda Jazz Festival."

"They're model employees," he explained, adjusting his silk tie. "They've been with me for years. I don't mind making an exception for dedicated staff."

"I'm glad you feel that way because *I've* been with the agency longer, and if you check my file you'll see that I've signed more clients."

Leo's mouth remained a taut scowl, but she could hear whispering in the background.

Undeterred, Sage continued. "I'm entitled to four weeks paid vacation and I'm taking it effective Monday."

"What is she up to?" asked a voice that didn't belong to her boss.

"Know this," Leo spat out between clenched teeth, "if you're not back here by March first I'll be mailing out your severance pay."

Not bothering to reply to his threat, she closed her laptop. Dropping her head on the desk, she closed her eyes and soaked up the quiet sounds of the morning. Sage felt like a ship without a compass floating aimlessly at sea. She thought she'd made progress with Marshall, but Leo had made her feel inadequate. The problem was she hadn't been aggressive enough. Standing, she packed up her laptop, tucked it under her arm and dashed into the bedroom. Sometimes to win you had to break the rules and that's exactly what she intended to do. Game on!

Two hours later, Sage stepped onto the Westchester Academy football field. Her eyes watered, her teeth chattered and her body shivered against the punishing arctic wind. Rubbing her hands together, she hustled across the field, searching the bleachers for Marshall.

Spotting him, she wet her lips and ignored the sharp tingling sensation between her legs. Clad in a toque, a button-down jacket and jeans, Marshall towered head and shoulders above the spectators standing beside him. What was with this guy and plaid? she wondered, shaking her head in distaste. Didn't he realize that it had never, ever been in style? Marshall had wide shoulders, a powerful chest and was a staggering six feet six inches tall, but he wore the ugliest clothes. He was an attractive guy; he just didn't know how to dress. A trip to Nordstrom would cure him of his comfort-over-style mindset and not a moment too soon. Khari was going to be a superstar athlete and the quicker Marshall got with the program the better. Goodbye Eddie Bauer stores, hello Hermès boutiques!

Anxious to talk to the single father, she climbed the steps and squeezed herself onto the crowded bench, almost knocking over a kid in the process. By the time Marshall noticed her she was standing beside him. "Hey, Marshall. What's up?"

"Sage? What are you doing here?" he asked, his face lined with confusion.

His words slammed into her chest. There was no mistaking the edge in his voice. He was not happy to see her. Fussing with her scarf, she glanced out onto the football field. "I—I, um, it's a funny thing…" she stammered, unsure of what to say.

"I invited her," Khari said, tossing a handful of popcorn into his open mouth.

Swiveling around, Sage offered the teen a gracious smile. Making a mental note to thank him privately later, she turned back to Marshall. "I hope you don't mind me joining you. I don't know anyone else here and I'd feel silly sitting alone."

His smile returned. "Are you here to solicit business for World Mission?"

"No, not today, but I'm always on the lookout for generous donors. Do you have any rich friends in the parent association that you'd like to introduce me to?"

Marshall curved an arm around her waist and stared deep into her eyes. "No, Ms. Collins. I think I'll keep you all to myself."

The roar of the crowd drowned out Sage's girlish laughter.

During the game, they talked about their respective jobs and their mutual love of sports. And when Marshall went down to the canteen to buy her a cup of hot chocolate, Sage couldn't help thinking he was unlike anyone she'd ever met. Though the at-risk-community youth director wasn't her usual type, she found herself attracted to him. His quiet, calm demeanor was a great compliment to her assertive personality. There was an air of humility about him, but he didn't put up with any crap, either. He struck a fine balance of being cool and firm, and if he wasn't from small-town Indiana, she'd be all over him.

"You like my dad, huh?"

Sage looked over at Khari. The teen was watching her, an amused expression on his slim face. "Your father's a very nice man."

"That's not what I asked you."

"He's all right, I guess."

Khari grinned. "Yeah, okay. You *definitely* like him."

"No, I don't." Despite her better judgment, she asked the questions circling her mind. "Is he dating anyone right now?"

"No, never, but since I—" he corrected himself. "I mean,

since the team started playing better, more women have been pushing up on Dad."

Shame wedged in her throat, preventing her from speaking.

"I was the one interviewed on ESPN, but my pop's the one getting crazy play!" Khari confessed with a chuckle.

"You don't say?" Now Sage understood why Khari was attracting nation-wide attention. Every sports agent in the country had seen him on TV and had descended on the city like a pack of vultures. "You've become a celebrity overnight and now everyone feels like they know you, huh?"

"Yeah," he replied quietly. "I just hope no one's trying to play my dad."

Sage gulped. "Me too, Khari. Me too."

Sage bit into her Meat Lover's pizza, her gaze fixed on Marshall and the woman in the tight baby-blue sweater. Gulping down a mouthful of Cherry Coke, she wondered if everything Khari told her about his dad was true. Marshall might not be dating anyone, but he sure liked to flirt.

"More soda?" The sound of the waiter's voice drew her attention.

Nodding, she raised her glass. "Thanks."

After Westchester Academy won in double overtime, the football team and their fans had crammed into Dominos to celebrate the hard-fought win. But with teachers, parents and students all talking at once, it was hard for Sage to spend more than a minute with Marshall.

Taking another bite of pizza, she took notes on her competition. The blonde had delicate features and long flowing hair that kissed her shoulders. There was no denying her beauty, and when Marshall refilled her water glass, Sage felt a stab of envy.

Disappointed that a man as intuitive as Marshall Grant could fall for such a plastic-looking woman, she sighed inwardly. Sitting back in her chair, she allowed her gaze to wander. Sage was surrounded by people, amid laughter, smiles and jokes, but she felt oddly alone.

"Want me to go over there and tell my dad you want to talk to him?"

Sage didn't bother to look at Khari. "No. I already told you, I don't like him that way."

"Then why are you eyeballing him so hard?"

Stuffing a meatball into her mouth, she avoided the teen's intense gaze. He was an engaging kid, but his constant queries were more irritating than nails on a chalkboard.

"You're feeling my dad. I can tell."

Sage choked on her Italian sausage. Rubbing the ache in her chest, she shot a look at Khari, who was slumped back in his seat, chuckling. "Are you trying to kill me?"

"Admit you like pops and I'll leave you alone."

"Your dad's too serious for me," she argued, cleaning her hands on a napkin. "I bet he color codes his socks, irons his boxer shorts and listens to Mozart."

"That's cold, Sage! Pops isn't *that* bad."

"I'm right, though, aren't I?"

His smile was answer enough, but he said, "See, you guys just met and you already know him so well! I'm telling you, Sage, y'all were meant to be together."

"Drop it, Khari."

"I'm not a kid. I see the way you guys look at each other. I know what's up."

Sage bit back a smile. She'd caught Marshall staring at her a few times, but thought nothing of it. Besides, if he was interested in her, why had he spent all night flirting with Malibu Barbie? "Why are you sitting here with me?" she asked, turning the tables on him. "You should be eating with your friends."

"I invited you, remember? I can't leave you alone. You're my personal guest." Khari folded his pizza in half and took a bite. "Besides, it's fun giving you a hard time."

"I can see that." Sage sipped her drink, the cold, sweet liquid alleviating the sudden tightness in her throat. Anxious to change the subject, she maneuvered the conversation away from Marshall and asked Khari about school. "What are your plans after graduation?"

His face brightened. "I'm going pro."

"But your dad wants you to study medicine."

"That's his dream, not mine. I'm entering the NBA draft and nothing's going to stop me."

Sage was surprised, but kept her tone even. "Does your father know?"

"I'll be eighteen soon. I don't need his approval." Squaring his shoulders, he thumped a hand to his chest. "I know what I'm doing. I can take care of myself."

"Khari, it's not that simple," she told him. "You're going to need a manager, an agent, a publicist and a damn good lawyer to make it happen."

"I am?"

Sage nodded. "And the sooner you find representation the better. The draft is still months away, but your first order of business will be to set up a meeting with the NBA's Board of Directors. The committee will determine whether or not you can handle the pressure of playing in the league. If they think you can cut it, they'll give you the go-ahead and you can write an official letter declaring your eligibility."

"Really?" Eyes wide, Khari scratched the top of his head. "I— I thought I just entered the draft and waited for the offers to roll in."

"The NBA is the most lucrative sports organization in the world," she explained. "Commissioner Stern isn't going to let money-hungry, high school players destroy the league, no matter how high they can jump."

"Shoot! What am I going to do now?"

Sage patted his shoulder. "You can start by calming down," she joked, laughing. "It'll be fine, just do your research and—"

"Hey, you're from Las Vegas. I know you work in the nonprofit world, but you must know someone I can talk to. Someone who might be interested in taking me on as a client. I only have five hundred dollars in my bank account, but I'm good for it. I swear."

Sage wrestled with her conscience. She was supposed to be having this conversation with Marshall, not Khari. Sure, he was almost an adult, but in this situation, almost didn't count. Unsure of what to do, she slipped a hand into her purse, pulled out a pen and notepad and wrote down her contact information. Sage didn't know if Khari was ready for the NBA, but she didn't want him to be taken advantage of by the wrong person. "All my information's on here," she said, sliding him the piece of paper. "If you need anything, or just want to talk, call me."

Khari pocketed the sheet, a look of relief on his face. "Thanks, Sage. I won't forget this. When I turn pro, I'm compin' you a car!"

His declaration compounded her guilt. "Khari, I don't need you to buy me anything." Sage studied him closely for a few seconds, then wondered why he wanted to turn pro. "You're entering the draft because of your love of the game, not because of the money, right?"

"It's a bit of both," he admitted. "It would be nice to make my own decisions and not have to ask anyone for money."

"Khari, you don't have to enter the NBA to exert your independence. Move out, get your own place, and buy your *own* car."

"How am I gonna do that? I get two hundred bucks a month in allowance, and I don't have a social insurance number or a license."

Bug-eyed, her mouth fell open wordlessly. Sage knew Marshall was strict, but this was ridiculous. Khari still got an allowance? He didn't have a driver's permit? And even more shocking, he'd never had a part-time job? "But you're almost eighteen. I'd been working for three years by the time I was your age!"

"Tell him that," he said, motioning with his head toward his dad. "I want to work at Footlocker, but Dad won't let me. He's scared my grades will slip. I'm the only one in my group who doesn't have a job. You know how that makes me feel?"

"Would it help if I tried to talk to your dad?"

"You'd do that for me?" he asked excitedly. "Thank, Sage. You're the best!"

Her eyes twinkled with mischief. "I am, aren't I?"

Chapter 6

Beer in hand, Marshall strolled into the living room, sat down on the couch and waited for *Prison Break* to return from commercial. As he tasted his beer, his thoughts returned to the football game. It was a riveting, action-packed match, but it was the plays off the field that left his mind reeling.

He'd lost his head when Sage slipped onto the bench, wearing her wide, camera-ready smile. Seeing her again made him realize just how unique she was. There was a sense of governance about her, but she was fun and spontaneous and ridiculously sexy. Personable, engaging, interested in everything he had to say.

Raising Khari to be a smart, responsible young man had been his focus for years, but he was intrigued by the attractive World Mission executive.

An image of Sage decked out in a baseball cap, sweater and blue jeans surfaced. Every time she looked at him he felt like he lost his cool a little bit. He was unflappable when it came to the opposite sex. Nothing fazed him. But that belief went straight out the window the night he ran into Sage at Champions Sports Bar.

Stretching out on the couch, Marshall wondered if he'd see Sage again before she left town. He wanted to, even if it was just for a cup of coffee. Being with a woman who enjoyed talking about cars and sports was a welcome change.

He'd overheard Khari tell Sage about the cheerleader he

wanted to ask to the prom. Listening to them made Marshall realize how much Khari appreciated having a woman to talk to. He spent a lot of time with his grandmother, but she didn't understand the challenges and pressures he faced. But Sage did. And she obviously had a soft spot for teens.

"Dad?"

Marshall turned at the sound of his son's voice. "Hey. What's up?"

"Nothing. I was, ah, wondering if I could go to Oakley's."

"Now?" he asked, glancing at the clock. "It's nine-fifteen."

"I know, but some of the guys are hanging out over there."

"Hanging out? What are they doing?"

Khari shrugged. "I don't know. Watching movies and stuff."

"Are Oakley's parents home?"

"I guess."

"You guess?" Marshall put down his beer. "Forget it. It's late, they're probably over there drinking and his folks aren't home."

"Come on, Dad. The guys will think I'm—"

"I don't care what those clowns think. You're staying home and that's final. Besides, don't you have an essay due on Monday?"

"I have the entire weekend to get it done."

"Get started on it now."

"Everyone will be at Oakley's house but me." Face pinched, lips tight, he pleaded his case. "Destiny will think I'm a baby and go with someone else to the prom. Is that what you want? For me to lose all my friends?"

Marshall picked up the remote control, signaling the end of the discussion. "It's your turn to walk the boys."

Khari stood in place. His arms hung stiffly at his sides and the veins in his neck were popping.

"What are you waiting for? I said get going. You want your allowance next week, don't you?"

The doorbell chimed. Before Marshall could tell Khari to get the door, he stomped out of the room and upstairs. Shaking his head, Marshall got up from the couch. He hoped it wasn't one of Khari's friends. He didn't want to argue with his son, but he wasn't going anywhere tonight. At nine-thirty at night, the only place he should be was at home, working on his essay.

"Who is it?" Marshall called.

"Open up and you'll see."

Marshall frowned. It sounded like Sage. He pulled open the door, and when he saw her standing there, broke out into a smile. "You're not selling Girl Scout cookies this time, are you?"

"What if I was? Would you buy some?"

"I sure would."

"Prove it," she challenged, sticking out her hand. "Put your money where your mouth is, Big Guy."

Feeling benevolent, he reached into his back pocket. When he didn't find his wallet, he patted the front of his shirt. Nothing. Eyes blinking with fear, he rubbed a hand over his jeans. His mouth fell open, but the cold air drifting inside didn't squelch the burning sensation in his throat.

"Looking for this?" Sage waved the brown leather wallet under his nose. "I thought this might be yours."

Face awash with relief, he said, "What are you, Houdini?"

"Something like that. You should see what I can do with a blindfold!"

Marshall chuckled. "How did you get my wallet?"

"I crawled through the window, crept upstairs and plucked it out of your top drawer." She laughed easily. "You left it back at the restaurant."

"I did?"

Sage nodded. What she didn't tell him was that she swiped it off the table when he wasn't looking. In the commotion of squaring the bill, seeing to it that everybody had a ride home and carrying a box of leftover pizza, Marshall didn't even notice he'd left his wallet behind. "You must have been distracted, again, by my Vegas beauty," she quipped.

"It sounds like maybe *you* were the one who was distracted. By me."

"Perhaps. Or maybe I was waiting for you to make the first move."

"I did. You turned me down." His voice was thick with insinuation.

"We keep running into each other. I'm surprised you're not sick of me."

"Sick of you? I'd never get tired of having you around. You're great company." He added, "Why would I call, if I didn't want to see you?"

"Aw, that's sweet. Too bad I don't believe you!"

They laughed.

"Thanks for bringing this by," Marshall said, slipping his wallet into his back pocket. "I owe you."

"When I called and didn't get an answer, I decided to swing by." Seduced by his smile and scared the wind had stolen her once-tight curls, she ran a hand through her hair. "I hope that was okay."

"Not a problem. Khari must have been on the phone when you called. I don't know how many times I've told him to answer the line when it beeps. Or better yet, to make his calls on his cell phone. That's why I got one for him in the first place."

"That's okay. You got your wallet. That's all that matters." Waving goodbye, she turned and took a step off the porch. "Anyways, I have to run. See you later!"

"Don't go. I was just about to—" he paused "—make some popcorn. *Set It Off* is on TBS tonight, ever seen it?"

"Only a million times! I love that movie, especially the part where Jada Pinkett Smith and Blair Underwood get it on." Sage fanned a hand in front of her face, soliciting a chuckle from Marshall. "Talk about hot!"

"That's your favorite part, huh? The part where they get busy?"

"Pretty much." Sage and Marshall were so busy flirting with each other, they didn't notice Khari until he was in the foyer.

"Hey, Sage. What are you doing here? I thought you were going home to watch *Dancing With the Stars*."

"And I thought you were going to Oakley's." Sage stepped inside, relieved to escape the ice-cold weather. The warmth of the house quickly thawed her fingers and toes. "Did you change your mind?"

"Dad said I can't go."

"Why not?"

Khari stared down at his shoes.

Sensing the friction between father and son, her gaze bounced from Khari to Marshall. "Why can't he hang out with his friends?"

"Khari has an essay to write."

"No, seriously. Why can't he go?"

"I just told you," Marshall explained, a hard edge in his voice. "Khari got a C minus on his last assignment and did poorly on his midyear exam. If he's going to get into Harvard, he needs to get his mind off his friends and focus on his studies, starting with that *Hamlet* essay that's due on Monday."

He was about to tell her to mind her own business when it came to his son, but he remembered how glad Khari seemed to be whenever the teenager talked to Sage.

Sage turned to Khari. "I aced English, and *Hamlet* was my favorite play. If it's all right with your dad, I can come over on Sunday to help you with your essay."

His face brightened. "You will? I suck at writing. Even my e-mails sound like something a third-grader wrote!"

"Sure. It'll be fun."

"Aren't you leaving tomorrow?" Marshall asked, touching her forearm. His eyes were riveted on her lips, and for a moment he almost forgot Khari was in the room.

"Looks like I'll be sticking around a little longer."

"That's good news."

"Really? And why's that?"

Khari waved his hands. "Hello? Back to me. I'm still here."

Sage and Marshall laughed.

"Dad, is it okay if I go to Oakley's? I promise to be back by curfew."

Marshall reconsidered his son's request. If he said no, Sage would think he was unreasonable, but if he let Khari go and something bad happened, he'd never be able to forgive himself. Weary of Khari's friends, but willing to trust his son, he decided to call Mr. Chapman to put his mind at ease. "All right, but no drugs, no alcohol and no sex."

"I know, I know," Khari repeated, rolling his eyes. "My friends and I aren't into that stuff. I don't know how many times I have to tell you before you'll believe me."

"You can leave after you walk the boys."

"Boys?" Sage asked, turning toward Marshall.

"We have two Alaskan huskies out back," he explained. "Khari gets five dollars every time he walks them."

Sage pinched Marshall's arm.

"Ouch! What was that for?" Frowning, he rubbed the tender spot with his thumb.

"Five dollars? Those are slave wages! I'll walk them." Shaking her head, she turned back to Khari, a smile on her lips. The thought of going back outside made every nerve in her body scream out in protest. "You go have fun with your friends and I'll talk to your dad about raising your allowance."

"Thanks, Sage! See you on Sunday!" he called over his shoulder, sprinting out of the room. Seconds later, they heard the back door slam.

"I have a bad feeling about this," Marshall admitted, releasing a deep, troubled sigh. "You don't know his friends like I do. Oakley's older brother used to deal drugs. He might pressure Khari to join his gang or something."

"Marshall, I know you want the best for your son, but you have to loosen up. He'll be eighteen in a few weeks." Sage tugged on her suede gloves. "Trust that you raised him to be a sensible, responsible young man and he'll be fine."

"One wrong move is all it takes. I've worked with troubled youth for seven and a half years, and I see kids like Khari every day. Intelligent, young, black men who should be studying for their SATs or getting ready for the prom. Instead, they're stuck behind bars earning thirty cents an hour." The expression on his face was grim. "I love Khari and I'm proud of him, but he's a follower. He needs a rocket to blast him into maturity, and not a moment too soon."

"I'm just an outsider looking in, but I think you're too hard on him. Khari's got his head on straight. He's a smart kid."

"All he cares about is girls and basketball."

"What did you think about when you were his age?"

Marshall stepped forward. "A better question is what am I thinking right now?"

"Let's walk the boys," she told him, sideswiping the question. "Then you can share all of your dirty thoughts."

He dropped an arm around her shoulder. "Sounds like a plan to me."

Chapter 7

A harsh, bitter breeze greeted Marshall and Sage when they stepped onto Irvington Lane. The wind hissed in the trees, whipping branches, swirling leaves and shaking bushes in its fury. Quivering with cold, her coattail slapping her thighs mercilessly, Sage nestled her face in her cashmere scarf, imagining it was a soft, fluffy, king-size pillow.

Layered in winter gear made it difficult to move, but Sage snuck a look at Marshall. His bubble jacket added bulk to his already thick frame, a thermal toque protected his head and brown hiking boots made his feet look twice their size. Marshall hadn't said a word since they left the house, but the silence didn't bother her. As a child, she'd often lived in solitude for days at a time and had learned how to entertain herself. Like now. She imagined that she was sprawled out on the beach, surrounded by palm trees and sunshine, and a tall, muscular man who looked oddly like Marshall Grant was feeding her papaya.

It was dark outside, the sky a deep, angry gray, but Sage could still see the troubled expression on Marshall's face. Tension radiated from his body and his mouth was a firm line. Worried about his son, his overactive mind was likely imagining all the possible things that could go wrong at Oakley's.

Unsure of how long they had been gone, but convinced an

hour had gone by, Sage rubbed the iciness from her fingers. "How long have you had the dogs?"

"Three years. Pippen and Malone were a gift from my parents. Khari usually takes great care of them, but he's got so many things on the go right now, he doesn't have time. I try to help out when I can."

Hearing their names, the dogs barked voraciously, tugging wildly on the leash. Sage was glad she didn't have pets, especially ones who enjoyed the great outdoors. Pippen and Malone stopped every few minutes to sniff the ground, and moved at a slow, leisurely pace. It was below zero, but the freezing temperature didn't seem to faze them.

Chilled to the bone, but intent on bringing Marshall out of his funk, Sage asked him about his family. "Khari mentioned that your dad played professional baseball in the late sixties. Is it true he played with Hank Aaron?"

Marshall cleared his throat. "Yes, he played thirteen seasons with the Braves before calling it quits."

Detecting a subtle shift in his tone, she glanced over at him, hoping to spot the source of the change. Nothing. Confident she hadn't imagined it, she asked, "Why did he leave the game? Was he injured?"

"No. The team acquired a younger, more athletic pitcher and decided not to re-sign him." Marshall tugged on the leash, pulling the dogs away from a metal garbage bin. "My dad didn't have any formal education, so the years after he left the league were hell. Both of my parents worked, but there was never enough money. Thankfully, they live here in the city and we're closer."

"Is that why you want Khari to go to Harvard? So he'll have something to fall back on in case things don't go as planned?"

"Exactly!" The word burst out of his mouth like a cheer. "Finally, someone who agrees with me." Marshall looked down at her, his eyes full of gratitude. "As a parent, there's no greater joy than seeing your child fulfill their dreams. Up until last year, all Khari could talk about was being a surgeon, but now he's lost his focus. It's up to me to get Khari back on track."

"What does the rest of your family think?"

"That I should let Khari decide what to do." He added, "But he's too young to make the right decision."

"And the right decision is to go to Harvard?"

"Right." Smiling at her, he said, "You're a wise young woman."

Sage didn't know what to say. Marshall thought she was an ally. Definitely progress, from a deranged psycho beating up on a vending machine. She wanted him to trust her, but she didn't want to betray Khari, either. She saw both sides of the argument, but now was not the time to present the other side. "Please don't start using words like *wise* and *prudent*," she told him with a laugh. "I'm only twenty-eight! You're making me feel old."

Marshall stumbled but didn't fall. He cranked his head to the right, his eyes the size of tennis balls. "You're only twenty-eight?"

Nodding, she favored him with a smile. "You thought I was older, right?"

"Yeah, I did," he confessed. In the accompanying silence, he stared at her as if seeing her for the first time. She was as sleek and as elegant as a fifties actress, but had the buoyancy and youthfulness of a woman half her age. Marshall couldn't believe she was so young. There was almost a decade of life experiences between them.

If she was older, even a year or two, he would have no qualms about asking her out. Most men would jump at the chance to date a young girl. Not him. He liked older women, someone he wouldn't have to explain the significance of the civil rights movement, the purpose of the Million Man March, or why he lived and breathed seventies music. He was looking for a mature woman. Someone intellectual and well schooled. And as appealing and intelligent as Sage was, she was much too young and much too inexperienced for him.

Feeling letdown, he abandoned his thoughts and said, "You mentioned that you moved to Las Vegas as a teen. Where's home?"

"Sacramento."

"Does your family still live there, or did they make the move too?"

"I don't have a family."

Startled by the edge in her voice, he said, "Everyone has a family."

"Everyone but me."

"You were raised in foster care."

Now it was her turn to be surprised. "How did you know?"

"I worked in a prison for a while, and troubled youth is my career. You learn to pick up on things." He smiled, hoping she saw the genuine look of concern in his eyes. "I take it you didn't end up with the Huxtables."

Sage sucked her teeth. "The Addams Family would have been an improvement." They turned the corner and the pitiless force of the wind almost knocked her over. Sage felt like she was walking on quicksand with stilettos on. The crunch of leaves and snow under her feet brought her back fifteen years.

Piling up the leaves in the middle of the backyard. Taking turns with Tangela doing back flips and somersaults into the pile. It was one of the few happy memories she had of her childhood, and thinking of her best friend made her homesick.

"It's funny. We've been talking all this time and I still don't know what you do."

"What I do?" she repeated, her teeth chattering.

"Yeah. I mean besides going door-to-door."

"I'm in marketing." It was true. She was. Celebrity managers had to market, package and sell their clients to the public. "I travel regularly to promote the organization, acquire new business and I spend a lot of time recruiting volunteers."

"Meeting you confirms it."

"Confirms what?"

"Charitable organizations hire the most beautiful women." His eyes shone with sincerity and his smile was sweet.

What was meant to be a compliment submerged her in a pool of guilt. Sage had often wondered if Leo hired her because of her drive or because of her looks. Inexperienced in the field but eager to learn, she had talked him into allowing her to intern at the agency. A month later, Leo offered her an entry-level position.

"I love what I do. Working at World Mission has opened a lot of doors for me, and I feel I'm making a difference in the lives of needy children," she said, her eyes bright with enthusiasm. "I'd work for free if they couldn't afford to pay me."

"You would? That's amazing. Few people can say that."

To steady her balance on the ice-encrusted sidewalk, she reached out and gripped his forearm. When he stared down at her, his lips shaped into a small smile, her legs turned to mush. Finding her voice, she asked him more about his job. "Do you like running the youth center?"

"I was born to be a marine. Protecting America and their allies, rebuilding war-torn communities and offering hope to third world countries has always been my passion. If it wasn't for Khari and all my responsibilities here, I'd still be in the service. So the center seemed like the perfect transition."

Skipping effortlessly from one subject to the next, they talked with the ease and familiarity of lifelong friends. They discussed their childhoods, and the positive and negative experiences that had helped shape their lives. Sage was having so much fun listening to all the trouble Marshall and his buddies had caused during basic training, she didn't realize they were back at the house until he said, "Follow me around back so I can get the boys settled in for the night."

"They don't sleep inside?"

Shaking his head, he unlatched the fence and led Pippen and Malone into the yard. Among the solid oak trees and snow-covered garden was a wooden deck. Once his pets were inside the doghouse, he climbed the steps and sat down on the bench. The wind wasn't as sharp and cruel as it had been when they'd first left the house, but it was still cold. Much too cold to be sitting outside shooting the breeze. But when Marshall said, "Why don't you take a load off?" She took the seat beside him.

"Are you all right?"

Sage didn't want to complain, so she nodded. The arctic wind made her eyes water and her feet felt like two slabs of ice, but she was enjoying his company. Drawn to his conservative nature and engaging personality, Sage wondered why he'd never remarried. Sisters all over the country crammed into churches Sunday after Sunday, begging God to send them a man as tall and handsome as Marshall Grant. A hardworking single father with more stories than the presidential library, he'd packed a world of excitement and danger into his thirty-seven years. Camel trekking in the Thar Desert. Scuba diving in Belize. Running with the bulls. "How will you feel if Khari doesn't go to Harvard?"

"Harvard is one of the finest schools in the country and it's important to me that Khari gets the best education available. If he doesn't go to Harvard to study medicine, I'll feel like I failed him as a parent."

"Marshall, that's crazy. We just met, but even I can see what a great father you are." Her voice was firm, strong, convincing, full of admiration and praise. "You've raised Khari single-handedly and you've done a kick-ass job."

"You're just trying to make me feel better."

"No. It's the God's-honest truth."

He didn't say anything for several moments. "You really think so?"

"Khari's an amazing kid, and it's all because he has you as a role model. Few kids can say that their parents are their best friends, but that's what Khari says about you."

"Thanks for sharing that with me." He hesitated, then after an elongated pause, said, "You're an intriguing woman, Sage Collins. If you weren't so young I'd…" The wind snatched the rest of his sentence.

"You'd what?" she challenged, her voice low and sexy.

"I'd pursue you until you were mine." His tone was rife with sensual undercurrents and warmed her from the inside out. Five minutes ago she was convinced she'd freeze to death, and now she was so hot, she could fry an egg on her forehead. Tongue-tied and out of focus, she licked the dryness from her lips. Marshall was talking, but between the wind, the voices in her head and the clattering roof shingles, she couldn't hear a word. He must have sensed her confusion, because he leaned over. His mouth was just a breath away from her ear. "Let's go inside," he suggested, the heat in his eyes exposing his desire.

"But we're having so much fun out here." Sage gave him a teasing smile. "Why ruin a perfectly good thing?"

"Because if we stay out here any longer I'm going to end up kissing you." The look on his face was intense. "Is that what you want, Sage? For me to do what I've been dying to do since we met?"

Astonished by his admission, and surprisingly aroused, she racked her brain for an appropriate response. Words didn't come. Her throat was dry, her tongue was limp and the desire to kiss him was crushing. As uncomfortable as she was, she couldn't stop her eyes from zeroing in on his lips. They beckoned, called, promising an experience she'd never forget. To keep from reaching out and tracing a finger over the curve of his mouth, she buried her hands in her jacket pocket.

"I've been too busy raising Khari to even think about dating, but you're hard to resist," he told her, his sensuous voice ripe with lust. "You're right, though. It's better we stay out here because I don't trust myself inside with you."

Sage prided herself on being tough under pressure, but when Marshall brushed his lips across her cheek, her mind went blank. If a police officer had walked up and asked her name, she'd stutter like a fool.

"This'll never work," she announced, forcing her wayward mind to focus.

"You're right. It won't."

"I'm glad we agree."

"I do. You're young. Much too young for me."

Sage puckered her lips. "Is that what you think?"

"I'm nine years older than you."

"Is that all?" she scoffed. "I've dated older."

"You have?"

"Yeah, and *he* didn't think I was immature."

He edged closer. "That's not what I said."

"You didn't have to say it. It was implied."

"Why did you break up?"

"What makes you think we did?"

His eyes probed her face, searching, wishing, hoping. "If you had a boyfriend, you wouldn't be here with me." His breathing was heavy, labored, jagged, like he'd raced up ten flights of stairs. "What happened?"

"I got bored and broke it off. I told you, I'm a chameleon. I didn't keep one look or one man for too long. That's why we'd never work, Marshall, because I'm not into long-term relationships. It has nothing to do with our age difference." Hurt by his remarks and disappointed in him for the second time that evening, she pretended not to notice the contrite expression on his face. She felt insulted. What did he think she was, a kid? Sage opened her mouth to say goodbye, but before the words left her mouth, he kissed her.

Heat rushed to her face. All the verbal banter, flirtatious smiles and sly looks had finally done her in. Her eyes instinctively closed, sealing her in the moment. His touch and the tenderness of his embrace stoked her body's fire. Knowing this was the first and only time they'd ever be this close, this connected, this intimate, she savored the beauty of the kiss. Abandoning herself to the pleasure of his lips, she blocked out all negative thoughts and ignored the knifelike pricks jabbing her conscience.

Wishing they weren't wearing so many clothes, but thankful for the physical barriers between them, she inclined her head to the left, teasing Marshall's tongue from his mouth. Murmuring softly, pleading feebly for him to stop, but unable to move from the comfort of his arms, she slid closer on the bench. Gone was the bravado, the humor, the cheekiness. All she wanted was for him to touch her. Sage had an uncontrollable craving for Marshall, and her feelings quickly veered from tenderness to full-blown lust. She wanted him. Now.

Drawing her to him, he loved her mouth with a gentleness she had never known, but wanted to explore at the deepest, most intimate level. Enraptured in the moment and wanting to give herself completely to him, she considered coming clean about who she really was. Telling the truth would alleviate her guilt, but Sage didn't trust that Marshall would understand. She had done a lot of things she wasn't proud of and there was a good chance he wouldn't forgive her. Sage turned away from her thoughts. This was business, nothing personal. If she could keep her eyes on the prize, and off Marshall, there'd be no stopping her. She'd have the signing bonus *and* the executive manager position, shocking her boss, her coworkers, and her competitors. Coming to her senses, she turned away, breaking off the kiss. "I gotta go."

"Stay." He looked like a sad kid who'd dropped his ice-cream cone on the pavement. "We're going to watch *Set It Off,* remember?"

Sage had done a lot of underhanded things while working at Sapphire Entertainment, but she had never mixed business with pleasure. Not even when Damien Jaymes, a platinum-selling R & B crooner had pursued her. Gifts were returned unopened, flowers were trashed and she never answered any of his calls. She had been tempted before and withstood the heat, so why couldn't she do that with Marshall? "I don't want to overstay my welcome," she said.

She tried to stand, but her legs felt like sandbags.

"You don't really believe that, do you?" he asked, his eyes skimming her face. "I want you to stay. We're having a good time, aren't we?"

His voice dripped with arrogance, infuriating her. "Two hours ago you were flirting with that hoochie at the pizza parlor, and now you're out here kissing me. You must think you're slick."

Marshall shook his head slowly, the intensity of his gaze beating down on her like the tropical sun. "Khari said you were jealous, but I didn't believe him."

"I'm not. I don't get jealous. I'm bigger than that."

"Then stay."

"No, thanks."

Marshall had heard the sarcasm in her voice, but didn't react. "You look mad. Is everything okay?"

"Just peachy."

"No hard feelings?"

She faked a smile. "None whatsoever."

"Good," he said, standing. "I'll walk you to your car."

"That's not necessary. I know where it is," she snapped.

"I want to see you off. It's the gentlemanly thing to do."

"A gentleman would never insult his guest."

Marshall decided to play his hunch. If he was wrong, he'd just have to apologize later. "Are you mad because I said you were young, because we kissed or because you wanted more? Which one is it?"

"None of the above." Her voice was loud, squeaky like a ventriloquist.

"That kiss was something though, wasn't it?"

Sage opened her mouth to clarify who kissed who, but it was Khari's voice she heard behind her. "I could hear you guys yelling from up the block!"

For the first time ever, Marshall was not happy to see his son. "You're home early," he said, consulting his watch. "You have half an hour left on your curfew."

"I know, but they were watching *Friday After Next,* and I've seen that movie a thousand times." Khari tried to wipe the smirk from off his face, but it only got wider. "Dad, you must be real angry. Your left eye is twitching."

Sage felt a strange compulsion to giggle, so she turned away.

"What were you guys arguing about?" Khari asked, a knowing look on his face. "Sage, are you still mad at Pops because he dissed you at Dominos pizza joint?"

A grin eclipsed Marshall's face. "Speak up, Sage. Inquiring minds want to know."

Shock prevented her from speaking. Sage had never been so embarrassed. Getting drunk at the agency's New Year's Eve party two years ago and dirty dancing with the lead singer of the calypso band paled in comparison. Seeing Marshall's smug I'm-the-man expression infuriated her to the bone. "No one's angry, and I'm not jealous." *Or am I?* The question reverberated in her mind as loud as a megaphone. To deflect attention from herself, she turned to Khari and asked, "How was Oakley's?"

"It was cool. We just hung out in his basement listening to music and talking about the senior trip. Everyone's really hyped about it." Eyes narrowed in thought, he snapped his fingers. "Hey, Dad, why don't you invite Sage? She could keep you company on the slopes."

Marshall gestured toward Sage. "She's right here, son. Why don't you ask her yourself? It's *your* big weekend."

"Okay, I will." Smile in place, Khari sat down beside Sage on the bench. "Next Friday, the senior class is going to North Hill Ski Lodge. There'll be snowboarding, skiing and hiking. Saturday night is the dinner and award show. Guess who's up for Athlete of the Year?"

"That's great, Khari!" she said, with a bright smile. "Is Destiny going to be your date for the party?"

"I don't know yet."

"What did she say when you asked her?"

"I sent her a text message when I was at Oakley's, but she hasn't replied yet."

Sage frowned. "A text? Why didn't you call her?"

Khari shook his head. "Naw, it's not that serious."

"Is that what you boys do nowadays? Send girls text messages asking them out?" Marshall asked, bewildered. "You have a cell phone. Use it to talk."

"Talk? I don't have time to sit on the phone yapping. That's girl stuff. Back in your day they sent telegrams, huh, Dad?" he quipped.

Sage howled. Her uncharacteristic laugh drew the attention of both father and son. Cupping a hand over her mouth to stifle her chuckles, she jabbed Khari playfully in the ribs. "That was a good one, Khari. You're hilarious!"

"It wasn't that funny," Marshall grumbled, pulling up his jacket collar.

"Will you come? Please?" Khari begged, a hopeful look on his face.

"I'm sure your dad already invited the woman from the pizza joint, and I don't want to ruin their romantic weekend."

"Dad's on his own, unless he wants to hang out with the other chaperones, but most of them are middle-aged soccer moms."

"Then he should fit right in. He loves *older* women."

Marshall's face shriveled up like a nudist in a meat locker.

"You prefer women who bake bread from scratch and still do the Bump, don't you?" she jeered, ignoring the fiery glaze in his eyes.

"That's right. I do. Older women don't play games."

If Khari wasn't listening in, Sage would have cursed Marshall out, but since she was the mature one, she decided to take the high road. "Khari, I really hope you win Athlete of the Year. You deserve it."

"Please come," he begged, sliding down to one knee, and clasping his hands. "This year's going to be off the hook and I want you and Dad there on my big night."

Sage paused. Spending the weekend with Khari without any other sports agents popping up or calling was a golden opportunity. Her intuition told her if she went on the trip, she'd sign him. But Marshall would be there, watching her with the keen eyes of a hawk. He'd insulted her, kissed her until she saw stars, then laughed in her face. Defiance hardened her features. It was a risk, but why should she miss hanging out with Khari because Marshall didn't want her there?

Instead of accepting the invitation and thumbing her nose at Marshall, she told Khari to have a good time. "When you get back, I'll take you out to celebrate." Standing, she descended the steps, waved goodbye and hurried through the side gate.

Chapter 8

Shopping bags in hand and a catchy reggae tune in her head, Sage sailed through the sliding-glass doors of The Four Seasons Hotel. Catching sight of her reflection in the square antique mirror, she ran a hand through her hair. She looked every bit as fabulous as she felt. Her belted red coat emphasized her slender waist, and skinny jeans elongated her legs. Razor-cut bangs and the golden highlights throughout her locks emphasized her bold, trendy, uptown look.

Pausing at the front desk, she surveyed the opulent lobby. Natural sunlight splashed on the gleaming floors, water gushed from a bronze fountain and the bucketed armchairs and sofas in the waiting area invited rest and conversation.

An ultratanned woman sat near the fireplace, men clustered by the hotel bar and a family of five waited for the elevator. The doors slid open and a well-groomed man in a tailored suit emerged. Thick black hair, which Sage could imagine spilling between her fingers, tumbled across his forehead, and behind his designer eyeglasses were the bluest, richest eyes she'd ever seen.

He caught her staring, and the corners of his mouth rose in greeting. His smile pierced her like an arrow to the heart. Licking her lips, she grunted quietly. Now, that was the kind of man she should be with—someone who would wine her and dine her and look good doing it. He was obviously successful. A mover, a shaker, a man who carried plastic, not cash. Unlike that buffoon Marshall, the stranger had finesse, class, style. And she'd bet he didn't own plaid shirts or scuffed shoes.

All Marshall had going for him was that he was tall. And that he knew how to kiss. Her eyes drifted shut as memories of last night consumed her. Who knew perfection came in six-foot-six packages? And more importantly, where in the world did an ex-marine learn to kiss like that? When their lips came together she'd heard sparks crackle. It was a powerful jolt. She wanted to push him off, wanted to curse him out for touching her, but desire overpowered her like an assailant lurking in the shadows. Climbing Mount Kilimanjaro in her Jimmy Choos would've been easier than resisting his moist, supple lips and strong, eager hands.

Forcing her eyes open, she glanced around the reception area. The handsome stranger was gone. Damn that Marshall! Fantasizing about him had cost her a date with a Greek stallion. In her mind, she had pitted the two men against each other. Marshall didn't have an expense account, he couldn't whisk her away to St. Barts for the weekend and he didn't own a summer home. But what really stood out about him was not the way his eyes glowed when he was amused or his thick lips, but how much he loved his son, his family and his community.

Sage didn't know anything about the Greek stallion, but she doubted he was generous with his time or money. Jet-setting around the world, brokering deals and wooing investors left little time for humanitarian work. Or relationships. Look at Tangela. Her best friend was in love with a man who was too busy to marry her.

Inhaling the subtle scent of ginger drifting over from the hotel bar, she considered her last serious relationship. Dating accomplished men certainly had its privileges. Spur-of-the-moment trips, fine dining at celebrity hotspots and jewelry. It was too bad Antwan worked twelve-hour days and could only see her once a week. Is that what she wanted? A life of wealth and luxury but no one to share it with?

"Miss?"

"Hell, no!"

"Excuse me?"

Sage blinked. The astute-looking man behind the marble counter was frowning at her. "I'm in the Ashor suite," she explained, hoping to expunge his scowl with her smile. "Are there any messages for me?"

He consulted the computer. "No telephone messages, but there is a note here about your room. Your employer paid the charges for last week, so we will need a new credit card to bill for the remainder of your stay."

"I don't understand. Sapphire Entertainment is paying the bill."

"Correction, they were paying for it. According to our records, a Ms. Josie Unger called to say you are on your holidays and the company is no longer responsible for your lodging. You do know Ms. Unger, don't you?"

Sage nodded, realization dawning like a new day. Leo had been true to his word and had ordered his secretary to call and remove the company credit card from the bill. Great for him, but trouble for her. While the concierge answered the phone, Sage considered what to do. After blowing a thousand dollars on winter clothes, boots and accessories, she couldn't afford to charge anything else on her American Express card. And a one-month bill at an upscale hotel could buy her a used car. She thought of phoning Leo, but rejected the idea. Her boss wouldn't take her call, and even if he did, what would she say? "Pay my hotel bill. I'm broke." She didn't have a case, so why even bother?

"Do you have a corporate rate?" she asked, hopeful something could be worked out. Favoring the older gentleman with a smile, Sage twirled a lock of hair around her forefinger. "This is such a lovely hotel and the staff is so efficient. I'd hate to have to check out, but two hundred dollars a night is a little steep."

"How long do you anticipate staying?"

"Three weeks."

"Very well, then, let me see what I can do for you." Eyes focused on the computer screen, his nimble fingers flittered over the keyboard. "My apologies for the delay, Ms. Collins, but our server has been on the blink all morning."

"No problem," she told him, lowering her bags to her feet. But after three nerve-racking minutes, Sage bent over the counter and pointed at the monitor. "Is that the total?" she asked, convinced her prayers had been answered. "Two thousand dollars and eighty-two cents?"

His smile was guarded but polite. "Ms. Unger said you were on vacation."

"That's right. I am."

"Then I can't charge you the corporate rate. It's for business travelers."

"It's a working vacation," she explained, feeling the reduced rate slipping from her grasp. "You can call my boss, Mr. Leo Varick, to verify my story," she said. Aware that her boss didn't answer unknown calls, she rattled off the number to his private line and thanked the concierge profusely when he dialed.

"Hello. This is Pascal Ferdinand from The Four Seasons hotel in downtown Indianapolis. Is this Mr. Varick?" A pause, then, "He's not available. I understand. Might you be able to answer a question for me, Mr. Woodrow?"

Sage wanted to scream. Throw her head back, open her mouth and let one rip. God must have it in for her. Or get a laugh out of her misfortunes. Why else would that jerk Brian have intercepted the call?

"I'm here with one of his employees. Ms. Collins would like the corporate rate on the Astor suite, but I have to confirm that she's indeed in town on business."

Her stomach twisted in knots.

"Oh—" he lifted his eyebrows and raised his voice in surprise "—she's not here on business. She's on a *personal* holiday."

Cheeks burning with humiliation, Sage opened her wallet, extracted her Visa credit card and slapped it down on the counter. "Forget it. I don't have time to haggle over a few bucks."

To her shock, the concierge cupped a hand over the mouthpiece and said, "One moment. I'll be right with you." In response to something said, the man laughed loud and hardy. "Is that right, Mr. Woodrow?"

Another round of chuckles.

Aggravated that he was talking to Woodrow and that she was

the butt of their jokes, Sage reached across the counter, disconnected the call and leveled him with a smoldering gaze. "You
were saying?"

Lugging her suitcase from the elevator, Sage was so tired and
so hungry that her legs were beginning to give way. In her haste
to check out of the Four Seasons hotel and lug all her gear, she
had sore feet and a cramp in her left thigh.

Unsure of where her room was, she stopped in the middle of
the hall to catch her breath. Where the hell was the bellman? Five
hours ago, she had reclined in bed, eating crepes, watching the
cast of *Gossip Girl* on *The Tyra Show.* Now she was in a one-
star motel that reeked of fried chicken and Newport cigarettes.
When she pulled up to the motel entrance, there'd been no valet
to park her car. A crisp, suit-clad bellman didn't welcome her
and the overdeveloped teenage girl at the front desk was painting
her press-on nails.

Sage peered around the corner. The numbers were getting
smaller. Wrong way. Taking the right, she walked briskly down
the hall. Room doors were wide open, expelling nicotine and
cigar fumes, but she didn't dare look inside. Gangsters could be
in there plotting their next job, and Sage didn't want any trouble.

Her thoughts drifted back to that morning. When the desk
clerk had given her the total for a one-month stay, she swiped her
credit card from his hand and announced that she was checking
out. Between the hotel bill and the rental car, she was looking at
a five-thousand-dollar tab. Downgrading to a motel was the smart
thing to do, but that didn't mean she was happy with it.

Sage didn't think she could feel any worse, but after fighting
with the cheap lock and finally getting the door open, she saw a
mouse skip across the bedroom floor and dive underneath the
bed. Swallowing a scream, she took a deep, calming breath and
told herself to get a grip. She had to look at the bigger picture.
This time next month, she'd be executive manager at Sapphire
Entertainment and thousands of dollars richer. Resigned to being
miserable for the rest of her time in Indianapolis, but more confident than ever that she would be promoted, she examined the
room for any other unwelcome creatures.

Leaving her things in the hall, but keeping an eye out for thugs, gangsters and thieves, she marched over to the rickety-looking desk, snatched up the phone and dialed the operator. On the sixth ring, a man with a heavy southern accent answered. "Luxe Motel. Chip speaking."

His voice was thick with sleep. Or boredom. Sage couldn't say for sure. "I just saw a mouse skid—"

"Room number?"

"Um—" Sage peered at the gold plates on the door. "Three twenty-eight."

In the silence, she heard muffled voices and the faint sound of country music. "Come back down to the front desk and I'll give you a new room key."

"Can't you send the bellboy up?"

He chuckled. "The bellboy? We don't have a bellboy, ma'am. This isn't one of those fancy-shmancy downtown hotels."

"Who are you tellin'?" she mumbled, wishing she could click her heels three times and end this nightmare. "I'll be right down."

Thirty minutes later, Sage threw herself across the tacky, heart-shaped bed in the honeymoon suite. It had taken some convincing, but after threatening to call city building inspectors, Chip had agreed to upgrade her room free of charge. There were no Belgian chocolates on the desk, or crisp, fluffy towels in the bathroom, but she was saving money by staying at the motel, and that was all that mattered.

Sighing deeply, she wondered how things could have gone so terribly wrong. Two weeks ago, she was at Tangela and Warrick's house, sipping a fruit smoothie by the pool, and now she was in blistery, cold Indianapolis with frostbitten ears, three thousand dollars poorer. She hadn't signed Khari yet, other celeb managers were breathing down her neck like damn bloodhounds and to make matters worse, she had played tongue hockey with Marshall Grant. Could things get any uglier?

Sage took in her surroundings. Apart from the bed and the chair standing beside the TV, the room was empty. No fridge, no DVD player, no walk-in closet. Depressed at the thought of spending a month in this unsightly room, Sage stared outside the window. From the third floor, she had a clear view of Pacific Laundromat. She sighed.

Fleecy clouds sailed across the sky and the sun was making its descent. Without warning, her thoughts turned to Marshall. And if that wasn't bad enough, she could smell his cologne, hear his deep, rumbling laugh and feel his lips against her ear.

Rolling onto her back, she forced him from her mind. But memories of the Las Vegas sunshine, the Greek stallion from the Four Seasons hotel, and even scrubbing toilets at Ms. Claxton's house, didn't erase his image. He haunted her like Patrick Swayze in *Ghost,* and looked damn good doing it.

Sitting up, she unzipped her boots and shrugged them off. She was in a dingy thirty-dollar-a-night motel, fantasizing about a surly parole officer who liked wearing plaid. How fitting.

Sleep tugged at her eyes, pulling them shut. Patting back a yawn, she checked the time on her watch. Eight-thirty. She'd sleep for an hour then see about getting dinner. Her days of ordering room service were over. And not just because the motel didn't have any. Her Sign Khari Grant Fund had been cut in half and she was in town for another month. Eating out and getting weekly pedicures was killing her bank account. From now on she'd have to learn to do without and be a lot smarter with her money.

The blanket felt like cardboard against her skin, but she wrapped it around her shoulders and snuggled against the pillows, pretending they were Marshall's arms.

The distinctive voice of Bob Marley and the pounding, scratchy rhythm of his guitar filled the room. The sun pressed against the curtains, bathing the motel room with its gentle rays. Momentarily disorientated, Sage opened her eyes and propped herself up on her elbows. A quick glance around the room confirmed she wasn't at the Four Seasons hotel and that her dream had been a cruel joke. Stretching her lazy muscles loose, she hummed along with the catchy ring tone. It didn't matter how low she felt, one Bob Marley song and she was ready to face the world. Spotting her handbag on the floor, she bent down and retrieved her ringing cell phone from the side pocket. "Hello?"

"Sage?"

"Khari?" she asked, immediately recognizing the teen's voice. "What's up?"

"Am I bothering you?"

"No, not at all. I was just getting up from my nap."

"Nap?" His tone was doubtful. "It's nine-thirty."

"In the morning?"

"Uh-huh."

"Shit! I slept in my makeup!" Phone at her ear, she threw off the blanket and flew into the bathroom. As suspected, her hair was sticking up in every direction, her eyelashes were clumped with mascara and she had drool stains on her wool House of Dereon sweater. "Great. Now I look like a stylish raccoon."

Khari laughed. "I'm just calling to remind you about today."

"What about it?"

"You're still coming, right?"

"Where?"

"To my house."

Sage frowned. "What for?"

"To help me with my essay, remember?"

"Shit, I forgot!"

"I could really use your help," he confessed, his voice losing its warmth. "I've been working on it all morning and all I have is the title."

"Where's your dad?"

"He's here. Do you want to talk to him?"

"No! I was just curious. And please don't tell him I asked."

"All right. But you're gonna come, right, Sage?"

"Sit tight, Khari. I'll be there in twenty minutes." Peering into the mirror, she inspected the pimple on her forehead. Last night, she'd felt too miserable and too lethargic to get up and shower and now her skin was paying the price. Grabbing the tube of toothpaste and squirting some on the blemish, she said, "Better make that an hour."

Chapter 9

"Read it," Sage ordered, shooting Khari a don't-mess-with-me look.

"No way. I've embarrassed myself enough for one day."

"I don't care how bad you think it is, I want to hear it."

"It sucks, trust me."

"Let me be the judge of that." Sage sipped her tea, savoring the heady aroma and rich taste. After a terse greeting, Marshall had placed a tray with tea and cookies on the dining-room table, then escaped upstairs. He'd struck the perfect blend of vanilla, cinnamon and nutmeg, resulting in one seriously delicious drink. "Khari, go on."

"Are you sure?" he questioned, rearranging the sheets of loose-leaf paper. "It still needs a lot of work. This is just a rough draft and—"

"Go on, boy. Let me hear it." Sage gave him a reassuring smile. When he started reading, she broke an oatmeal cookie in half and popped it in her mouth. She had arrived at the house hours ago, but she and Khari had done more talking than writing.

The scent of men's aftershave settled over the room. Sage heard footsteps behind her and turned around just in time to see Marshall exit the den. In a navy blue knit sweater and corduroy pants, he had the commanding presence of a general and had the stern, antagonistic expression to match. His bulging shoulders strained against the material, and wisps of hair sprinkled his forearms. Wallet in hand, he crossed the living-room floor and retrieved his jacket from the closet.

Staring openly, Sage revisited that head-spinning kiss. There was no way she had imagined that jolt, that spark, that fire. It was immediate and powerful, and she had never connected with anyone that intensely or that quickly before. Not even with Jeremy, and she'd thought he was "the one." But those were the foolish, whimsical thoughts of a nineteen-year-old girl looking for love in all the wrong places.

Examining the sensuous curve of his lips and his creamy brown skin, she toyed with the diamond bracelet on her wrist. If he felt something, which she was convinced he had, why hadn't he said anything? Outside on the deck after the kiss, she'd insulted him, but that wasn't reason enough for him to ignore her now. After all, she was a guest in his home. He should be hospitable, warm, charming, not mute, angry and cold. Pondering the reason behind his silence, she watched him lace up his boots. He had strong, slender fingers that she could feel flitting over her stomach and slipping between her legs. Sage grabbed ahold of her thoughts, but couldn't help noting the astonishing length of his feet. If her coworker, Cashmere, was here they'd be whispering behind their hands, debating the significance of a man's shoe size and his endowment. Passionate, opinionated and a self-proclaimed man-slayer, the petite powerhouse would argue fervently why she believed the myth to be true. And if Cashmere knew anything, it was about how to impress and seduce and trap the opposite sex.

Sage lifted her gaze to Marshall's face. He was watching her. Their eyes held, then greeted each other with a smile. If he thought he was going to pressure her into looking away, he was wrong. Men faltered under her gaze. Professional athletes, ruthless defense attorneys and some of Hollywood's leading men had fallen victim to her come-and-get-me stare in the past, and Marshall Grant was no exception.

The corners of his mouth flared into a slow, easy grin, lighting her inner fire and challenging her to respond to his invitation.

Bright-eyed with desire, she leaned forward, loving the way he was watching her.

"That's all I have so far. What did you think?"

Eyes set on Marshall, but responding to Khari's question she said, "You did a great job capturing the essence of Hamlet's character, and I like how you described him as being blinded by revenge. But you missed an important piece of the puzzle."

"I did?" he asked, pouring over his notes. "I covered all four themes. Deception, passion, corruption and revenge. I'm not missing anything."

"You are." Pausing for affect, she lifted the mug to her lips and took a sip. "Hamlet was crazier than Lorena Bobbitt with a pair of garden shears!"

Marshall's laugh rocked the room.

Khari scratched his head. "Who's Lorena Bobbitt?"

"Never mind that," Sage said, facing him now. "From the beginning of the play, Hamlet is melancholy and despondent, and he never really seems to break out of his funk. And the people around him are all vindictive opportunists who in some way or another contribute to his madness." Picking up one of the Shakespeare books spread out on the table, she slowly flipped through it. "Khari, don't ever underestimate the power of the human mind. Mess with a guy's head and you've halfway won the battle."

"Wow, that's deep." He scribbled furiously in his notebook.

A cell phone chimed. Khari pushed back his chair and stood. "I'll be right back."

Sage watched Khari leave the room, then turned her sights back on Marshall. "You were so quiet I almost forgot you were here," she lied, dusting cookie crumbs off the table. "Have anything to add to the discussion?"

"Do you really believe that?" he asked, folding his arms across his chest.

"Believe what?"

"Mess with a guy's head and you've halfway won the battle."

"Always works for me." Allowing herself a wry smile, she shrugged her shoulders nonchalantly. "I don't make the rules, Marshall. I just call it as I see it."

"You strike me as a woman who's played a mind game or two."

"Haven't we all?"

Marshall laughed.

"Where are you heading off to? Got a hot date?"

"Not unless it's with you."

Sage didn't know what to say. Awareness dawned, forcing her to reevaluate her plan. This was it. Her last chance to make something happen. She had to sign Khari this week or her reputation was toast. "So, no hot date."

"Not at my Wal-Mart store." He broke into a laugh. "I'm going to get some stuff for Senior Weekend. Do you want to tag along?"

"I can't. We're not finished up here and I promised Khari I'd take him to the mall and help him pick out a gift for Destiny's birthday."

"I really appreciate you helping Khari. He's never had a woman he could talk to about girls and stuff." Marshall wore a thoughtful look. "You're in town on business, but instead of relaxing at the hotel this weekend, or hustling the guys down at Champions for donations and talking about the importance of philanthropy, you're helping my son with his homework. Thanks, Sage. It means a lot to me."

Sage laughed. "You don't have to thank me. Khari's a great kid. And for the record, I'm not a hustler. I just like to win at darts!"

Laughter passed between them and swallowed up the sexual tension hovering over the living room.

Standing, her gaze fell across the window. Snow flurries blanketed the sky, coating the trees and bushes. Icicles glistened from rooftops and Irvington Lane was encrusted in a thin layer of ice. "I can't believe it's snowing again," she scoffed. The rental car was submerged under a mountain of snow and the entire neighborhood was covered with the white, fluffy powder. "Does it ever not snow in this town?"

"No."

"Is that why you live here, because you like the cold weather? I'd think, after living in somewhere as hot as Kuwait, you'd hanker for the sunshine."

"I love winter sports. I learned to ski when I was around Khari's age and took up snowboarding a few years back. There's nothing like it. The speed, the buzz, the adrenaline rush." His voice grew deep. "But don't get me wrong. I love the heat too. The hotter the better."

Goose bumps pricked her arm. Sage glanced over her shoulder, expecting him to be behind her. He was. So close she could smell his minty breath. She felt naked, exposed, the heat of his gaze searing her with its intensity. Her first inclination was to kiss him, her second was to beg him to kiss her. Stepping forward, he reached out and touched a hand to her waist. Heart racing with anticipation, she leaned forward, grazing her chest purposely across his. If he could be aggressive, so could she.

"About last night…"

"What about it?" she challenged, her eyes lingering on his lips.

"I shouldn't have kissed you."

"You're right. You shouldn't have."

"I'm sorry."

"It was just a kiss." One scrumptious, delicious kiss. But that went unsaid. "It's no big deal. Forget it happened. I know I have."

"Do you usually go around kissing men you've just met?"

"No, of course not."

"Then why me?"

Sage felt cornered, trapped, confused, like a cub in a hunter's snare. "It was impulsive, stupid. It won't happen again."

"It won't?" His tone was thick, evocative, rich with suggestion.

The chemistry between them crackled like logs in a fireplace. Shocked by the sheer strength of their attraction, she stepped back, hopeful the physical distance would bring clarity. "Khari's going to be back any minute now."

"I doubt it. When that kid gets on the phone, there's no stopping him. Do you have any plans tonight?"

Her tongue went limp and she struggled to make it work again. What was it about this man that made her want to dive under the coffee table for cover? "No, no plans. Just back to the hotel to sleep." She added, "Alone. Back to the hotel to sleep *alone.*"

"Do you want some company?"

"No!" flew out of her mouth, but when she saw the startled expression on his face, she wore a small smile. "That's a bad idea."

"It is? Two friends can't hang out after dark?"

She hedged, her thoughts circling out of control, stealing her resolve. This was all too much. Marshall smelled divine, his eyes were filled with promise and he was stroking her arm. There was only so much a woman could take. Temptation was a bitch, toying with her mind, inciting her desire, leaving her hot and bothered. "Marshall…we can't do this. Not today. Not ever." Every word was a fight, a fight to do the right thing, a fight to preserve what little dignity she had left.

"Are you sure I can't stop by later? For a nightcap?"

Sage wanted to be alone with him, wanted to feel his touch, wanted to experience another one of those sweet, sensuous kisses, but she couldn't invite him to her nasty, fried-chicken-smelling motel. One whiff of the Luxe Motel and he'd crash through the emergency doors. It would be a different story if she was still at the Four Seasons hotel. Or would it? Biting down on her bottom lip, she shook off the thought. No Marshall, no nightcap and no more kisses. It was bad enough she'd lied and schemed her way into his life. Having a tryst with him now would complicate matters and compound her guilt. She was living a whopper of a lie and it was only a matter of time before the truth caught up with her. "Quit hanging out with Denzel," she said, sweeping her bangs off her forehead. "His bad habits are starting to rub off on you."

Marshall chuckled. "If you want to blame somebody for my behavior, blame yourself. I haven't been the same since we met."

Sage wore a provocative smile. "Is that right?"

Nodding, he brushed his mouth against her cheek, blazing a trail down her warm skin. "We both agree. We're completely wrong for each other. But that doesn't mean we can't hang out while you're in town."

"And what exactly does hanging out entail?"

"Dinners, movies and chaperoning Senior Weekend."

"I can't."

"Do you have to work?"

"No." Sage fumbled for an excuse. Better not to encourage

him, or make him think she liked him. Even if she did. A little.
"I don't know how to ski."

"There's more to do at North Hill than ski. You can go hiking,
lounge at the fireplace with a good book or treat yourself to a
massage in the spa."

Now, *that* sounded like a plan. Chaperoning Senior Weekend
was risky, but her weatherbeaten body was crying out for some
R & R. Unaccustomed to frostbite and arctic temperatures, she
desperately needed the skilled hands of a masseuse, an estheti-
cian and a manicurist. And if she accompanied the senior class
to North Hill, there was no question in her mind that she'd sign
Khari. "How much?"

"That's the best part. Chaperones are free. Your meals and
lodging are taken care of for the entire weekend. All you're responsible for is your entertainment and any extras you want."
Sage angled her shoulders in his direction and Marshall drew her
close. "But just so you know, I give one hell of a hot oil massage.
And it will only cost you—"

He lifted his gaze to the kitchen door.

"It'll only cost me what?" she asked, resisting the urge to
drape her arms around his neck. One kiss and she was panting like
a Doberman in heat. Her intuition told her Marshall didn't want
money, but something more private, more personal, more
intimate.

Chapter 10

At 5:00 a.m. on Friday morning, ten luxury buses bearing the Sky Light Tours logo stood outside of Westchester Academy, lined up against the snow-packed curb. In the adjoining parking lot, kids bolted from cars, bleary-eyed fathers heaved luggage, skis and snowboards onto the pavement and a band of teenage boys tossed around a football.

"See you guys later!" Khari jumped out of the Jeep SUV. He was sprinting toward the school before either of them could reply.

"Isn't this trip just for seniors?" Sage asked, clicking off her seat belt and glancing at Marshall. "It looks like the whole school is here!"

"Ready for the trip?" he asked, relinquishing his hold on the steering wheel.

"You have no idea. Today couldn't come fast enough." It was another wickedly cold day in Indianapolis, but nothing could dampen her spirits. The orange-hued sun was creeping over the horizon and vibrant shades of burgundy, pink and magenta were splashed across the morning sky. "You were holding out on me, Marshall. I looked up the resort on my laptop last night, and not only is it the only five-star ski lodge in the state, it's only an hour and a half from Chicago. We should zip down to the Windy City and have lunch at Pizzeria Due restaurant."

"You'd drive ninety minutes for pizza?"

"Sure would." His eyes widened in shock and Sage laughed. "Don't look at me like I'm crazy. Wait until you try their Chicken Fajita Deep Dish Pizza. One bite and you'll be begging for more!"

"I'll have to take your word for it." His words, though innocent, made her body weak in all the right places. Sitting in the car a mere breath away from him was a temptation she just didn't need. She was staring openly and there was no mistaking the sheer, magnetic hunger in his gorgeous, almond-brown eyes.

"Oh, I almost forgot." Marshall took out his wallet, produced a slip of paper and handed it to her. "Here's your confirmation number. I tried to get you a room on the same floor as the group, but the lodge is fully booked."

"No problem. That means I won't have to listen to giggly teenage girls all night."

Laughing, Sage opened the passenger door and stepped out of the Jeep SUV. If she was going to keep her head and not repeat the scene out on the porch, she had to put physical space between them. And if that didn't work, she'd sprint like hell. There was no shame in running, especially when lust had you in its erotic grip.

Sage went around to the trunk and grabbed her suitcase. Appearing beside her, Marshall reached in, covering her hand with his own. "Let me. A woman as beautiful as you has no business carrying her own luggage."

A bolt of excitement zipped up her back. Sage lifted her eyes to meet his gaze, convinced that he had felt it too. Her whole body ached to touch him, to feel the tenderness of his kiss and the warmth of his hands. It was all she could think about these days. "I'm used to taking care of myself," she told him, her eyes circling the parking lot. "I've been doing it since I was a kid."

"I know, but let me help you out. Makes me feel useful," he said with a chuckle. "It won't be long before Khari's carting me off to some old folks home."

Sage smiled up at him, loving the twinkle in his eyes, his scent and the delicious sound of his laugh. "You're talking crazy. You're only thirty-seven. That's not old."

"Oh, yes, it is. I have the gray hairs to prove it!"

They laughed together.

"Do you mind taking my bags to the bus? I've gotta go to the ladies room."

"No problem." He checked his watch. "We're on bus number eight and it leaves in fifteen minutes."

"I'll meet you there."

Inside the school washroom, Sage studied her reflection in the mirror. Popping a peppermint candy into her mouth, she sprayed a vanilla-scented mist onto her brush and dragged it through her hair. She and Marshall would be in close quarters for the next five hours and she wanted to make sure her breath smelled minty fresh and every hair was in place. Her whole career was riding on this weekend. It was do or die, and she had no intention of failing. If she signed Khari, she would use her raise to square her debts and to buy a house. No more renting. Finally she would have a place to call her own. She didn't want a mansion, just a spacious master bedroom, a handsome kitchen and a wide-open porch like the one Marshall had.

Marshall. There he was invading her thoughts again. Refusing to revisit their kiss, she grabbed her handbag, threw open the bathroom door and walked briskly down the hall. The once-crowded field was virtually empty, and only two buses remained in the parking lot. Wishing her purse wasn't weighed down with fashion magazines and CDs, she increased her pace. On the bus, she took the empty seat beside Marshall.

"Want some?" Marshall held a Kit Kat candy bar in his outstretched hand.

"No, thanks."

"Come on," he urged, his lips twisted in a crooked smile. "You know you want some. Two weeks ago you beat the crap out of the vending machine for one of these. It's your favorite."

"I can't eat that now. It isn't even nine o'clock!"

"Has that ever stopped you before?" He ripped off the wrapper and waved a stick under her nose. "Smells good, doesn't it?"

"Since you insist," she replied, snatching it from his hands and devouring a stick in three giant bites. "Mmm..." she cooed, licking the chocolate from her fingers. "I hope you have more, because once I get started, I just can't stop!"

Marshall swallowed a groan. Her mouth was smeared with chocolate and he could smell the sweet aroma on her lips. Imagining her naked, sprawled out on his platform bed, lathered in chocolate syrup, made his throat tight and his palms slick. Why was he tormenting himself like this? Not only was she accustomed to a life of wealth, she lived in Las Vegas, viewed long-term relationships as a death trap and she didn't have a college degree. Four credits shy of graduation, she had dropped out of school, moved to Sin City and took a job at a marketing agency. It was hard to believe that a girl from the ghetto, who grew up in foster care, had grown up to be a flamboyant spender with expensive tastes. Sage liked designer clothes, fast cars and living on the edge. And according to the self-proclaimed thrill-seeker, the riskier the adventure, the better.

Marshall used to live on the edge, but those days were long behind him. He was a father, an upstanding citizen, a do-gooder. What would his family and friends think if they knew he was cavorting with a younger woman? Okay, so he wasn't Hugh Heffner and she wasn't forty years his junior, but there were years and years of life experience between them. And he now had Khari to think about and set an example for; he didn't want any distractions.

Eyebrows spiked when he had introduced Sage to the other parent volunteers, and Mrs. Abongwa, a sharp-tongued mother of two, had muttered under her breath. Peering at the front of the bus, where the woman now sat, Marshall wondered if she was whispering about him to the chemistry teacher. Eighty-seven students, parents and teachers filled the luxury buses, and aside from Steve Harvey's animated voice streaming out of the driver's radio, the cabin was quiet. Khari sat two rows ahead, but like the other passengers onboard, he was snoring to the gentle chug of the bus.

"Thanks, Marshall. That really hit the spot."

He brought his gaze back to her. A chocolate stain dotted her chin.

"What? Why are you staring at me like that?"

Plagued by a sheer, almost primitive desire, he stamped out

the sinful thoughts ruling his mind and body. If he was going to make it through this weekend with his reputation intact, he had to stop daydreaming about making love to her.

"What? Do I have something on my face?" Licking her lips, she cleaned the corners of her mouth with her fingertips. "If Khari wakes up and sees me like this, he'll clown me for the rest of the trip. Is it gone?" she asked, presenting her face for inspection.

It was still there.

"Well?"

Not trusting himself to speak, he reached out and cleaned away the spot with his thumb. She didn't smack his hand away, didn't tell him to back off and didn't recoil in disgust. Marshall slipped a hand around her shoulders. It was meant to be a caring gesture, but it elevated his anxiety. They sat staring, locked in the moment, each intimately aware of the other. Time ceased to exist. Seconds slipped into minutes, but they remained fixated on each other, a pair of real-life statues. Moved by the strength of her perfume, he leaned over and stroked her cheek with his thumb, surprised that such a simple act could elevate his desire.

"Thanks, Marshall." Favoring him with a smile, she dropped her voice to a sultry whisper, her full lips grazing his ear. "Do you have any other hidden talents, because I sure could use a foot rub."

Proving to himself that he wasn't turned on by her blatant come-ons, he reached out and affectionately squeezed her thigh. "You know where to find me."

Chapter 11

Marshall watched Sage tie up her hiking boots. Her pants looked like they were holding on to her ass for dear life, and he wasn't the only one admiring her delicious shape. Three married men were practically frothing at the mouth. Their wives, perfectly plump stay-at-home moms, were at the back of the group, chatting merrily about baking recipes, the season finale of *Desperate Housewives* and their teenage daughters.

An ambitious group of nature lovers, high on fresh air and sunshine, were enjoying an afternoon hike on Black Bear Mountain. The must-see view, with its tall, majestic mountains and pristine wilderness was a real-life postcard. Marshall had explored the trail countless times over the years and had every intention of spending the afternoon out on the slopes, but when he saw Sage sign up for the hike, he'd quickly followed suit. The gondola ride was the highlight of the tour, and being alone with Sage in the most romantic place in the resort was too tempting to pass up.

Khari was snowboarding with his friends and Marshall didn't care if he saw his son again for the rest of the weekend. Usually, he kept a protective eye on Khari, but he'd never had a female guest before. And there was no mistake about it, Sage was *his* guest.

Owen Cunningham, the only other single father in the group,

had latched on to Sage the moment he saw her, and didn't seem to care what anyone thought. The man had the nose of a blood-hound when it came to sniffing out beautiful women. He'd already put the moves on the tour guide, a female ski instructor and now Sage.

Marshall eyed the pair and quickly surmised that Owen was a threat. A big threat. The divorced father was a self-made man who had made his millions the easy way. Born into a family of extreme wealth and prestige, the fortysomething entrepreneur owned a fleet of high-end apartment suites and office buildings. His name was synonymous with high living, and in the past Marshall had seen the businessman work his charms on several of the single mothers in the group.

Marshall thought of rescuing Sage, but decided against it. She'd think he was jealous. And he was. He just didn't want to show it. Besides, Owen Cunningham had a better chance of winning the state lottery than scoring with Sage. She had better taste than that. And it would take a lot more than smooth pickup lines and a flashy gold Rolex watch to win over the gorgeous World Mission executive. Or so he hoped.

With much difficulty, he tore his eyes away from her curva-ceous body and stared up at the clear, wide-open sky. But a second later, he was back at it. This time, he chose to admire her long, slim legs. Sage Collins was a contradiction. Tomboy and girlie at the same time. Chic but overdressed, the short, fur-hooded coat, body-molding pants and brown equestrian-type boots emphasized her youthfulness and expensive tastes.

Sage glanced over her shoulder, caught him staring at her and stuck out her tongue. Her eyes were bright with laughter and she wore a mischievous expression on her face. Smiling ruefully, he shook his head. Sage was fun, lively and no stranger to trouble. Everything his ex-wife used to be. And not only did both women have wide, sensuous lips and an infectious laugh, they had the same quirky mannerisms. Memories long buried surfaced.

He'd met Roxanne at the local bowling alley, and though they went to rival high schools, he'd fallen hard for her. Skipping class, making out in the backseat of his car and spending hours on the phone became a way of life. They were young and in love and all was right with the world. And when Marshall got a taste of his first orgasm, he was like a kid in a candy store. He couldn't get enough.

They even went to the same college. It was a humid afternoon the August before their sophomore year when he picked Roxanne up from her part-time job at Burger World and noticed her tear-stained cheeks. Long-faced and subdued, she stared out the passenger window, refusing to answer his questions. After pestering her for three quarters of an hour, she finally broke her silence. Eyes filled with tears, she cleaned her runny nose with the back of her hand and said, "I'm pregnant." He lost control of the car and ended up in the ditch.

Hoping and praying the home pregnancy test was wrong, he accompanied her to the walk-in clinic the following day. Convinced this was nothing more than a scare, he assured her she wasn't pregnant and vowed to be more careful from now on. But when the doctor entered the room, Marshall knew. Knew that Roxanne was pregnant, knew that he was going to be a father, knew that his life would never be the same. Then seeing Roxanne waste away. In the blink of an eye, he'd lost everything. His hopes, his dreams, his future. Gone. Like a puff of smoke.

For as long as Marshall lived, he'd never forget the look on his dad's face when he told him Roxanne was pregnant. Eyes filled with disappointment, shoulders slumped, he'd rubbed his hands over his weathered face. Even now, seventeen years later, Marshall could still hear the anguish in his father's voice when he said, "How could you have let something like this happen, son? Do you know what you've done?"

The ferocity of the wind and the sound of rustling trees jarred Marshall out of his thoughts. Sage and Owen were now at the front of the pack, miles ahead of the other hikers. Five more minutes and they'd be at the information center. Once the group stopped for water and bathroom breaks, he'd swoop down, steer Sage over to the tower and buy their tickets for the gondola ride.

Thought you said she was too young? Marshall ignored the voice, wishing he had never made her age, or rather, the lack of it, an issue. His problem was and always had been that he had a tendency to overanalyze situations, to dissect things from every angle and from every side, no matter how straightforward. It was a skill he had acquired as a sharpshooter, but it was a useless and taxing trait for everyday life and annoyed his friends and family to no end.

His gaze slid over her pretty mouth and delicate cheekbones. Even in fuzzy earmuffs and burly scarf she was still a beauty. And he wasn't scared to admit that he wanted her. And from now on, he wasn't going to analyze his feelings for her to death. Sage was a cosmopolitan woman, terribly independent and had the power to play men like the strings on a fiddle. Look at Owen. He was tripping over himself trying to impress her. But could he blame him? He'd be doing the same thing if he were in his shoes. Hell, he already had been! He'd fallen victim to his desire and kissed her and there was no question in his mind it would happen again.

"How'd you meet her?"

Marshall glanced to his left. It was Eddie Romano, one of the married gawkers.

"You find her on one of those online dating sites?"

Not wanting to divulge too much, he shrugged dismissively. "We met through friends." It was true. If Denzel hadn't approached Sage at Champions Sports Bar, he never would have seen her. *Are you sure?* his inner voice asked, challenging his recollection of the night in question. Why was he lying to himself? He'd noticed Sage the second he'd walked into the bar. How could anyone miss those smoky eyes, that Colgate-white smile and that bangin' body?

"The girl's young, huh? Can't be much older than your boy."

"She's legal, if that's what you're asking."

"You guys sharing a room?"

"No," Marshall replied, annoyed. Just because their son played basketball on the same team, it didn't give Eddie license to pry.

"Since she came with you, I assumed you were a couple."

"Well, we're not. And even if we were, we still wouldn't be sharing a room. What kind of message would I be sending my son if I spent the whole weekend holed up in a suite with a woman?"

"Back in the day, I would have acted a fool for a honey like that." He glanced around for his wife. "I still do sometimes. Just don't tell Ana."

"Married or not, she's way too young for you. Didn't you just turn forty?"

"And?" Eddie scratched his bearded chin. "Young girls are the best girls. Their biological clocks aren't ticking, they don't have an agenda, and as long as you wine 'em and dine 'em, they're happier than a married man at a strip club!"

"Your point is?" Marshall asked, knowing full well what Eddie was getting at, but wanting to hear the construction foreman say it.

"I have to spell it out?" he retorted, furrowing his bushy eyebrows. "You better jump on that before someone else does! Owen didn't waste any time stepping to her, and now she's laughing at his stale jokes."

Marshall had been so busy talking to Eddie, he'd lost sight of Sage. His eyes panned the crowd outside of the information center, but came up empty. Huffing vigorously, he increased his pace and climbed to the top of the hill. Hikers stood in clumps, guzzling water, children raced around tables, and tour guides shepherded sightseers through the woods.

Inside the information center, he combed the main floor for Sage. As he exited the second-floor gift shop, he spotted her in the slow-moving line for the gondola ride. In a fuchsia jacket, and oversize hoop earrings, she stood out like a beauty contestant in a Wal-Mart store. Owen was beside her, a grin on his lips and a hand on the slope of her back. The notorious skirt-chaser had designs on Sage, and though Marshall didn't like it, there was nothing he could do. He couldn't storm over and pull her away, no matter how much he wanted to.

There was nothing like a young, spontaneous woman to make a man feel alive. Marshall didn't know if it was fact or fiction, but he intended to find out.

"Paging Sage Collins to the information booth. Sage Collins."

"Shoot, that's me!" Sage turned to Owen. "I gotta go."

"I'll come with you."

"No need. You're at the front of the line. Go on. I'll see you later," she said, slipping out of the line and shouldering her way through the crowd. Her thoughts went to Tangela. They had talked yesterday, and though her friend sounded good, things had gotten worse with Warrick. Her heart hammered in fear. Something was wrong. It had to be. Why else would Tangela call the resort? Was this her punishment for lying to Marshall? Convinced that her best friend had met with an accident and was hooked up to machines and monitors in a Las Vegas hospital, she dashed into the already jam-packed elevator.

"I'm Sage Collins. Someone just paged me," she said breathlessly, reaching the information desk.

The redhead behind the counter pointed to the right. "That guy over there in the bomber jacket was looking for you."

Sage did a slow turn. Marshall was sitting in the coffee shop, wearing a sheepish grin. Shock quickly gave way to relief. Her overactive mind had scared the living daylights out of her. No one was hurt and no one was dying. Tangela was alive and well, but could she say the same about herself?

Marshall was making it increasingly difficult for her to keep her eyes on the prize. First, he'd flirted with her at Champions Sports Bar, then he'd kissed her, and last Sunday at dinner, he'd made her laugh so hard, she'd popped the button on her jeans. How was she supposed to resist him when he kept pursuing her?

"What was that all about?" she asked, approaching the table. "When I heard my name over the intercom I thought it was an emergency."

"I'm sorry. I didn't mean to scare you. Why don't you sit and take a load off for a while?" He motioned to the mugs topped with whipped cream and the plate of gooey pastries. "I thought you might enjoy a midmorning snack."

She inhaled the fragrant aroma of cinnamon and sugar, and right on cue, her stomach grumbled. Eyeing him warily, she took a seat across from him and helped herself to an apple turnover. "You know, I was about to go for a gondola ride when you paged me."

Feigning surprise, he selected a multigrain bagel and took a hearty bite. "I didn't realize you and Owen had made plans."

"No plans. He asked and I said yes." Seconds passed before

either one of them spoke. "I didn't realize you were keeping tabs on me."

"Is Owen the kind of guy you usually date?"

"I'd hate to think I have a specific type, but I am attracted to educated, ambitious men." Smiling like she'd just won a million dollars, she said innocently, "Why? Does seeing me with Owen bother you?"

"That man is old enough to be your father," he grumbled. "And I bet Mr. Hot Shot didn't tell you he has a daughter your age or that he's had a string of trophy wives."

"Careful, Marshall," she warned in a singsong voice, "you're starting to sound like a knife-wielding ex. You're not jealous, are you?"

"Should I be?"

"Didn't your mother ever tell you not to answer a question with a question?"

"I must have missed that lesson."

"Remind me to slap you later," she joked, kicking him playfully under the table.

Marshall busted a gut. Relieved that she wasn't angry about the stunt he'd pulled, he moved his chair closer to hers. Twenty minutes ago, paging her to the information booth had seemed like an ingenious idea, but now he saw the plot for what it was: a silly ploy to win the girl. What was it about Sage that made him lose his God-given sense?

They sat in the coffee shop for the rest of the morning, drinking, eating and swapping childhood stories. A casual observer would have mistaken them for newlyweds and the thought made Marshall smile. Her assertive, gutsy attitude got to him every time, and it wasn't long before he was reaching across the table and caressing her hands. Wanting more of her sweet, enticing scent, he leaned closer to her over the table. He loved the way she smelled. The feminine fragrance overwhelmed him, but he didn't pull away.

"I'm going to need your help with something," he announced, wishing she didn't look and sound and smell so much like the woman of his dreams. "I was hoping you could help me plan Khari's surprise birthday party."

"Me?" she asked, jabbing a finger to her chest. "Surely there's someone else more qualified for the job."

"My mom offered to give me a hand, but when she suggested we do a Spider-Man theme, I knew I had to ask you. Besides, I bet you've organized hundreds of fund-raising events for World Mission. This will be a piece of cake for someone with your experience."

Sage smiled. "I'm flattered."

"Does that mean you'll do it?"

"Sure, why not?" Leaning forward in her chair, she put down her mug and asked him about the time and venue. Full of enthusiasm and energy, Sage chatted about the menu, the music and decorations. Marshall was impressed. He'd asked for her help five minutes ago and she already had a wealth of ideas brewing in her mind. "What's the budget for the party?"

"How does two hundred sound?"

"Like a backyard barbecue with fries and hotdogs."

"That's not enough?" he questioned.

"Make it five hundred and we're in business."

"That's a lot of money for one night."

"You only turn eighteen once, right?"

As Marshall listened to her, he found himself thinking about that kiss. Desire pulsed through his veins, stealing his concentration. His eyes lingered on her lips, then slipped down to her chest and crept down her legs. Sage Collins was the ultimate femme fatale. She was sexy, erotic and hopelessly naughty. Every man's dream and every woman's nightmare. And she was with him.

Meeting a woman as free-spirited as Sage was a welcome change. Vivacious was the perfect word to describe her, and the thought of making love to someone bold and daring thrilled him. As much as he hated to agree with Eddie, the construction foreman was right. Women his age had weddings, babies and nurseries on the brain. Who cared if she was younger? They were here, together, enjoying each other's company. Why not make the most of the opportunity? She was only in town to find corporate donors for World Mission, but she had agreed to chaperone Senior Weekend at a moment's notice. That *had* to count for something.

Rising from his chair, he helped Sage with her coat. He concealed a slow-forming grin. This was good, clean, harmless fun, and Marshall had a sneaking suspicion she'd love the chase.

Chapter 12

The gondola chugged out of the tower, climbing steadily toward the heavens. Eagles soared boldly in the sky, flaunting their speed and matchless grace. Small, confined spaces usually terrified Sage, but with Marshall beside her, surrounded by the snow-capped mountains, thick fleecy clouds and crystal blue skies, it created a peaceful background.

Dumbstruck by the breathtaking view, Sage peered out the side window. "It's gorgeous," she gushed, pressing her hands against the glass. "Isn't it the most beautiful thing you've ever seen?"

"It pales in comparison to you."

Sage didn't dare turn around. His voice had deepened to a rich, silky hue and she could feel the smoke in his eyes. The tantalizing mixture of their fragrances filled the cramped space. Driving out all thoughts of kissing him, she focused her gaze on the twisting hillsides and ice-slick trails. "We're hundreds of feet up, but everything looks so clear. I can see skiers, a kid eating snow and even—"

Marshall reached for her, stealing the rest of her sentence with his touch. It was time to step up his offense. He was tired of waiting for things happen; it was time he *made* things happen. "You're right. Seeing you with Owen does make me jealous."

"Why? I'm a young girl who has nothing going for me, remember?"

"I never said that."

"You didn't have to. I can read between the lines."

Drawing her to him, his gaze penetrating her anger, he brushed his lips across her ear. His touch set off ripples of pleasure through her body. "Why would I insult such a gorgeous and captivating woman?" He put a hand on her waist. "You're making a difference in the lives of orphaned children and I greatly admire you."

"What happened to us being completely wrong for each other?" she asked, pressing a hand against his chest to ward him off. Despite his bulky jacket and all the layers of clothes, she could feel the strength of his upper body and found herself fantasizing about kissing him from head to toe. "You said I was too young."

"You are."

"What does that mean?" she demanded, thoroughly confused. "You're talking in circles, Marshall."

"It means I'm not going to fight our attraction for each other anymore and you shouldn't, either." He had an urge to kiss her, but something held him back. "You do feel this thing between us, right? This chemistry? I'm not imagining it, am I?"

Sage sequestered a smile. Could this man be any sweeter? For all his talk, he was as nervous and as confused as she was. Doubt flickered in his eyes and he had a scared-little-boy look on his face. "I agreed to be your date for the awards dinner. Isn't that answer enough?"

"You haven't changed your mind?"

"Why would I?"

"I thought maybe you were going with Mr. Hot Shot."

She gave him a long, searching look, admiring the thickness of his lips and the delicious width of his mouth. "Marshall, I'm as good as my word. You should know that by now. I never go back on a promise."

"Is that right?"

"Sure is."

Marshall stared at her for a quiet moment, then said, "Not messing with my head, are you?"

"And why would I do that?"

"'Mess with a guy's head and you've halfway won the battle,'" he quoted, wearing an easy grin. "Sound familiar?"

"The rule only applies to scoundrels and jerks."

Marshall chuckled long and hard. Their verbal banter was as erotic as foreplay and just as dangerous. "You're starting to grow on me," he confessed, reaching for her.

"What am I, fungus or something?"

His laughter rocked the cable car. Startled, she reached out, clinging to him like grapevines. "Careful, big guy, you almost sent this thing flying!"

"You're not scared, are you?"

"Of course not." Releasing him, she turned and pointed out the window. "We're almost at the tower. Do you still want to check out the Native American art gallery?"

He answered her with a kiss. A deep, sumptuous kiss that made her head throb and her legs tingle. Her heart was heavy, a pungent cocktail of guilt, lust and fear. But she couldn't ignore the truth any longer. They had a great vibe, laughed easily together, and his kisses left her delirious and desperate for more. Like a gambler enticed by casino lights and slot machines, she was powerless to resist. Stroking the back of his head, she pressed her body against him, swallowing the space between them. Closing her eyes, she allowed herself to be swept up in the excitement of the moment.

Marshall kissed her perfectly, expertly, like they'd been here a million times before. He knew exactly how to touch her, how to hold her, where to grab. Surrendering to her need, she locked her arms around his head, drawing him close. Wishing they were in the privacy of her suite, rather than the tiny cable car, but refusing to deny the pleasure of his touch, she steered his hands around her waist. Their coming together was so intense, so spellbinding, so wickedly naughty that she didn't realize the gondola had stopped until she heard a knock on the glass. Breaking off the kiss, she glanced over her shoulder, her face wrinkled with annoyance. Everyone on the observation deck, from seniors to toddlers, stood watching them, openmouthed.

"We should go," Sage said, pecking Marshall on the cheek, "before we *really* give them a show!"

Three hours later, Sage hobbled into the ski lodge. Hair speckled with snow, twigs, grass and leaves, she tried not to make eye contact with anyone in the lobby. Spotting Owen, she ducked behind a eucalyptus plant. The garrulous attorney was standing beside the elevators, chatting with a brunette with fake boobs. Unable to climb the stairs to her suite, and scared Owen might ditch his companion for her, she lowered herself into a cushy armchair. The main floor lounge was dotted with couches, sofas, ceiling-high bookshelves and a cozy fireplace that shared its heat.

Extracting dirt from her locks, Sage cursed herself for behaving in such a sad, pitiful way. In the hopes of impressing Marshall, she had donned a pair of skis, shot him a saucy smile and took off down the mountain. *What was I thinking? Am I out of my freakin' mind?*

Yeah with lust, she thought, unzipping her jacket. One minute she was watching Marshall do his thing out on the slopes and the next her big mouth was getting her in trouble. A male bystander had challenged her to give it a try, and soon she was flip-flopping all over the place like a straight man in stilettos.

Getting a bikini wax was less painful. Her arms screamed with pain, her back muscles were wire-tight, and it hurt to blink. She crossed one aching foot over the other, images of her tumble down Black Bear Mountain flashing in her mind like slides on a Jumbo Tron screen. Sage couldn't believe she had wiped out in front of the entire resort. If Khari hadn't rushed to her aid, she'd still be face-deep in snow, clawing her way out. Why couldn't she be graceful like all the other skiers?

Feeling dejected, and worried what Marshall and the other parent volunteers must think of her, she stared out one of the arched windows. From her seat, she had a clear view of Black Bear Mountain. Spotting Marshall's orange-stripped ski suit, she leaned forward in her seat, her mouth wet with desire. He was talking to a short, portly man, puffs of cold air passing between them. The temperature had hovered in the high twenties all afternoon, but that didn't keep the crowds inside. A second later, Marshall flew down the mountain, his arms swinging powerfully, his poles stabbing the snow, his boots slicing the ground like shears. The slopes were chock-full of skiers and several cute instructors, but no one looked better or moved better than Marshall Grant.

Sinking farther into her seat, she threw her head back and stretched out her legs. It was the first time since they'd arrived in North Hill that she'd put her feet up, and it felt good. *So much for pampering,* she thought, shaking her head. This was supposed to be a stress-free weekend filled with rest and relaxation. Instead, she'd got busted making out with Marshall and had stumbled down Black Bear Mountain like a damn rag doll.

If she hadn't been consumed with thoughts of Marshall and that hot, torrid kiss, she wouldn't have wiped out on the slopes. Thank goodness she didn't twist or break anything. How would she look, hobbling into the awards banquet in three-inch heels? Like an airhead, that's what. She needed ice and lots of it. Ice would reduce the swelling, relieve the pain, and if she was lucky, cool her desire for Marshall. She was playing with fire, and if she wasn't careful, she'd lose everything she'd worked so hard for.

Rubbing the sting in her arms, she moaned, wishing her mind would stop tormenting her. Had they really gone at it in the cable car? Marshall had teased her with his smile, then kissed her until she saw stars. His hands had been everywhere, and even now, hours later, she could still taste the sweetness of his lips, the gentleness of his touch, and every time she closed her eyes, she saw his smiling face. How had this happened? How had she gone from thinking he was a horrible dresser to making out with him a thousand feet in the air? And even more troubling, she wanted more. More kisses, more touches, more everything. Maybe tomorrow night after the awards show she'd invite him back to her suite and…and what? Sage let the thought linger, not trusting her feelings, a helpless slave to her emotions. *Have you forgotten why you're here?* her inner voice asked. The poignant question circled her mind, stealing her peace and intensifying her doubts. It was time to regroup, to refocus, to push Marshall's kisses out of her mind and replace them with thoughts of signing Khari. That was what mattered. That was what was important. Not how great a kisser Marshall was, or how soft his hands were or how damn good it had felt when he'd nibbled on her ear.

"Are you okay?"

Sage opened her eyes. Khari. He was standing in front of her, decked out in his red-and-black snowsuit, holding two mugs.

"No, I feel terrible. I'd kill for a hot oil massage, but the spa's closed for the day."

"That's a bummer." He offered her a cup. When she took it, he sat down on the chair beside her. "I've never seen anyone wipe out that bad on Black Bear Mountain. For a minute there I thought we'd have to call the paramedics."

"Thanks a lot, Khari. Now I feel even worse."

"No more showing off in front of Dad," he scolded, wagging a finger in her face. "I don't think your body could handle another beating like that."

Sage thought of refuting his claim, but if she lied, he'd press the issue, confirming the truth in the end. "Shouldn't you be snowboarding with your friends?"

"I told the guys I'd meet up with them later. What kind of guy would I be if I didn't come check up on my future stepmom," he teased, wiggling his eyebrows.

"Stop saying that," Sage ordered, glancing around. "Someone might hear you."

"I don't care. It's true."

"Khari, I'm hardly old enough to be your mom."

"Says who?" She heard the smile in his voice and laughed when he made a silly face. "I don't care how old you are. As long as my pop's feelin' you, I'm feelin' you."

Sage laughed. Khari was a great kid, and when she told him just that, he popped his collar and quipped, "I know, I know. That's what all the honeys say!"

Over hot chocolate and sugar cookies, Sage and Khari talked about the awards banquet, his feelings for Destiny and his fears of graduating. When the conversation turned to his plans for the summer, his eyes lit up with excitement.

"My friends and I are going to Cancun for a week. Kind of like a guys-only trip." He added, "And this time there'll be no nosy chaperones spoiling our fun."

"Khari, I wouldn't make plans to go anywhere in June. If you decide to enter the draft, you'll be busy for weeks leading up to the big night. It's a whirlwind of interviews, meetings, team tryouts and—"

"But I'll only be gone for a week," he protested.

"I know, but in the world of sports every day counts." Feeling guilty for ruining his mood, she smiled. "What else is on your mind?"

"Nothing. You probably wouldn't understand. Nobody does."

"Try me."

"I want to play in the NBA, but I don't want to miss out on all the cool things my friends will be doing." He paused, a somber expression on his face. "Destiny's going to UCLA and Oakley and Tevin both got full scholarships to California State University."

"And how does that make you feel?"

"I don't know. I wish I'd applied to some universities, just to see if I would have been accepted."

Sage frowned. Stringent, concise and methodical, it was hard to believe Marshall hadn't sat down with Khari and handpicked the schools. Before she could ask the question running through her mind, he said, "Dad helped me fill out the application forms, but Coach is stalling on his recommendations."

"What?" Her voice carried around the room, drawing the attention of everyone in the lounge. "Why?"

Khari shrugged. "He said I was born to play ball, and that a university degree wasn't going to do anything for me. He said I should go right into the draft."

An overlay of calm concealed her rage. Coach Conway was poisoning Khari's mind. "Khari, have you changed your mind about going to Harvard?"

"I don't want to study medicine."

"What else do you like doing besides playing basketball?" she asked, smiling over at him, noting how much he resembled his father.

"Lots of things. Playing baseball, football and—"

"I mean besides sports. If you couldn't play ball, what would you do?"

"You'll laugh if I tell you."

"I won't. I swear on my Jimmy Choos."

Khari laughed and the tension on his face vanished.

"I'm not going to laugh at anything you say. You have my word." She touched his leg, offering reassurance and support.

"We're friends, remember? And friends don't make fun of each other."

After a brief pause, he said, "I think it would be kind of cool to be a music producer. You know, like Timberland and Diddy."

"There's nothing funny about that. All you need is an ear for music, a strong work ethic and a desire to learn. I know a lot about the entertainment industry, Khari, and a four-year business degree could really take you places."

"That's what Oakley said."

Nodding, she poked him in the shoulder. "Smart kid. You should listen to him."

"I still want to play in the NBA though."

"I know." Sage didn't want to influence Khari's decision, but she had to tell him the truth. "You can always turn pro after you graduate. Then you'd have the best of both worlds. A university degree *and* a professional basketball career."

"But Coach said— "

"Never mind what he said. You need to do what's right for you and only you."

"I hear you." Khari covered his head with his hands. "This is crazy. I've never been so confused."

"No one said you had to decide today."

"I should've sent off those applications, but now it's too late to—"

"No, it's not. It's only February."

His eyes shone like two coins. "Do you think I still have a chance?"

"For sure. Not only are you an amazing basketball player, you have a pristine academic record and you're an A student. You could get a full scholarship to any school of your choosing."

"You really think so?" he asked, his voice hopeful. "I was doing some checking online, but UCLA doesn't accept late applications."

"Come by my suite in the morning and we'll get down to work. Maybe we can do it online."

"Thanks, Sage! You're the best." Khari jumped to his feet. "I'm going to tell Oakley. We could end up playing ball at the same school!" His smile brightened the entire room. "We could live in the dorms. Or get an apartment off campus. Wait until Oakley hears this!"

Sage laughed. She watched Khari sprint through the door and disappear outside.

Chapter 13

Saturday was spent ice-skating, snowboarding and tobogganing. Bent on redeeming herself, Sage signed up for ski lessons and practiced all afternoon out on the slopes. She still wasn't as graceful or as majestic as the other skiers, but she didn't fall as much.

By six o'clock that evening, Sage was waiting at the door of her suite, dressed and ready to go. When Marshall didn't arrive at six-thirty, she phoned his room. No answer. She thought of calling his cell, but didn't want to seem anxious. She was, but when it came to the opposite sex, it was always wise to play it cool. Her foster mom had always told her to act like a lady, but think like a man. It was the only useful piece of advice Ms. Claxton had given her and Sage credited the adage for protecting her from heartbreak.

Sage stood and walked over to the balcony. Streaks of sunlight flittered into the room through the blinds. The sky was a flattering turquoise-blue and the mountains were as high as the heavens.

A smile danced across her face as she thought about Marshall. He'd showed up at her room last night with club sandwiches and fries, a pile of DVDs and a pack of brownies for dessert. Marshall looked crestfallen when she told her she was going to the all-night slumber party on the first floor. Sage was sorry to see him go, but being alone with Marshall in her hotel suite was a temptation she just couldn't handle. If she wanted to keep her head, she had to stay far, *far* away from Marshall.

Bob Marley's voice broke into her reprise. Sage unzipped her purse and retrieved her cell phone. She didn't have to check the number to know it was Tangela. "Hey, girl, what's good?"

"Nothing. I'm just calling to check up on you. How's it going?"

"I love it up here! The scenery, the mountains, even skiing. Isn't that crazy? Five years ago you had to teach me to walk in high heels and now I'm on skis!"

"But you hate cold weather," Tangela pointed out. "And you bitch and moan whenever it's less than fifty degrees here!"

"Like I said, crazy."

Tangela laughed. "Your renewed love of the great outdoors doesn't have anything to do with Marshall Grant, does it?"

"Maybe a little."

"You slept with him, didn't you!"

"No." Sage started to protest, but stopped herself from saying anything that Tangela could use against her later. "We haven't slept together."

"But you want to."

"It's not going to happen," she insisted, hoping to convince herself in the process. Glancing at the clock, she decided to go on without Marshall. On her way to the reception hall, she'd stop by the front desk and leave a message for him. "How are things going with Warrick? Did he apologize for not coming home the other night?"

As she listened to Tangela's latest tale of woe, she picked up her clutch purse and sailed through the front door. Remembering that she wanted to bring her digital camera, she spun on her heels and hurried back into the bedroom. There was no doubt in her mind Khari would be named Athlete of the Year, and she wanted to capture every moment.

"Enough about my problems. Tell me more about Marshall."

Images of their tryst on the gondola surfaced. "Girl, you won't believe what happened yesterday," she began, unzipping her bag. She was in the middle of telling Tangela about their kiss, when she heard Marshall's voice beyond the bedroom door.

"Sage?"

"In here," she replied, butterflies pelting her stomach. Not wanting Marshall to think she was a slob, she snatched up her underwear from off the floor and stuffed them under the pillow. "I'll be right—"

Marshall strode through the open door. Bug-eyed, her cell phone slipped out of her hand and fell to the carpet. Was this the same man who lived in plaid?

His white dress shirt was ironed to perfection and his striped black-and-gray sweater vest made him seem even taller. It wasn't an Armani suit, but it didn't matter. He was a certified hunk. Handsome without even trying. His chain glimmered and his shoes were so shiny, she could see her reflection. Marshall Grant sure knew how to clean up! And she thought he didn't know how to dress. He'd done it again. Surprised her. Yesterday he'd stolen her away from Owen and now he strolled into her hotel room looking every bit her type.

Moved by the strength of his cologne and his buoyant smile, she cancelled her search for the digital camera. His smile lured her away from the closet and images of their kiss flashed in her mind. She preferred a clean-shaven face, but his newly acquired goatee was growing on her. Hands fixed to her hips, she arched her eyebrows skeptically, affecting a look of disbelief. "You're an imposter. What have you done with Marshall?"

Chuckling, he stared down at the cell phone lying helplessly between them. "Looks like you lost something." Swiping it off the floor, he spoke into the receiver. "Hello?" After a brief pause, he said, "Can she call you right back? She's, ah, tied up at the moment." Marshall ended the call, tossed the cell phone on the bed and surprised his date with a kiss. A knee-knocking embrace that made her feel like she was floating high up in the sky. A nervous mess, Sage fought the urge to break free, scamper into the bathroom and lock the door.

She wasn't going to let Marshall have his way with her again. All these sexy, heated exchanges and wild, frenzied kisses had to stop. Resisting him was harder than she had imagined. Rebelling against his touch, she stepped back. He pursued. Like a ravenous beast, he stalked her, claiming her with his lips and seducing her with his hands. His mouth paid homage to her lips, sucking, nibbling, caressing. He hit the sweet spot on her neck and she bit back a moan. Savoring her taste, he buried his hands in her free-falling hair. Sage was the one battling her conscience, but Marshall was the one who finally broke off the kiss. "You're going to knock 'em dead tonight."

Throwing her hands out at her sides, and doing a slow, sexy turn, she modeled her outfit. "Like the back?" she asked, staring at him coyly over her shoulder.

"Do I ever." His low, husky voice underlined his need. "If Khari wasn't up for an award tonight, I'd—"

"What? Ditch the party and stay here with me?" she finished, batting her thick, extralong eyelashes. "You and I both know that would be a mistake."

"Never figured you were the kind of girl to follow the rules." His hands curled around her waist. Marshall traced a finger down her arm. Loaded with shine and subtle waves, her hair coursed over her bare shoulders, skimming her elbows. And tonight, he wanted her all to himself. "Don't make any plans for later. We'll have drinks after the party wraps up. No excuses this time."

"I like a man who knows how to take charge."

"You do, huh?" Licking his lips, his gaze rested on the ruffles along the plunging V-neck blouse. He copped an eyeful of her cleavage, wishing he could nestle his head there for the rest of the night. Her skirt clung to her hips and the dangerously high slit flaunted the silky slope of her legs. The red-painted toes that poked out of her black sandals were bathed in an array of rhine-stones. Blown away by the simplicity of her look and her stag-gering beauty, he took her hand and led her out of the bedroom. "We better get out of here before we miss dinner!"

Cone-shaped lights, and round tables showered with silverware, candles and appetizer trays pilled high with finger foods filled the second-floor banquet hall. Guests had been greeted by uniformed servers, offered a glass of sparkling club soda and accompanied to their seats. After a brief welcome from the vice principal and a toast to the graduating class, people made their way to their tables.

"Dessert, Ms.?"

Sage glanced up from her coffee cup. Lowering it, she inspected the plates on the dainty silver tray. Amaretto cream cake, pecan pie and cherry crisp were on the menu and she could already taste the vanilla icing in her mouth. After a grueling hike, wiping out repeatedly on the slopes and breaking two fingernails, she deserved a treat. It didn't matter that she'd had two plates of food. What was the point of exercising if you couldn't indulge every now and then?

"I'll have the double-decker chocolate fudge cake," she told the waiter, handing him her empty dinner plate. "And if it's not too much trouble, can I have another glass of wine and a couple more of those lemon pie tarts?"

Nodding, he put down the dessert and marched off.

"I hate you."

Conversation ceased around the table. Staring wordlessly at Geraldine Buford, a mother of four with Goddess braids, Sage pointed a finger at her chest. "Me?"

"Yes, you! I can't stand women like you."

Sage laughed to cover her embarrassment. "Why? What did I do?"

"You can eat whatever you want without fear of gaining weight." The humor in her voice shone through. "If I so much as look at a piece of chocolate, I gain ten pounds!"

Laughter rang out. Sage turned to Geraldine's husband, a short, tubby, balding man in his fifties. "You better keep a close eye on your wife because she was wooing them out on the slopes today. I caught a male instructor hitting on her!"

More chuckles. Geraldine may have been born in the sixties, but she had the face, the body and the vigor of a thirty-year-old. The motivational speaker had been the one to organize the senior girls' slumber party, and when the teens conked out at midnight, she'd ordered dessert and cocktails for the chaperones. Four apple martinis and a New York cheesecake later, and the women were dishing the dirt about the men in their lives.

"I don't have to ask if you're having a good time," Marshall said, touching the back of her neck. "You've charmed everyone, even Principal Rupert, and that old man never smiles!"

"I'm not the only one making an impression. I didn't know you used to be a chef," she said, wishing he didn't look so damn sexy. They had turned heads when they'd entered the reception hall and Sage had caught the jealous stares of the female guests. There was nothing sexier than a handsome, extratall brother, and tonight Marshall Grant was every woman's dream. "Why didn't you tell me you know how to cook? You know I love to eat!"

"I've had every job under the sun." Shaking his head wistfully at memories of the past, he said, "Before I joined the marines, I did everything and anything to make ends meet. I washed windows, walked dogs, delivered newspapers, I even drove a school bus. You name it, I did it."

"A jack of all trades, huh?"

"A man's gotta do what a man's gotta do."

"I hear you," she agreed, nodding her head. "I had dozens of crappy, low-paying jobs before I got hired on at World Mission. Now, I finally have a satisfying, rewarding career, but I'll never forget what a struggle it was back in the day."

Sage tasted her dessert. The cake was light and fluffy and lathered in icing. "Mmm. This is so good, I'll probably be dreaming about it tonight."

Marshall broke into a smile. "I should cook for you. Then maybe you'll stop dreaming about food and start thinking about me."

If only you knew, she thought, her eyes tracing the outline of his mouth. The soft, juicy mouth that left her breathless and yearning for more every time they kissed.

"What do you want me to make?" His smile teased her, hinting at things to come. Her heart leaped in her chest when he trailed a finger down her shoulder. "I hate to toot my own horn, but I can throw down in the kitchen."

"Really? What's your best dish?"

Marshall momentarily lost his concentration when she licked her spoon. Thoughts of making love to Sage plagued his mind, but he forced them away. Later, when the time was right and the mood was set, he'd love her until she begged him to stop. "My jambalaya. Khari says it's so good it'll make you slap your momma!"

They laughed together.

"But it's not about me, it's about you."

She signified her approval with a smile. Had she ever met a man this caring, this selfless, this anxious to please her? "It's been ages since I had Moroccan food. I'd kill for some chicken Tagine and spicy pilaf. Think you can manage that?"

"A five-course meal and wine coming right up!"

High on food, laughter and wine, Sage looped an arm around his. The cut of his shoulders, and the sheer strength of his upper body sent her mind into an erotic tailspin. Flirting with him weakened her resolve and intensified her desire, but she just couldn't help herself. With Marshall everything was so easy, so natural, so right. And just because she'd made up her mind not to sleep with him, didn't mean she was going to kill all her fun. "You're not going to order in and pass it off as your own, are you?"

"I don't need to, girl. I'm the black Wolfgang Puck!" Chuckling, he bent down and kissed her cheek. "It's all set. I'll cook a feast for you on Tuesday night."

Sage couldn't think of anything she'd like more, but having dinner with Marshall was a recipe for disaster. Consumed with second thoughts, she racked her brain for an excuse to get her out of the date. A last-minute appointment. An overlooked meeting. Something, anything to soften the glow of her rejection. What was wrong with her? One minute she was agreeing to dinner and the next she was pushing him away. When had she become an insecure, wishy-washy tease? "I don't know," she began. "I work really late on weekdays."

Marshall knocked back his wine in two swallows. "I'm flexible. What time do you finish up at the office?"

"It depends. Sometimes, I don't leave until six or seven." Sage had always been an up-for-anything type of girl, but this time she had to proceed with caution. Over her head and sinking fast, she had to get her mind off Marshall and back to signing Khari. "I'll be leaving for Vegas by the end of the month and I have a lot to do between now and then."

"I didn't realize you were leaving so soon." Leaning over, he touched her cheek in a gentle caress. "We're getting together this week. I won't take no for an answer."

Sage moaned inwardly. An aggressive, take-charge kind of

man got to her every time and the fiery heat in Marshall's eyes made him irresistible. "I'll check my schedule and give you a call later in the week."

"I don't know if I can wait that long."

His cologne aroused her senses and his kisses set her body on fire. Roping in her thoughts before she got carried away, she spooned more cake into her mouth. It was time she put on the brakes and got off this sexually charged ride.

"Tuesday, seven-thirty, my place."

Secretly pleased that he'd stood his ground, she yielded to his request. "Okay, okay. Quit twisting my arm. I'll come."

"After you taste my cooking, you'll be glad I talked you into it."

She held his gaze, seduced by his smile and the sudden thickness of his voice. His hand had started on her legs and then slipped up to her thighs. She knew exactly where it was going next. Her body throbbed with hungry anticipation.

"A romantic dinner for two. Just in time for Valentine's."

Sage scoffed. "I've never liked Valentine's Day."

"Right, I'm sure brothers are lined up outside your house, waiting for you to get home."

"Hardly. Most of the men I meet are more interested in playing games than dating. Good thing I have my own personal pleasure chest or I'd be one lonely girl!"

Marshall rocked with laughter. "Why do you have to make us brothers sound so cold? Like I told you that night at Champions, not all men are dogs."

"Not all," she conceded, "just most."

He stared at her for a long moment. "I guess it's up to me to show you how *real* men treat their women. It's a challenge I'll take great pleasure carrying out."

Sage leaned into him, inhaling his rich, invigorating scent. Marshall had a calm, grounding effect on her, but she loved that he had a fun side too. His voice was buttery smooth and the fire in his eyes could torch her panties.

"I'll have everything ready by seven, so don't keep me waiting." Marshall paused, a reflective expression on his face. "Better yet, maybe I should bring dinner to your hotel. You must be sick of ordering room service."

Games of the Heart

"I am, but I'd rather come over. Will your parents be there too?"

"No, I want you all to myself." His voice was a deep, husky whisper. "There'll be no distractions this time. I'll pay Khari to get lost if I have to." His words were filled with promise, eliciting sexy thoughts Sage had no business having. Thoughts of kissing and loving and caressing. The voices in her head told her to stop, so she put her desires on ice and eyed Marshall with interest. "Can I ask you something? Something personal?"

"What's on your mind?"

Geraldine was the only other person at their table, but she was too busy devouring the dessert tray to pay them any mind. "What happened with your ex-wife?"

His features darkened. Glancing around the room, she smoothed a hand over his chin. "We were young. Kids. Babies having babies, as my mom used to say."

"And?"

"And while I was in Kuwait, Roxanne was running the streets with her friends. She'd drop Khari off with my parents, then take off for three or four days. No one knew where she was or who she was with. Roxanne would resurface days later, copping an attitude and arguing vehemently that she was working."

Dance music filled the room. Dinner was finished and guests were ambling around the hall, talking, laughing and posing for pictures. Sage suggested they go out into the lobby, but Marshall declined. She suspected he wanted this conversation to end as quickly as possible and the more he tugged on his collar, the more convinced she was.

"Neither of us wanted to get married, but our parents applied the pressure and we eventually caved. I fainted twice at the church, which should have been a sign, but I went through with the wedding anyways. She was having my baby. It was the right thing to do. The only thing to do," he stressed, leaning forward in his chair. "I would have done anything for her, but she changed. Hell, we both did."

"Did she cheat on you? Is that why you broke up?" Sage took in everything—the sorrow in his eyes, the sudden tightness in his jaw, the restless way he adjusted his watch. It didn't matter what he said, because she saw the truth in his eyes. He'd loved Roxanne and her betrayal had cut him deep.

"We both made a lot of mistakes. I wasn't a perfect husband. I worked long hours, came down hard on her at times, and it wasn't long before we both fell out of love."

"Where is she now?"

He averted his eyes. "I have no idea." His gaze wandered around the room, drifting aimlessly from one table to the next before settling on Khari's face. He wasn't ready to talk about that with Sage. Not yet.

"I don't know about you," she began, hoping to alleviate the tension, "but I've eaten enough food to last me a week."

"You're right, you have." Marshall chuckled heartily. "You don't mind if I go check in with Khari, do you?"

"Of course not."

He stood. Sage reached out and stroked her fingers along his forearm. "Hurry back, or I'll be forced to find another dance partner."

"Keep my seat warm," he instructed, winking at her.

The rest of the night was spent watching an uproarious slide show of pictures captured from the weekend—including a shot of Sage face down in the snow—and honoring the academic and humanitarian achievements of the senior class. It was no surprise when Khari was named Athlete of the Year, but Sage and Marshall jumped to their feet, hooting and hollering, leading the audience in fervent applause. Khari graciously thanked his teammates, the coaching staff and his teachers, but reserved the highest praise for his dad. Sage couldn't tell the last time she cried, but when Khari hopped off the stage, strode over to their table and hugged Marshall, she blinked back tears. And as she watched father and son embrace, a sudden, intense panic gripped her. The moment passed quickly, but for the rest of the night Sage had a cold, sinking feeling in the pit of her stomach she just couldn't shake.

Chapter 14

When Marshall turned onto Irvington Lane on Sunday afternoon, Sage released a low, pitiful groan. Her rental car was buried under a heap of snow and her tires were coated with ice. Dreading the inevitable clean up, she zipped up her jacket and put on her hood. "Is it okay if I use your bathroom?" she asked, releasing her seat belt. "I think I had one too many of those hot chocolates on the bus."

Marshall chuckled. "Khari, take Sage inside while I unload the truck."

"Do you still want to see my trophy wall?" Khari asked, as they climbed the steps. He was cradling his athlete of the year tropy in his hands, a proud smile on his face. "While you're checking out my awards, I can upload the pictures on your camera to my computer."

Minutes later, Sage was in Khari's bedroom, perusing the wooden shelves teeming with awards, trophies and framed newspaper and magazine clippings. Life-size posters of professional athletes were splashed on the walls, T-shirts and jeans poked out of the dresser drawer, and a blue duvet was tossed carelessly on the king-size bed.

"Are you going to be in town a little while longer?" Khari asked, plopping down on his computer chair. When Sage told him she would, he looked relieved. "Great, then you can help dad and grandma plan my surprise party. Make sure they don't do one of those corny slide shows with my baby pictures and whatever you do, please don't let Grandma choose the music. My friends won't be jamming to Little Richard."

Sage faced the window so he wouldn't see her smile. "What makes you think they're throwing you a party?"

"Nothing gets past me," he boasted. "I know everything that goes on around here. Everything," he said, stressing the word.

"You have a lot of baseball awards, Khari. Ever thought of playing in the junior league?" she asked, maneuvering the conversation to a safer topic.

"Basketball's my first love. I'm always looking for ways to improve my game. I'm even inventing plays in my sleep!" Khari chuckled. "But if it doesn't work out, I'd definitely play baseball." Connecting the cord from the computer to her digital camera, he rolled the wireless mouse on the pad, laughing out loud at the images filling the screen. "Senior Weekend was off the hook! Especially the toboggan race. Me and Oakley killed all of the other groups!"

Laughing, she glanced at Khari, astride a wooden chair, a gigantic smile on his face. As she turned away, her eyes caught sight of the wrinkled black-and-white photograph tacked above his desk. Sage peered at the photo, convinced the slender woman in the multicolored sundress was Marshall's ex-wife. "Is this your mom?"

Khari lifted his head. "Yeah, that's my mom, Roxanne Narissa Grant."

"She's beautiful. You look just like her."

"You think so?"

"Definitely," she agreed. "You have the same dark eyes, and nose. And she's tall too."

"My mom was the best. Everyone loved her. My friends used to beg to come over to my house for dinner, just so they could hang out with mom."

"It sounds like you have a lot of fond memories of her."

"I remember one time I came home for lunch and she wasn't there to meet me. I must have been around five. I cried all the way back to school. During art, mom tiptoed into the classroom with McDonald's! I sat at my desk, eating my French fries, feeling like the luckiest kid alive!"

Sage leaned against the wall, her conversation with Marshall at the awards dinner coming to mind. Marshall had painted Roxanne as a negligent mother, but Khari spoke of her with love and respect. Two very different portraits of the same woman. "Was your mom gone a lot?"

"Yeah, she worked a lot, but on her days off, she'd take me to the park or to the mall."

Sage didn't want to pry, but her curiosity wouldn't leave it alone. "Your dad said your mom was in and out of your life."

"If it wasn't for Dad, she'd still be here. Every time she had a beer or a smoke, he'd yell at her." His words were lined with anger. "He drove her away."

"I know you miss your mom, Khari, but you're really lucky to have your dad. I know he's hard on you sometimes, but he only wants the best for you. I would have loved to have someone check my homework or come to my track meets. I had no one."

"Who raised you?"

"An assortment of foster moms, babysitters, child care workers and a few teachers here and there." Sage picked up one of the medals crowding the shelf, amazed that one kid could be good at everything. Baseball trophies, track-and-field medals and academic certificates spoke of Khari's dedication, athleticism and talent.

"One day I'm going to track my mom down." He paused for a moment before sharing his thoughts. "I was just a little kid when she left, but I still really miss her, you know?"

Sage nodded in understanding. "Is that why you're anxious to go pro, Khari? Because going pro will give you the money and resources you need to find her?"

"Well, that's part of it." He met her gaze, then shrugged. "All right, it's a big part."

"Khari, you're a great kid and I'd hate for you to make the wrong decision. You need to do what's right for you, and no one else." Standing beside him, she put a hand on his shoulder. "And you don't need to enter the draft to find your mom, either. There are lots of nonprofit agencies that specialize in reuniting lost family members. I'm sure they can help you."

"Thanks for everything, Sage. You've been a really good friend to me, and—" he paused for effect "—I think I know what I'm going to do after graduation."

Sage raised her eyebrows. "Care to share the big news?"

"Nope. You'll have to wait until my party to find out." Chuckling, he spread his eyes wide and said, "I better not say that too loud, huh? After all, it is a surprise party!"

Bob Marley's muffled voice filled the room. Sage retrieved her cell phone from her jacket pocket and was surprised to see her boss's name and number on the screen. "Leo?"

"What's the matter with you, Collins? Are you trying to ruin me?"

He was yelling so loud, the couple who lived next door could hear him. Scared Khari would overhear him, she slipped out of the bedroom and went downstairs. Relieved Marshall wasn't around, she asked Leo what was going on. "Calm down, boss. What's going on?"

"I just got off the phone with Khari's coach. I called to express my interest and said he can deliver the kid. What's the matter with you, Sage? You've been out there for weeks. Your first order of business should have been to talk to the coaching staff."

"Coach Conway likes to go around saying he's Khari's mentor because it makes him feel important. Don't believe him. He has absolutely no control over what Khari does."

Shovels scraped against the pavement, grating on her nerves and drawing her attention to the window. It wasn't some annoying neighbor who had nothing better to do than piss her off. It was Marshall. And not only had he cleared a path from the door to the sidewalk, he'd cleaned the snow off the car and was in the process of scraping the ice off her windshield. Overcome with gratitude, she knocked on the glass. When Marshall looked up, she waved. Sage didn't know too many brothers who'd brave minus-thirty weather to help her out. But Marshall Grant wasn't just any man. He treated her like gold, but she suspected he would have done the same thing for a friend, a coworker or a neighbor. That was just the kind of guy he was.

"Are you listening to me?"

Sighing deeply, she tucked her arm under her elbow. "Yeah, I heard you. You want me to call Coach Conway and set up a meeting."

"It's not a suggestion, Sage. It's an order." He raised his voice. "I'm the one who signs your checks. Don't ever forget."

Sage felt the hairs on the back of her neck rise. Wrestling with her conscience, she leaned against the windowsill. Why didn't things ever go her way? It didn't matter how hard she worked, at the end of the day she always had to choose between doing what was right and doing what would bring success. Fear drove her to be the best and she was desperate to make a name for herself. And she would, one blockbuster client at a time. Sage knew what she had to do, but she couldn't force the words out of her mouth. In her eight years at the agency, she'd snuck into private parties, hospital rooms and rehab centers, never giving a second thought about breaking the rules. She did whatever it took to land the client. Negotiating behind the scenes and scheming her way to victory had never bothered her before, so why now? Her guilt was so palpable she could taste it in her mouth.

"Meet with him tomorrow. I'll call you in the afternoon to see how it went."

"Khari's going to college," she blurted out.

"Why would he do that when there's a shitload of money to be made now?"

"Because he's a kid. He wants to hang out with his friends, attend wild frat parties and date. He's not ready to turn pro and he doesn't have to be." She added, "The NBA's not going anywhere. It'll be there when he graduates in four years."

"Shit. Now you're starting to sound like his old man."

"You spoke to Marshall?"

"Last week."

"And?"

"He hung up in my face."

Sage swallowed a laugh. "That's too bad, boss man."

"Talk the kid out of going to school. It's a bad idea. Stay as long as you have to, but…"

Her conversation with Khari came to mind. No one understood more than she did what a confusing time adolescence was. She'd had childhood fantasies of her parents coming back for her. Bearing gifts and profusely apologetic, her mom would kiss and embrace her. Sage didn't know how Marshall would feel about Khari tracking down Roxanne, but she made a mental note to talk to him about it. Cutting an end to her boss's rant, she said, "I'm not going to persuade Khari to turn pro. He has to make this decision on his own, without any interference from me, Coach Conway or anyone else."

"You're making a mistake," he warned. "One misstep in this business and you're done."

Sage paused. "That's a chance I'm just going to have to take. I owe it to Marshall and—"

The line went dead.

Chapter 15

Marshall hoisted the glass dish on top of the stove, closed the oven door with the back of his foot and switched off the timer. "We'll give Khari a few more minutes, but if he's not down here by seven-thirty, we're eating without him."

When Sage didn't respond, Marshall glanced over his shoulder. She was still perusing the Neiman Marcus department store catalogue. *Vogue, Cosmopolitan* and *Elle* magazines were sprawled out beside her, and she'd combed through each one with precise scrutiny. An hour ago, she had sashayed into the kitchen, hopped up onto the counter and read him an eyebrow-raising article about sex toys. If he didn't have gravy simmering on the stove, he would have taken her upstairs to practice some of the scintillating techniques.

For the last three weeks, they'd met for quick lunches, drinks at Champions Sports Bar and the evening kickboxing class at Gold's Gym. More flirting took place than working out, but Marshall always looked forward to seeing her there. It didn't matter if they were walking the dogs or experimenting in the kitchen, jokes flew, laughter abounded and kisses were plenty. They cheered for opposing football teams, couldn't decide what radio station to listen to in the car and argued about how he disciplined Khari, but they made each other laugh, could watch reruns of *Sanford and Son* for hours and both loved to travel. And it didn't hurt that she had an eye for fashion. Tonight she'd paired a tunic sweater with jeans and a chain-link belt. A headband held her curls off her face and her hair flowed down her back. *Who knew a shirt and jeans could be so sexy?* he thought, admiring her chic, sophisticated style. Sage looked so good with clothes on, he could only image how hot she'd look naked.

"What do you want to drink? We finished the amaretto last night, but I can run out and get another bottle."

Sage didn't answer.

Marshall dropped the oven mitts on the stove, then turned to admire his date. From a foster child abandoned by her mother to a big-city exec. Marshall admired her tenacious drive. And the more time they spent together, the stronger his feelings grew.

"Who are you drooling over now?" he teased, noting the gleam in her dark brown eyes. "Will Smith? Terrance Howard?"

"Hmm," she murmured, her gaze fixed on the magazine in her lap.

Since he didn't know if it was in response to his joke or what she was reading, he squeezed her thigh to get her attention. "Who's got you so mesmerized you forgot how to talk? It's Derrick Jeter, right?"

"It's not a who, it's a what," she corrected, holding up the magazine for him to see. "Isn't she gorgeous?"

The object of her affection was a purse. It had a star-shaped gold buckle and looked large enough to hold a twenty-inch TV. "You've seen one handbag, you've seen them all," he answered with a shrug.

His indifference didn't temper her excitement. "This is *the* purse to have this season. All the stars have them. Tyra, Rihanna, Beyoncé." She returned the catalogue to her lap. "I'm going to get one in every color."

"That must mean it's expensive," he observed, staring down at the glossy full-page ad. "How much do one of those bags go for? A couple hundred?"

"A couple hundred," she repeated, her tone rife with humor. "That might get you the buckle," she joked. "I have a friend who works at Neiman Marcus department store. If it wasn't for her discount, I'd be paying five grand like everybody else."

Marshall's eyes were the size of ping-pong balls. "Five thousand dollars for a purse? You're kidding, right?"

"It's a suede hobo bag. What do you expect?"

"Do you know what you could do with that kind of money? That's four months worth of mortgage payments and…"

"Beauty isn't cheap," she quipped, patting his cheek. "I deserve nice things. I work my ass off and then some. Besides, it's just money. Life's too short to pinch pennies. Sometimes you just have to live it up and worry about your bank account later!"

"Not when you have bills and a teenager who can eat you out of house and home!" He leaned against the counter. Their shoulders were touching, and the scent of her sweet feminine perfume incited a rumble from his empty stomach.

"Humor me, okay?" When Marshall nodded, she continued. "If you bought one of those scratch tickets at the gas station and won, what do you do with the money? And this money is for you, Marshall. Only you," she stressed, emphasizing her words. "What do you do with it?"

He thought for a moment.

"A down payment on a new Jeep truck? Home renovations? One of those big snow-blower things?" she offered, swinging her legs restlessly back and forth. Sage was wearing a wide smile, indicating just how much she was enjoying this fictional exercise. "Hurry up. The anticipation is killing me."

"I'd go to Kenya." He watched the expression on her face morph amusement into shock. "You probably think I'm crazy, but when I was a kid, I watched a documentary about Africa and I've been wanting to go there ever since."

"There's nothing crazy about wanting to know more about our history," she told him with a smile. "If we let some TV channels tell it, Africa is nothing but jungles, face-painting and witch doctors. But the Rift Valley in Kenya is practically the cradle of civilization."

"I didn't know that."

"Kenya is the jewel of Africa. Even Charles Darwin believed humankind originated in the region. I haven't been there yet, but I'm working on it."

"You're a wealth of information," he praised, careful to keep the surprise out of his voice. "What can I say? I'm impressed."

Sage winked. "I'm more than a pretty face, you know."

"I know."

Laughing, she stretched her arms over her shoulders, her shirt rising and revealing a sliver of her taut stomach.

Everything was about timing. When the moment came a man had to be ready.

Holding her gaze, he stepped forward, imprisoning her. Her eyes glowed. With desire or amusement? He couldn't be sure.

"Careful," she cautioned, leaning back. Her smile expanded into a full-fledged grin. "Come any closer and I'll be inside the cupboard!"

Marshall laughed.

Sage licked her full, wet lips and Marshall struggled to maintain control. He could feel his willpower oozing away, but there was nothing he could do. He'd been fighting his desire for her all week. On Monday, when they were playing a Scrabble game, two days later, when she showed up with Chinese takeout, last night, when they were in the living room, stretched out on the sofa, listening to Will Downing. His mind refused to give him a moment's peace, and every time he closed his eyes he saw her face.

Marshall stood frozen like a statue. The richness of her smile made his pulse quicken. Lust filled the air, suffocating him, enticing him with its thick, musky scent. Helpless to resist, he reached out and caressed her cheek.

Wrapping his arms around her, he buried his face in her hair, inhaling her floral scent. Their deep, all-consuming embrace was as sensuous as a kiss. Marshall didn't know who kissed whom first, and he didn't care. All he knew was that he couldn't get enough. Consumed by moans, groans and deep, sensual sighs, he kissed from her mouth to the apex of her breasts. Sage parted her legs, inviting him in, then clamped them possessively around his waist. Hands intertwined, he pressed her against the wall, loving her with his mouth, showering her with slow, hungry kisses.

He slipped his hands under her sweater, trailing his fingers along the front of her push-up bra. Her body was warm and her nipples rose to attention under his gentle stroking. Slipping off the counter, she locked her arms around his neck, creating a warm, cozy cocoon. Marshall had never known such hunger, such pleasure, such need. Desire engulfed him, punishing him like a surfer battled by an eighty-foot tidal wave. He couldn't stop. Wouldn't stop. He'd never wanted a woman this badly. Sage was his dream girl, his fantasy, his one and only. He loved spending time with her and wanted a relationship—but it wasn't love, was it? Love was an emotion, a feeling, a state of mind he wanted no part of. Falling in love had been his downfall before, and he'd be damned if he got bamboozled again. Sex was welcome—hell, *needed*—but he wasn't going to give up his heart.

His errant hands couldn't get enough of her breasts. Was he moving too fast? Was he pawing her? The voice in his head told him to stop, but her deep, throaty moan smothered his thoughts. This was a fantasy come true. And when she unbuckled his jeans and stuck a hand inside his boxer briefs, his head flopped back like a puppet. Bracing himself against the wall, he buried his hands into her hair. Sweat gathered on his brow and his heart raced with glorious anticipation. Groaning his pleasure, he eased his tongue into her mouth and gently nipped at her bottom lip.

Marshall felt like he was going to explode. She was stroking him into ecstasy, and when she gripped his shaft with both hands, his knees buckled. The phone rang, and for a second, his vision cleared and the haze lifted. Reason set in. He was playing with fire. Angry at himself for losing control, he turned back toward the stove. Eyes fixed on the kitchen door, he zipped up his jeans, exhaling a slow, ragged breath. He needed to stay focused on Khari. On not being distracted by this woman.

"What's the matter?"

Marshall leveled a hand over his shirt. His reflection bounced off the stainless-steel pots. He had the lazy, contented expression of a sexually satiated man, but his body was still dying for release. "We can't do this…here, Sage."

Her smile returned. "You're right. We can't." She grabbed his hand, practically dragging him across the kitchen floor. Pushing open the door, she peeked into the living room. "Think we can make it upstairs to your bedroom without Khari catching us?"

Marshall wanted nothing more than to take her upstairs and

love her all night long. But what kind of example would he be setting for Khari? He wanted Sage, but he couldn't make love to her while his son was doing his homework in the next room. And if he let Sage stay over, it would be just a matter of time before Khari was bringing girls inside the house, and Marshall would rather fantasize about what could have been than be hypocritical. It was bad enough they'd made out in the kitchen. He'd never be able to eat in there again without remembering what they'd done. Shaking the image of her red satin bra and the feel of her soft flesh, he forced his licentious body into submission. "We can't go upstairs, either. Khari's studying. That wouldn't be right."

"No problem. I don't mind a quickie." Her joke added much-needed levity to their conversation, but when she gripped his belt buckle, he realized she was serious.

"I want you, Sage. God knows I do, but we can't do this here."

"Why not?" Eyes wet with lust, she rubbed her hands over his chest, her lips perilously close to his ear. "I can be quiet, if that's what you're worried about."

Marshall chose his words carefully. He'd been in this predicament before, but he'd never cared so much what a woman thought of him. "I've been preaching abstinence to Khari since he had his first wet dream. I can't control everything he does, but I made it clear he's not allowed to bring a girl to this house. Ever."

"That's admirable," she praised, lovingly caressing his face.

Marshall had a hell of a time keeping his eyes open. He felt her warm hands under his shirt, her breath on his neck and a slow lick of her tongue across his lips. Her voice sounded sweeter than ever. Longing welled in his chest, but he turned his back on his emotions and forced his unruly body into submission. "I promised Khari I'd live by the same standards I set for him."

Her kiss was gentle. "I wish there were more fathers out there like you."

"I'm not as great as you're making me sound."

"Most men expect to have sex by the third date," she pointed out.

"I'm not most men." He measured his words and spoke before he lost his nerve. "You can't spend the night, Sage. I'm sorry."

Her hands fell to her sides. The expression on her face told him she was disappointed, but there was something else in her eyes he couldn't read. Five minutes ago, the sexual tension had been so thick he could cut it with a knife, and now embarrassment hovered like early-morning fog.

"I'm not blowing you off. I'd never do that. I want you. I *really* want you," he repeated, desperate to touch her. Fearing her rejection, he stuffed his hands into his pockets. "If we were anywhere else I'd…" He left her to fill in the blanks.

He could tell Sage was angry, but she didn't argue. Instead, she poured herself a glass of wine and stood beside the window, sipping slowly.

Feeling the need to explain further, he opened his mouth, but stopped himself from speaking when he heard footsteps beyond the kitchen door. Khari burst into the room, a ball of pent-up energy, rambling about the NBA All-Star Game. "Dad, is it all right if I eat in my room?" he asked, swiping a plate off the counter and heaving spoonfuls of spicy pilaf into his dish. "The game just went into second overtime!"

"You know the rules. We eat dinner together, at the—"

"Good Lord," Sage muttered, rolling her eyes. "Surely you can make an exception just this once."

Yup, she was mad at him all right. Her tone had a hard, bitter edge, and she was staring at him, a cool, hostile expression on her face. Marshall watched his son pour juice into a glass mug. If Khari ate upstairs, he'd have Sage all to himself. They'd enjoy a nice dinner and retire to the living room to have dessert. And if he was lucky, they'd pick up right where they left off. "Take a coaster with you," he told Khari, offering him one. "I won't have you spilling Kool-Aid juice on the carpets again."

"Thanks, Dad!"

Marshall smiled as he watched Khari disappear back through the kitchen door. Hoping to smooth things over with Sage, he grabbed the bottle of Merlot from off the table. He crossed the room and refilled her glass. "I guess it's just us tonight."

"Oh, no, it's not," she answered, brushing past him. "I'm out of here."

"Where are you going?"

"To watch the game with Khari."

"But I thought we were having dinner together."

Sage glanced over her shoulder. "I suddenly lost my appetite."

Chapter 16

Sage slapped cold cream onto her cheeks. *Damn him!* she thought, smearing the thick, foul-smelling green substance along her jaw line. *Damn Marshall and his stupid rules!*

Questions crowded her mind, deepening her frown and forming creases in the mask. Who ever heard of a man turning down sex? It didn't matter how religious, responsible or attached they claimed to be. In the heat of the moment, no one ever stopped to think about consequences or repercussions. They caved to their desires and didn't give a flying fig what happened later. Sage understood his reasons; in fact, she admired the example he was modeling for his son, but that didn't take the sting off his rejection.

She applied another coat of cream and rinsed her hands. Sighing deeply, she stared back at her reflection in the bathroom mirror. Her eyes narrowed. Doing the right thing sucked. Instead of spending the night with Marshall, kissing, laughing and making love, she'd returned to her nasty, mouse-ridden hotel, hornier than an inmate at the woman's central jail.

Slapping off the lights, she wandered into the living room, her steps slow and heavy. The curtains were drawn, revealing a full moon surrounded by a handful of stars. Swiping her water bottle off the dresser, she wondered what Marshall was doing. Her heart and mind were at odds. She'd be leaving Indianapolis next week. They'd spent every day together since Senior Weekend. Sometimes he took her out for dinner, other nights they relaxed at home, watching movies and playing cards. She'd purposely lose at strip poker and made sure she always looked great and smelled great, just in case Marshall was feeling frisky.

Rock-climbing at the Leisure Recreation Center. Exploring the Civil War Museum. People-watching at the Java Hut. She'd tried to keep things casual, but it was hard *not* to fall for him. What woman didn't like compliments, praise and elaborate gourmet dinners? Marshall told her she was sexy, baked her ginger cookies and didn't flip when she spent hours in Saks Fifth Avenue trying on clothes. He liked Bruce Lee movies, did a sidesplitting imitation of Rick James, and though she vehemently disagreed with his argument against rap music, she respected his wishes and didn't play it in the house.

Every week, they enjoyed Friday Fright Night with Khari and his friends. They popped a horror movie into the DVD player, dimmed the lights and waited to be scared senseless. Sage used every single jump-out-of-your skin moment to snuggle close. And when she screamed at the top of her lungs, Marshall wrapped his arms around her and held her tight.

Flopping down on the bed, she stretched her legs out in front of her, a sour expression on her face. Vanessa Williams was on TV, hawking skin care products that guaranteed miraclelike results. She bet Marshall wouldn't have rejected *her.* Sage checked the time. She wanted to talk to Tangela, but her best friend was en route to New York. And besides, Tangela had more problems than a Hollywood starlet, and was acting just as crazy. Convinced Warrick was cheating on her, she'd started trailing him in the evenings after work. Sage warned Tangela that she was playing with fire, but like a toddler in a toy store, she couldn't be reasoned with.

Switching off the TV, she turned on the radio and leaned back against the headboard. Sage closed her eyes and saw Marshall's handsome face smiling back at her. She'd stayed in town to sign Khari, not fall for Marshall. But that's exactly what she'd done. Fallen so hard that now she was in her hotel room, pouting because he'd kicked her to the curb.

Sage had been too embarrassed to eat dinner with Marshall, but when she got a whiff of the jambalaya, she sent Khari downstairs to fix her a plate. She might have been angry, but she wasn't stupid. Marshall was a culinary genius. It didn't matter what was on the menu—spaghetti Bolognese, vegetable curry, deep-dish brownies—he cooked it, and he cooked it well. So much so, she licked bowls, ate seconds and took containers of leftovers home.

Two plates and three glasses of merlot later, she returned to the hotel, where she'd been in a funk ever since.

She had no business influencing Khari's decision. It was the hardest phone call she'd ever have to make, but after leaving Westchester Academy, she ducked into the girls' washroom and phoned Leo. She told him Khari had decided not to enter the NBA draft. It was a lie, but she couldn't admit to Leo that she'd failed.

Sage was disappointed that she wouldn't be the next executive manager at Sapphire Entertainment, but after talking to her coworker, Dionne, she'd discovered that Leo had never intended to give her the job. He'd guaranteed the position to a less-qualified manager, who just happened to be a man. No surprise there. Leo claimed to be a progressive, open-minded boss, but he wasn't about to let a woman run the show. Leo might not be ready for a change, but she was.

When she got back to Las Vegas, she'd quietly shop around her résumé and see if there were any takers. From time to time, the idea of going back to school tugged at her thoughts, but she also had dreams of one day opening her own agency. She had been toying with the idea for months, and though Marshall promised to help her get started, just the thought of filling out loan applications gave her a migraine.

Her phone rang, but tonight Bob Marley's voice wasn't soothing or tranquil. It was carefree and buoyant and the lyrics mocked her. Everything *wasn't* going to be all right. She'd lost the executive manager position, a plaid-wearing community director had rejected her and her best friend was one triple latte away from a nervous breakdown. Sage had officially hit rock bottom and it was a very lonely place. Clearing her mind of Marshall and his kisses, she grabbed her cell phone.

"A blocked number," she said aloud, deciding whether or not to answer. She wouldn't be surprised if it was Tangela calling from the county jail, because if her best friend ever caught Warrick stepping out on her, there'd be hell to pay. But it wasn't Tangela. It was Marshall, sounding John Legend sexy and surprisingly contrite.

"Where are you?"

"That's none of your business." He'd rejected her, but had the nerve to act like a concerned boyfriend. Screw him and his questions. "It's nine o'clock, shouldn't you be ironing your socks?"

"Can we talk?"

"About what?"

"About what an ass I am. About how much I miss you."

If his voice was any smoother, it would be silk. His words caressed her ears like a kiss, but Sage wasn't ready to let him off the hook just yet. "You should have thought about that before you kicked me out."

"I didn't kick you out. You left."

"Because you didn't want me."

"That's impossible. I want you." He added, "I'll *always* want you."

His declaration inveigled a smile from her lips.

"I made you something."

"Keep it. I'm not interested."

"Does that mean you don't want to see me?"

He sounded so vulnerable, so remorseful, so sweet. Marshall was trouble and he was playing games; but instead of turning him down, she asked where he was taking her. "It better be somewhere nice. You owe me."

"We'll go wherever you want."

Leaping off the bed, she whipped off her robe and rushed over to the closet. "How long will it take you to get here?"

"I'm pulling into the parking lot as we speak."

"You're here, at the Luxe? I mean, at the Four Seasons hotel," she corrected, selecting a belted turtleneck dress and tan suede boots. "Sounds like someone's anxious to see me."

"Got that right! I was going to ask the desk clerk for your

room number, but figured I should call first and make sure it's okay." He paused. "We're okay, right?"

"That depends on what you bought me."

Marshall laughed. "Can I come up?"

"I don't know about you, but I could *really* use an Orgasm. Let's meet in the lounge," she suggested. Whipping the silk scarf off her head, she kicked off her slippers and flew into the bathroom like a bat out of hell. Her secret was safe. Now all she had to do was make it across town in the next fifteen minutes.

At midnight, Sage and Marshall stepped off the elevator onto the tenth floor.

"You didn't have to escort me to my suite," she said, feeling uncharacteristically shy. The hallway was lit with horn-shaped lights that illuminated framed paintings and pastel-blue walls. It was intended to evoke feelings of calm, but Sage was nervous. Marshall had been playful and affectionate in the lounge, and if she wasn't careful, he'd charm his way into her bed. "It's a short walk from the elevator to my suite."

"I know, but you're special to me and I couldn't live with myself if anything ever happened to you."

"I'm not in a witness-protection program," she joked, giving him a playful nudge. "Don't worry about me. I'm a big girl."

"I'm glad I came by. Did you have a good time?"

"You know I did. I always have fun when we're together. And those pie tarts you baked were delicious." Stopping outside room 1037, she retrieved her key card and clutched it in her damp palm. Checking into the hotel, while Marshall waited for her in the bar, had taken some expert maneuvering, but she'd rather be out another two hundred dollars than have him find out she was staying in a hideous one-star motel in the hood.

"I'll see you on Tuesday. Call if you need me to bring anything to the party."

"Khari's going to go berserk when he sees everyone." Marshall swept his hands over her shoulders, caressing them lightly. "I couldn't have pulled it off without you."

"Don't thank me yet," she cautioned. "A lot can happen between now and then. But you're right, Khari's going to love it."

Sage wanted to ask him to stay. If it wasn't for his stupid rules, she'd invite him inside, fix him a drink and ride him until the break of dawn. Purging her thoughts, she ignored the gleam in his eyes and his knowing smile. It didn't matter how handsome he looked or how delicious he smelled or that he'd made her laugh for the last two hours. There'd be no mattress marathon tonight. Everything she owned was back at the Luxe Motel. Sure, she could replace her deodorant and toothbrush, but the last time she checked, they weren't selling diaphrams at the local convenience store. "Good night, Marshall."

"So that's it. You're not going to invite me inside?"

Fortifying her will, she dug her heels into the carpet. She desired Marshall in ways he couldn't even imagine, but if he could play hard to get, so could she. "It's almost midnight."

"And?"

Sage took her time answering the question. "And we both know what'll happen if you come inside this late." This wasn't the Disneyland theme park and she didn't believe in fairy tales. It was time they stop skirting around the issue and put their cards on the table. "I don't understand your decision, but I respect it. I want you to stay, but I don't want to cause a rift between you and Khari. You're teaching him what it means to be a man and it's important to you to set the right example. You said so yourself."

"Khari's spending the night at Oakley's."

Sage frowned. "How'd that happen?"

"He asked and I said yes."

"Was that before or after you spoke to Oakley's parents?"

Marshall stroked a hand over his chin. "I had to make sure they'd be adequately supervised." He added, "You don't know these families like I do."

"Did you hear what you just said? Supervised? They're not four-year-olds!" Sage shook her head at him as if she was scolding a child. "Marshall, it's time you cut the cord. You've coddled Khari long enough."

His eyes were dark, cold stones. "What's that supposed to mean?"

"You've got to loosen up. Cut Khari some slack. He'll never

learn to think for himself if you're always telling him what to do. He's a bright, well-rounded kid who's never given you any trouble. Trust him to do the right thing."

"I'm trying."

"Well, that's a start." Standing on her tiptoes, she leaned over and pecked his cheek. "I'll talk to you tomorrow. Maybe we can do lunch or something."

He captured her waist. "I don't want you to go."

"I can see that," she teased, lifting her eyebrows. Sage didn't need a Breathalyzer test to know Marshall had ordered one too many beers. Loaded up on booze and ignorant of their surroundings, he lowered his mouth, pressing his lips against the slope of her ear. He hit the sweet spot on her neck and her eyes lulled shut. The right thing to do was to send him on his way. But Sage didn't want to do the right thing. She wanted to do *him*. "I think you're a little buzzed."

"I'm not drunk. Sometimes I just lose my head when I'm around beautiful women." Lavishing kisses on her lips and cheeks, he swept her up into his waiting arms. "The only way I'm leaving here tonight is if you come with me. Sage, one way or another, this is going to happen. I've been wanting you since the moment I saw you and I'm tired of waiting."

"Marshall, I want you too, but—"

"You can't fake chemistry," he told her, pressing her against the door. "This thing between us is very real and I don't want to run from it anymore. It's about living in the moment. Isn't that what you're always telling me?"

Aroused by his persuasive words, the width of his grin and his soothing touch, she circled her hands around his neck. Every kiss, every smile and every embrace had led them to this moment, and when he took the key card out of her hand, slipped it inside the slot and strode confidently into her suite, she followed, images of slow, sensuous lovemaking flooding her mind.

Chapter 17

Sage and Marshall lay in front of the fireplace, kissing. Desire hovered over the living room, smothering them with its thick, intoxicating perfume. The wine, the music and the outside city lights shining through the balcony doors heightened their growing passion.

Marshall swept her hair off her shoulders. His mouth was sweet, soft, pleasing. He pressed his lips against the slope of her neck and she moaned with pleasure. Sage had a strong sense of her own feminine power and sensuality, but Marshall's kisses turned her inside out. Overwhelmed by the intensity of his touch, she pitched her head back, words spilling from her lips between jagged breaths. Tracing his fingers along her back, in a loose zigzag pattern, he teased her earlobe with his tongue. "You like that?"

"Love it."

"Want more?"

"Grab a condom," she urged, tugging at his belt. "I have some in my purse."

"Slow down, baby. There's no rush. We have all night."

Marshall rolled on top of her and kissed her with such intensity, the room spun around her. Needing more of her, he unzipped her dress and tossed it onto the couch. The hot-pink bra and matching thong panties were nothing but scraps of fabric, but he liked the vibrant color against her brown skin. Twirling her hair between his fingers, he gazed lovingly at her, hoping she knew how much he cared about her. He wanted to know her deeply, intimately, the way a man should know a woman, and nothing mattered more than pleasing her. Grabbing a cushion off the couch and slipping it under her hips, he kissed from her navel to her thighs. His eyes took in her full lips, thick curves and long, sexy legs. Marshall ached for her. He had the erection to prove it. But he curbed his desire, and lowered his mouth between her legs.

Sage sucked in a breath. Lifting her head up off the cushion, she stared down at Marshall. No, she hadn't imagined him kissing her *there*. Most women had to beg, plead and cajole their partners into having oral sex. No one had ever volunteered before, and she'd never had the pleasure of being loved like this. For most men, foreplay was a means to an end. Give me what I want so you can get what you want. But Marshall was methodical, concise, absolute. He kissed from her ears to her toes and repeated the pattern until she was begging for him to be inside her.

Marshall sprayed light kisses down her waist, along the inside of her thighs and the back of her knees. His tongue licked the outer rim of her lips, before slipping inside. Her feelings for him were so deep, so intense, they scared her. Euphoria set in as his tongue pulsed inside her, moving in slow, intimate circles, lingering in her walls. He was unusually attuned to her desires and anxious to please her. Sensitive to his touch, she squirmed beneath him, her voice swelling from a moan to a full-fledged scream.

Cupping his head, she opened her legs wide and guided him to her center. He stirred his tongue inside her, kissing, prodding, stroking. She was anxious to feel his strength, his width, his power, but she didn't have the energy to move. She was caught in a trance. A sensuous, mind-numbing trance. He was loving her thoroughly, righteously, showing her just how beautiful true love could be. Her desire swelled, subduing her with its force. And when Marshall reached up and cupped her breasts possessively, she groaned so loud, the music faded into the background.

Sage had never known such pleasure. She'd had two orgasms and they hadn't even made love yet. Marshall was a passionate, generous lover...but her mind boggled at the thought of them being more than lovers. She wasn't a naive, love-seeking runaway anymore. This was just sex. Toe-curling, earth-shaking sex. Nothing more. They had agreed not to make any promises to each other, and that suited her fine. He wasn't looking for a commitment and neither was she. She'd never, not for one second, thought this could be love. But when he gripped her waist and plunged his tongue inside her, lavishing her center with wet, slick kisses, she only had one feeling, one thought, one emotion. Love rained down on her like snowflakes, filling her heart, overwhelming her mind and leaving her breathless.

Marshall yanked off his jeans and rejoined Sage on the bed. She brushed her full, wet lips against the hollow of his throat and pushed him playfully back against the silk pillows. Stretched out on his back, he watched in silent appreciation as she unraveled the condom on his erection. Streaks of moonlight fell across her naked body, intensifying his arousal and his need.

The lambency of the stars made for a tranquil scene, but his heart was thumping. Running her hands up and down his shaft, Sage rubbed her dark, erect nipples against his mouth, teasing him. Sucking both, he stroked the curve of her butt, loving the feel of her supple flesh in his large hands. Lost in lust, he explored every inch of her, petting, fondling, stroking her core with tender, loving care.

Sage blew into his ears and Marshall closed his eyes. Feet firmly planted on the bed, she clutched his shoulders, and lowered herself slowly onto his lap. Marshall sucked in a gulp of air. She raised her hips, making circles so wide, and so quick, a groan tumbled out of his open mouth. Her parted lips lingered on his neck, then closed around his nipples. Marshall craved a slow seduction, and what Sage was doing with her tongue was sweet torture.

"How did I get so lucky?" he rasped. "You're amazing, Sage Collins, truly amazing…"

"I'm the lucky one, Marshall." And to prove it, she licked from his ear to his nipple.

Marshall had an infinite amount of self-control, but he didn't know how much more of this he could take. He wanted their lovemaking to last forever, but his body was overheating and he couldn't think straight. There was nothing like loving her, nothing like tasting her, nothing like being inside her.

Sage rocked back and forth, in and out, thrusting her pelvis forward, drawing him into her tight, slick core. Pressure mounted, tearing through him with incredible force, leaving him worn-out and scatterbrained. Sage rode him like a bull rider—hard, wild and fast. Cupping her cheeks in his palm, he kissed her tenderly as she came and collapsed onto his chest.

Limbs heavy with sleep, Marshall rolled onto his side, gathering the woman he loved into his arms. "Uh-huh," she said, reclaiming her position and licking his ear. "There'll be plenty of time to sleep later, baby. Now, hand me another condom."

"Oh my God!" Ravaged by the intensity of her orgasm, Sage collapsed onto the bed, her hair a wild tangled mess, and her already-full lips swollen.

"You're huffing and puffing like you're about to give birth." The thick darkness of the night swallowed them up, but there was no mistaking the humor in Marshall's voice. "Are you okay?"

"Just peachy," she answered breathlessly. "I could do the fifty-yard dash."

It was a lie, but it earned her a laugh. "A foot race, huh?" he asked, staring at her with satisfaction in his eyes. "I'm not a doctor, but you're in no position to go anywhere."

Sage was lying comfortably on her back, and though it took all her strength, she rolled onto her side and propped a pillow behind her head. Sighing with contentment, she pushed a hand through her hair. Life was good. Better than it had ever been.

His body enveloped her and her mouth reached hungrily for his. The kiss was full of heat and love, and she melted under his touch. They were emotionally and physically connected now, and there was nothing better than being in his arms.

A hurricane of emotions whipped through her. She felt happy and guilty at the same time. On one hand, she was thrilled that they'd finally made love, but on the other hand, she hated that this intimate, private moment was marred by lies and half-truths. It was time she take stock of where she was in life and where she wanted to go. One thing she knew for sure was that she loved Marshall. He was reasonable and understanding, but if he found out she'd been lying to him all these weeks, he'd… Spurning her thoughts, she curved her body into his, tightening her grip around his waist. Why ruin a perfectly good moment by worrying about the future? She could make things right tomorrow. Tonight, she just wanted to be with her man.

Outside, dawn bathed the sky in a bold stream of pastel colors. The sun crept over the horizon, promising warmth and sunshine. Unlike the Luxe Motel, the hotel was quiet and peaceful. Babies weren't screaming. Radios weren't blaring. And the air wasn't saturated with the scent of fried chicken. They could lounge in bed for as long as they wanted, or get up and have breakfast at one of the trendy bistros along Twelfth Avenue. Marshall had to work in the afternoon, but maybe she could persuade him to call in sick. They'd finally made love, and she wasn't prepared to let him go.

"What's on your mind?"

The question caught her off guard, but she answered truthfully. "You." Safe in his arms, she snuggled close, reflecting on how far they'd come. Had it only been six weeks ago that he'd run up on her walloping the school vending machine? "I'm wondering what I'd have to do to convince you to stay."

"All you have to do is ask."

"I'm having déjà vu," she joked. "Isn't that the same line you used on me that night at Champions?"

"It wasn't a line," he protested, trailing a finger down her shoulder. "I meant it. And I mean it now."

Panic set in. This was wrong. Very, very wrong. How could she say she cared about him if she was living a lie? If they were ever going to have a chance at a relationship, she had to tell him the truth about who she was and where she'd come from. Sage started to speak, but stopped when Marshall told her he was going to be in L.A. next month. "I thought you guys were going camping for spring break?"

"Khari wants to check out UCLA and some other schools in the area." He drummed his fingers on her thigh. "Maybe you can drive up and spend the weekend with us."

"Sounds good." She looked up at him. "What happened to Harvard?"

"I still want him to study medicine, but I'm not going to push it anymore. I'm trying to be more supportive. It's like someone said, I just have to trust that he'll make the right decisions." He squeezed her shoulders, drawing a laugh from Sage. "I'm just glad he's showing interest in going to college again. For the last six months, all he's talked about is turning pro. I figured to relent a little."

"Marshall, you're an amazing father. Maybe if we had more positive images of black men stepping up to the plate, sisters wouldn't be so quick to label brothers lazy, good-for-nothing jerks. It's sad, but you're the minority, not the majority."

"That's just it. Where I come from, I *am* the majority. You know what my earliest childhood memories are of? Playing football with my uncles. Dad teaching me how to hit a baseball. My granddad taking me fishing. The brothers I know are all strong, successful men who put their families first."

"You and I couldn't have come from more different worlds. Where I come from, women are mother and father to their children. They don't sit around waiting for their ex-husbands or baby daddies to get with the program. These women do it all. *They* take their sons fishing, *they* play basketball with them, *they* teach them what it means to be a man. They have the support of their girlfriends, and that's all they need."

"That's the problem. Sisters have been shouldering the burden for so long, they don't know how to step aside and let their men take the reins." He cleared his throat, and after a brief pause spoke about being deployed to Kuwait. "I never imagined the evil I'd encounter in the Middle East. Soldiers were dying all around me, and I had such horrific nightmares, I was afraid to go to sleep. But you know what kept me going?"

Sage anticipated his response, but shook her head. "No, what?"

"Khari. I dreamed of teaching him all the things my father taught me. But when I returned home, everything fell apart. It was like meeting Roxanne for the first time. She got so used to me not being around, she didn't need me anymore. In her eyes, I wasn't worth shit, and she wasn't afraid to say it. I missed birthdays, anniversaries and recitals. It didn't matter that I'd been defending our country, I wasn't there when she needed me. We argued constantly and a few times things even got physical. Once a neighbor heard us going at it and called the police."

"You hit her?" she asked, flabbergasted.

Marshall looked embarrassed. "I wasn't the perfect husband, and I screwed up more than I care to admit, but I never hit her."

No stranger to drama, she listened without prejudice, wondering why he'd never said anything before. "You still love her, don't you?"

"Roxanne was my first love, and we had a lot of great times together, but I'm not in love with her, if that's what you're asking." He leaned forward and kissed Sage hard on the lips. "Trust, respect and loyalty are at the heart of every good relationship, and you can't recapture what's been lost, no matter how hard you try."

Sage inhaled sharply. What was she supposed to do now? Keep quiet or come clean and risk him blowing up at her? Either way, she was screwed. Listening to Marshall not only made her feel guilty and ashamed, but dirty. Like she'd just finished a set at a seedy, hole-in-the-wall strip club. Just because she didn't grow up with the Partridge Family didn't mean she could slip and slide around the truth. Being in a relationship, beckoned by support, love and respect, made her feel like she could do anything, including owning up to her mistakes and telling Marshall the truth. He had made himself vulnerable tonight and she didn't want any secrets between them. If they were ever going to have something real, she had to *be* real, starting now.

Sage didn't believe in beating around the bush, but she didn't have the guts to come straight out and tell him. Better she ease into it. "There's something I have to tell you," she began, moving out of his arms. "Something you're not going to like."

"Go on, I'm listening."

She took a deep breath.

"I'm a celebrity manager, not a marketing executive for World Mission."

His jaw was tighter than barbwire.

"I basically discover new talent and guide them through all facets of the entertainment business. I do everything from brokering deals, to arranging interviews and attending awards shows." Fearing she'd lose her nerve, she rushed on. "I was only three credits away from getting my business degree when I lost everything. And I mean everything. I was living in a housing project and some idiot fell asleep with the stove on. I had no insurance, no money, and if it wasn't for my best friend, I'd still be living on the streets. Tangela pulled some strings for me and I got a job working in the mailroom at Sapphire Entertainment, a talent agency. I worked my ass off for three years and then got promoted to junior agent. The rest is history."

The expression on Marshall's face was serious. "I bet you're one hell of a manager, because from what I've seen, you sure know how to talk a good game."

"I didn't come here to sign Khari. My boss brought me on this trip."

"But when you learned that he could be the next NBA superstar, you wasted no time joining the pursuit." Marshall sat up and swung his feet over the side of the bed.

"Okay, I admit I got a little caught up in the competition. I wanted to prove to my boss that I have what it takes to be an executive manager." Sage searched for the right words. She felt her heart race and her voice tremble. "After spending time with you and Khari, I forgot all about the signing bonus. I swear."

"Sure you did." Marshall stood and yanked on his boxer shorts. "I had a feeling you were one of them. I should have trusted my instincts."

"You did? How?"

"I put two and two together when you showed up at the track."

"But I wasn't there to spy on you. I—"

"Let me finish. I was born at night, not last night," he snapped, turning to face her. Sunlight splashed across his chiseled chest. Sage forced herself to concentrate. His body was perfect in every way. Physically strong and healthy, there was a light dusting of hair on his chest that trailed down to his stomach. His arms were firm and muscular, and just a few minutes ago they'd been wrapped around her in a lover's embrace. Now he looked like he wanted to throttle her.

"I like to think I'm a good brother, but I don't look like those actors and models you're always drooling over. I'm a regular guy, with a regular job."

"Regular?" Frowning, she shook her head. "Marshall, there's

nothing *regular* about you. You're a man of integrity who puts his family first, and I feel honored to know you and—"

"Is that a line from the employee handbook?" he asked, interrupting. "You deserve an Oscar for your performance, Sage. It's truly remarkable. I just have one other question. Do you get a bonus for bedding your clients?"

Sage lost her composure. "I hope you're not implying that I used you, Marshall. Or slept with you to gain an advantage over the competition."

"I don't have to be a brain surgeon to know something's up. When you showed up at the track, I knew it wasn't a coincidence."

"It wasn't like that."

"But it is." His eyes were empty and his tone was flat. "We had a good time. Let's keep it at that. You were paid to do a job. You did what you had to do, right?"

The jab was like a needle to her spine.

"I'm just disappointed that it took you this long to tell me. I thought we were onto something." Releasing a slow, ragged breath, he rubbed a hand over his head and down his neck. After a lengthy pause, he said, "I'd appreciate if you didn't say anything about this to Khari. He really likes you and he'd be hurt if he knew the truth."

"I never meant to hurt either one of you." Her voice cracked. "I'm sorry."

"I'm sorry too." He took a long, hard look at her, then strode into the bathroom and slammed the door. A second later, the sound of gushing water filled the silence.

Sage flopped onto the bed, feeling like the weight of the world was on her shoulders. Things couldn't have gone any worse. Her head was swimming and her eyes burned. Tears threatened to come, but she pushed them away. It had been years since she cried.

Pride pushed Sage to her feet. This wasn't over. A plot brewing in her mind, she scooped up his clothes, crossed the living room and stuffed them under the mattress. She was going to make him listen to her, even if it meant holding him hostage. Dry-eyed and composed, she slipped on his shirt, careful to leave the first three buttons undone, and smoothed a hand over her hair. Pausing outside the bathroom door, she took a deep breath, hoping against all hope that he would hear her out.

Butterflies danced in her stomach and her palms were slick with sweat. It was now or never. Gripping the door handle, she ordered herself to remain calm in spite of the awful scenarios running through her mind. Marshall yelling at her, calling her vicious names, walking out on her for a second time. Ready to face her problems head-on, she stepped inside the bathroom and said, "Marshall, we need to talk."

Chapter 18

The whirl of the electric razor interrupted Sage's heartfelt speech. She considered yanking the cord out of the wall and flinging the device into the jet tub, but she didn't want to antagonize Marshall. Annoyed that he wouldn't look at her, she stared at him through the gold-rimmed mirror. When the silence became unbearable, she slowly came up behind him. Peering over his shoulder, she met his gaze, and smiled apologetically. Still nothing. To appeal to his soft side, Sage leaned over and kissed his neck.

Marshall flinched. "Don't touch me."

"Fine. I won't touch you, but at least give me a chance to—"

"I'm not interested in hearing any more of your lies."

Staggered by the hostility of his voice, she grappled over what to do next. Determined to make things right, she sucked in her cheeks, and blew out a breath. "Marshall, at least let me explain. I know it looks bad, but once I tell you how this whole thing got started, you'll see that I'm not a malicious person."

He pointed at the open door. "Get out."

"I'm not leaving until you hear me out."

"Sage, you're a skilled liar and I don't want someone like you around my son."

"Someone like me?" she repeated, touching a hand to her

chest. "I've done nothing but help Khari. And contrary to what you think, I'd never do anything intentionally to hurt him."

"Right." His humorless laugh filled the silence. "It's funny. I always tell the kids at the center to trust their instincts, but this time I didn't take my own advice. I knew you were trouble from the moment I saw you, but I was too blind to see the truth."

Marshall brushed past her, and she reached for his hand. His eyes narrowed in a malevolent glare. "Let go of me."

"I screwed up, is that what you want to hear? I never considered the consequences of my deception and I'm sorry." Sage stood quietly, silently, praying that her words were penetrating his heart. "If I had to do it all over again, I never would've played this game. I would have been up-front from day one, instead of building our relationship on lies and half-truths."

"Drop the act, Sage. You're not fooling anybody." Head slanted, he rubbed the back of his neck, his hard, cold eyes roving over her face. "Is Sage Collins even your real name? I mean, you lied about everything else. So, come on, tell me," he jeered. "What is it?"

Her legs were rubber and her entire body was shaking. Sage felt powerless to do anything and feared that if she didn't make things right, he'd be gone, out of her life forever. Fighting back tears, she pleaded for a second chance. "I know I hurt you, Marshall, but don't throw away what we have. You're special to me, and I'll do anything to regain your trust."

Marshall raked his teeth over his lips.

"I care about you, babe, and—"

"Well, I don't care about you."

Shrugging off her hand, he turned and stalked back into the living room. His words hurt and she bent over as if she'd been socked in the gut. Sage heard Marshall stomping around the suite and knew what was coming next. "Where the hell are my clothes?"

Wincing, she hung her head. Gnawing on her bottom lip, Sage reluctantly returned to the scene of the crime. Feeling small and foolish, she trudged over to the bed, retrieved his jeans and handed them to him. Glad he didn't ask for his shirt, she gazed out the balcony window, wishing there was something she could say to fix this. "Marshall, I am deeply sorry for the pain I've caused you and your entire family."

Wallet in hand, he crossed the room and yanked open the suite door. "Don't come to Khari's party," he told her. "You're no longer welcome in my home."

Marshall flipped off the living-room lights, raised his hands in the air and led his guests in singing "Happy Birthday" to his now eighteen-year-old son. His mom carried the chocolate cake into the room, drawing cheers and whistles from Khari's friends. A photo of Khari, taken at North Hill, standing proudly at the top of Black Bear Mountain, had been recreated in the shape of a basketball. It had been Sage's idea, and though Marshall had balked at the price, it looked great. But as his eyes settled on the Las Vegas beauty, he still couldn't believe she'd defied his orders and showed up at Khari's birthday party.

After cake and ice cream were handed out, his mom said, "Time to open the gifts. Everyone gather around the birthday boy!"

Within minutes, an iPhone, a bomber jacket and a pair of Nike's were piled onto the recliner, and when Sage saw Khari pick up her card, her mouth went dry. She stood at the back, alone, feeling like an outsider. Marshall hadn't so much as looked at her when she walked in, and he seemed to be going out of his way to avoid her. If not for Khari's phone call an hour ago, she never would have showed up.

Eyeing the teen now, she smiled to herself. Khari was going to flip when he saw the concert tickets. Glad she'd had the foresight to slip the Kanye West tickets into a blank birthday card, she watched with bated breath as the teen ripped open the blue envelope.

"Wow, front row seats!" Waving the tickets high in the air, he met her gaze and winked. "Thanks, Sage. I knew you'd come through!"

A giggle bubbled in Sage's throat and she laughed out loud. There was no fooling Khari and as she watched him examining the backstage passes, she felt a deep ache in her chest. How could Marshall think that she'd ever hurt his son? Wasn't it obvious that she adored Khari? Her heart and mind were in turmoil, and suddenly being in the room with the Grant family was too much for her to bear.

Behind her, someone cleared their throat. Knowing instinctively that it was Marshall, she turned around and faced the man she loved. "We need to talk. Follow me."

"I want to see Khari open the rest of his—"

Marshall interrupted. "I don't care what you want. You're not even supposed to be here, remember? Now come on."

Irritated by his tone, but not wanting to make a scene, she followed him grudgingly out into the hall. Inside the kitchen, Sage let him have it. "What's your problem? Why are you trying to embarrass me?"

"I thought I made myself clear when I left the hotel suite this morning. This is a family function and you're not welcome."

"Khari asked me to come and I didn't have the heart to disappoint him."

"So, you can manipulate him for months, but you can't tell him no?"

Offended, she reeled back as if she'd been struck.

"Sage, do me a favor and just leave. No one wants you here."

"Hear me out," she pleaded, her voice a soft whisper. She wanted to touch him, wanted to apologize with her hands and lips and mouth, but wisely kept her distance. Any closer and she might lose her dignity. "All I want is an opportunity to make things right. What can I do to show you that I'm truly sorry?"

"Nothing, Sage. There's nothing you can do." His words cut her deep and underlined his bitter animosity. "Now, grab your things and get out."

Incensed that he could be so cruel, she said, "I thought by coming here today you'd see how much I care about you, but all you want to do is hurt me."

Marshall lowered his head. Her words gave him pause. Was he taking this too far? Hadn't he punished her enough? But as he thought back over the last six weeks he felt the veins in his neck tighten. Used to working with entertainers, she'd perfected that sad, woeful look and as he stared at her now, he wondered how he could have allowed himself to be conned by her. "Have you ever worked for World Mission or was that all part of the ruse?"

Swallowing hard, she channeled her gaze.

Shaking his head in disbelief, he slowly clapped his hands together. "I have to commend you on a job well done, Sage. You certainly had me fooled."

"I'm sorry I came here. I'll leave." Unstable on her legs, she straightened her shoulders and walked out of the kitchen with her head held high. Intent on making a clean getaway, Sage snatched her purse up off the living-room floor without slowing.

"Sage, where are you going?" Khari's voice carried over the chatter. "You can't leave now. You're going to miss my big announcement!"

Her feet slowed. Turning, she forced a wide, lopsided smile. "All right, now. Don't keep us in suspense, Khari. What is it?"

Guests chuckled.

A pause, then, "I'm going to forego this year's draft and go to college!"

Marshall embraced Khari in a fierce hug, bringing tears to everyone's eyes. Cheers broke out and it took several seconds for the noise to die down. "I haven't decided on a school yet, but I'm going to get a double major in business and music. One day, I'll be producing the biggest and baddest names in music." He added, "That is, *after* my illustrious NBA career!"

Proud of Khari, Sage joined in the applause. Careful not to make eye contact with anyone, she backed out of the room and crept stealthily down the hall.

"I owe a big thanks to one very special person."

Sage had one foot out the sliding glass door, when she heard Khari say her name. Legs quivering, she stopped dead in her tracks, listening intently.

"I was really confused about what to do after graduation, but Sage helped steer me in the right direction. She told me to calm down and think things through. And whenever I started trippin', she'd give me a shot in the arm!"

In a desperate attempt to clear the tears from her eyes, Sage blinked hard and smoothed a hand over her flushed cheeks. She felt like laughing and crying at the same time. Overwhelmed with feelings of pity, Sage realized there was one bright spot in all this. She'd screwed things up with Marshall, but at least Khari didn't hate her too. Worried the teen might come looking for her, she hurried into the backyard and disappeared out of sight.

Chapter 19

The Las Vegas sunshine greeted Sage when she emerged from her condo on Monday morning. Strolling down the flower-lined walkway, she took a long, slow, deep breath. After weeks of arctic winds and bone-chilling temperatures, she loved feeling the breeze in her hair and the sun on her face. Eagles soared in the rich, blue sky, crickets chattered and palm trees curved their stems like ballerinas.

Sunshine rained down on her, warming her body and showering her with its tranquility. Easing her car out of the driveway, she took off down the block and made a sharp turn at the stop sign. The lanky police officer directing traffic on Eastern Avenue indicated for her to proceed and Sage waved her thanks.

As her car cruised through the intersection, Sage was reminded of another tall, handsome man with a commanding presence. An image of Marshall sprang into her thoughts and she felt her palms sweat. Their connection had been instantaneous, and she'd never imagined that they would hit it off so well. And the night he'd surprised her with that romantic sleigh ride at North Hill, she knew they had something special. Marshall listened to her, treated her with respect and within a matter of weeks, she'd fallen hard.

Her cell phone rang. Assuming it was Tangela calling to

check in, Sage pressed Talk on her ear piece and greeted her best friend. "I can't believe you're up this early," she teased, maneuvering her car around the oil spill on the road. "I figured you and Warrick would still be in bed."

"Hi, Sage," the caller said. "How are you?"

Her face flushed. Perspiring profusely, she squirmed uncomfortably in her seat. This was the voice she'd been longing to hear. Straightening, Sage tightened her grip on the steering wheel to steady her shaking hands. Breathing deeply, she forced herself to calm down. "Marshall, hi, how are you? How's everything?" she rambled.

"I can't complain. The kids at the center are keeping me busy, and Khari and I have been looking over university brochures for the last few days."

"That sounds exciting."

Silence plagued the line and Marshall knew if he didn't say something quick, this conversation would be over. He'd told himself he just wanted to hear her voice, but deep down he knew it was a lie. And after working up the courage to call, he wasn't ready to let her go.

Pacing the length of his bedroom, he searched his heart for the right words. Soon, Khari would be heading off to college and he'd be alone, with no one to hang out with but the dogs. And they were no real company. Having Sage around made his life fuller, richer and more complete since she'd left, he hadn't had a good night's sleep. Accustomed to having her in his arms, he tossed and turned all night, thoughts and images of her playing in his mind. "Are you doing okay?" he asked. "I mean, are you happy to be back home?"

"Yeah, I am. Tangela picked me up from the airport on Friday night and we sat in our favorite lounge for hours just talking. I guess I didn't realize how much I'd missed her."

I know what that's like, he thought, flopping down on his unmade bed.

"Has Khari narrowed down his university choices?"

"No, not yet, but I thought it might help if he saw a few of the schools and hung out on campus. Khari has two weeks off during spring break, so we're planning a little trip out west."

Sage concealed her disappointment with false enthusiasm.

"Oh, of course, that's why you called. You want me to recommend some hotels and—"

"No, Sage, that's not why I called. I wanted to apologize for how I acted at Khari's party." After a moment of profound silence, he continued, "I lost my head and I'm sorry. You've been an incredible help to Khari, and if it weren't for you, he probably wouldn't have decided to go to college."

Sage wanted to believe him, wanted to believe that he'd forgiven her, but knew in her heart that Marshall hadn't. Khari had probably put him up to calling her, and she could hear the tension in his voice. Unmoved by his apology and anxious to end the call, she said, "I hope you guys have a great time on your trip. Take care."

"Any chance of us seeing you while we're in L.A.?"

"I can't. I burned all of my vacation time when I was in Indianapolis." Feeling guilty for lying, she extended an olive branch. "Feel free to call me if you have any questions about L.A. Things can be a bit confusing for first-time visitors."

"Sage, can you just give me a few more minutes of your time? I've missed hearing your voice and there's so much more I have to say."

"Like what, Marshall? It's over between us and—"

"Is it?"

Her heart sighed at the gentle yearning of his voice. After a moment of soul searching, Sage decided to hear him out. They'd both made mistakes and hurt each other deeply, but she couldn't ignore what she was feeling inside. Marshall was the man she wanted, the man she needed and she didn't want to have to let him go.

"Sage, I've done a lot of thinking these last few days. Despite everything that's happened, I want us to try and work things out." Marshall paused. That was an understatement. He wanted her back in his life, and the sooner the better. A sister like Sage wouldn't be single long, and he didn't want to have to compete with anyone else for her heart. "Things aren't going to change overnight, but I believe over time they'll get better. We'll just take things slow and see what happens. Does that sound fair?"

Sage didn't know what to say. It was the first time she'd ever heard Marshall sound so contrite and for some strange reason, hearing the vulnerability in his voice made her desire him more than ever. Keeping her cool, she listened to him say how much he missed her and felt her lips curl into a girlish smile. "I miss you and Khari too."

"What, are we a packaged deal?" he joked.

"Yup. A two-for-one special!"

They shared a laugh.

"Is it okay if I call you later? Say around six?"

"I'd like that."

"Bye, beautiful. Have a great day."

Sage disconnected the call and took off her earpiece. *I don't know what just happened,* she thought, punching up the volume on the radio, *but this day is definitely off to the right start!*

Sapphire Entertainment sat perched in the middle of Chedway Street, flanked by a sushi restaurant and an accounting firm. The long, wide windows gave passersby a clear view into the enormous, sun-lit reception area. Photographs of celebrity clients were paraded on the walls, gardenias sat in decorative pots and the coffee percolating in the main-floor conference room filled the air. Sage sailed through the door and broke into a grin when her coworker and friend, Cashmere Michaels, squealed.

"Sage!" Cashmere sprang to her feet and threw her arms around Sage. "It's about time you got your ass back here. This place isn't the same without you!"

"Thanks, girl, I missed y'all too."

"You look amazing!" Examining her closely, she picked up a lock of Sage's wavy hair. "Where did you go? Back to that resort in Antigua, or somewhere new?"

"I, ah, was in Indianapolis."

"What the hell for?"

Sage pretended not to hear the question. "It's a great city, but the weather is a bitch. The first thing I did when I got back was head over to Serendipity spa. My skin was drier than sandpaper!" She broke into a laugh. "I got a facial and a pedicure, and now I feel like a million bucks."

"And you look it too." The phone rang, but Cashmere made

no move to answer it. "What's Indianapolis like? Is it true that they have blizzards and snowstorms and stuff?"

Before Sage could answer, Nadine Tompkins, Human Resources Director, shuffled into the reception area carrying a stack of files. "Look who the cat dragged in," she said, eyebrows raised in appraisal. "It's been quiet around here, but like they say, all good things must come to an end."

Sage didn't know her well, but she was thankful for the interruption her presence provided, even if she was having an attitude.

Nadine came closer, a question in her hazel eyes. "Where have you been?" she asked. "And more importantly, who have you been doing?"

Cashmere giggled.

"There's something different about you," Nadine insisted, tossing the mail on the reception desk. "Do tell."

Sage stuck out her right leg and wiggled her foot. "I got these babies last night at the Armani store. Pretty, huh?"

"You're glowing and it has nothing to do with the shoes. The only time a woman glows is when she's pregnant or in love, so which one is it?" She couldn't explain why she looked good. After all that had happened, she felt like crap.

"I-I don't know what you're talking about," the words stumbled out of Sage's mouth. "And I'm not pregnant, so don't go starting any rumors about me."

Leo appeared. "Doesn't anybody around here work anymore?"

Sage didn't think she'd ever be this happy to see him. Another minute of Nadine's intrusive questions and she would have cracked under the pressure. She hadn't sorted out her feelings for Marshall yet, and she didn't want to talk about him with anyone, especially her nosey-ass coworkers. "Hey, boss man, what's up? You're looking good."

Cashmere rushed back to her desk and Nadine marched briskly into the conference room, leaving Sage alone with their boss.

"Collins, my office, now."

Following her boss down the hall, toward his office, she wondered if she really was glowing or if Nadine was just running her mouth again. Deciding to stop at the ladies' room to see for herself later, she took a seat in front of Leo's desk and helped herself to the chocolate mints in the glass jar. "What's up, boss man?"

"Renegade has an interview with *Source* magazine at eleven o'clock and I want you there. Make sure he doesn't hit on the editor again or say anything stupid."

"Come on, Leo. The guy's a pig. Why don't you send Tobias, or one of the other junior talent scouts?"

"Because I'm sending you. Renegade likes you, and you're the only one who can keep him in line." He tapped his gold pen on the desk. "Didn't you read the tabloids while you were away?"

Sage shook her head.

"He slugged a camera man and got busted for drinking and driving again."

"Oh, shit." Now she understood why her boss was in a sour mood. Renegade, a one-time rapper with a legion of teenage fans was a pain in the ass. Thanks to Sapphire Entertainment, he had a clothing line, a production company and was up for a part in the next Spielberg movie. The Grammy-Award winner was indulgent, arrogant and hot-tempered, but everything he did turned to gold. "So much for a welcome," she muttered, pushing herself up off the chair. "I should have stayed back east. It was crazy cold up there, but at least no one was ordering me around."

"Quit pouting," he snapped. "We're a team, and everyone has to do their part, including you."

"Is this my punishment for not signing Khari Grant?"

"I'm sending you to the Renegade interview because you're the best celebrity manager I got. I trust you, Sage." Leo cracked a sly smile. "But it's too bad Khari Grant's not going pro. I was going to use that commission to get a new Jag."

"Poor you," she drawled, rolling her eyes. "I guess you'll have to cruise around in last year's model a little while longer."

Chuckling, he leaned back in his chair and propped his feet up on the side of the desk. "It's good to have you back, kid."

Sage suppressed a smile as she sailed through his office door. Her boss was right. It was good to be back. Las Vegas was home. She missed lounging in bed with Marshall and goofing around with Khari, but this is where she belonged. She loved her job, her clients and her fast-paced lifestyle and she wouldn't trade her life for anything.

Three hours later, Sage was singing another tune. Not only had Renegade showed up forty minutes late for the interview, but he'd called the editor a racist, spilled his Pepsi drink on the plush white carpet and had the nerve to ask to be on the cover of the magazine. When he insulted the female reporter, Sage thought of faking a panic attack or playing dead, but since she didn't think she could pull it off, she just sat on the couch, seething. By the time she returned to the office, her head was pounding, her feet hurt from chasing around the ill-tempered rapper and thoughts of quitting circled her mind.

"Ready for lunch?"

Sage lifted her head up off her desk and faced Cashmere. Her coworker stood in the entranceway of her cubicle, waiting impatiently.

"I can't. I have a ton of paperwork to do." She motioned to the files piled up on her desk like phone books. "It's hard to believe I've only been gone for six weeks. It feels more like six months!"

"Let's go. The group's meeting at the sushi bar in ten minutes." Cashmere dragged Sage off her chair, swiped her purse off the desk and pushed her out into the hall. "I want to hear all about your new man." She winked. "You might be able to fool Nadine, but I've been around the block a few times and I'm way too smart for that."

A man in a blue delivery uniform turned the corner and stopped abruptly. He was holding a bouquet of flowers in one hand and a clipboard in the other. "Do either of you know where I can find Sage Collins?" he asked, glancing around the room.

"I'm Sage. Are those for me?" she asked, pointing at the roses.

"They sure are."

"They're gorgeous!"

Cashmere jabbed Sage with her elbow. "My boyfriend sent me roses for my birthday and you said that was cliché."

"A girl can change her mind, can't she?" Sage slipped a hand into her purse and handed the delivery boy a twenty-dollar bill.

"Thanks, kid," she said, practically ripping the package from his hands.

He stuffed the money into his front pocket. "Don't move. I'll be right back."

"There's more?" Cashmere asked, her eyebrows pinched in confusion.

"Oh, yeah," he said, turning away. "A lot more."

It took three trips to bring all the flowers inside and when the deliveryman was done, her cubicle resembled a botanical garden. Plump pink roses sat in sleek crystal vases all around her office. On her desk, beside the computer, above the bookshelf. The entire agency was perfumed with their scent, and when word got out that someone had sent her dozens of roses, her female co-workers rushed over to see for themselves. Her boyfriend's extravagant display of affection was the talk of the agency, and although Sage tried to downplay all the attention, she couldn't help feeling incredibly special.

Each bouquet had come with a card, and as she read the last one, she broke out into a girly smile. The message was short, simple and sweet. "A rose for every time you made me laugh, for every time you brightened my day and for just being you." Heart overwhelmed with love, she rested back in her chair, a soft sigh on her lips. Who knew Marshall had it in him? He was an old-fashioned, school-of-hard-knocks kind of guy, but that didn't stop him from romancing her. A month ago, she had bawled him out for not leaving a tip at Pasqual's, a posh European restaurant, and now he'd spent hundreds of dollars on flowers. *If only I could do something about those ugly plaid shirts,* she thought, laughing to herself.

"Sage Collins?"

She turned toward the voice. A guy with thinning hair and a crooked nose was smiling at her. Replacing the receiver, she stood, towering over the slight wisp of a man. "Can I help you with something?"

"This is for you." Sage was so caught off guard by his arrival, she hadn't noticed the white plastic bags in his hands. The scent of mozzarella cheese and green peppers made her mouth wet with hunger. She'd had a big lunch, but that didn't stop her stomach from roaring like a lion. "I didn't order this."

"A gentleman did on your behalf."

Before she could question him, he was gone.

"It couldn't be," she said aloud, shaking her head. The lip-smacking aroma of veal piccata incited more groans from her unruly stomach. Resting the plastic bags on her desk, she opened them and peeked inside. Glass bowls topped with mushroom fried rice, prawns and avocado salad had been ordered from Glory of Morocco, one of her all-time favorite restaurants.

Sage sank down on her chair. *Unbelievable,* she thought, awed that Marshall had pulled this off from a thousand miles away. He'd done it again. Wowed her. Spoiled her. Impressed her. Made her feel beautiful without ever saying a word. His actions underlined his feelings, and Sage felt incredibly loved and cared for. No one had ever surprised her like this. Sure, past boyfriends had bought her flowers and jewelry, but Marshall had gone above and beyond. Having lunch delivered to her at work was first-class all the way.

Smiling wide, she scooped up the phone and dialed his number. He answered on the first ring. His deep baritone voice, which had the power to seduce her, filled the line and she felt her temperature spike.

"I've been waiting for this call."

"How did you know it was me?"

"A guy can hope, can't he?"

Coiling the phone cord around her finger, she leaned back in her chair, crossing her legs under the desk. "I got the flowers."

"You did?"

"All six dozen."

"And?" he prompted, waiting expectantly. "How did I do?"

"I love them and I love you." The words spilled out of her mouth, shocking them both. *Shit! What'd I say that for?* Bolting upright, she coughed to conceal the long, awkward silence. Words tumbled out of her mouth, one after another. "I, ah, the lunch arrived a few minutes ago. Everything looks yummy, especially the veal."

"Did I get it right? I couldn't remember if you were allergic to walnuts, so I ordered the avocado salad. I hope that's okay."

"It's perfect, Marshall. Everything's perfect. Thank you."

"You deserve it, and more."

Marshall insisted they get off the phone so she could eat, but Sage wouldn't hear of it. They talked about the weather, the harrowing adventure of Khari's first driving lesson, and they discussed what to do when they met in L.A in three weeks.

"Now that Khari's taking driving lessons and working on the yearbook committee, he's busier than ever. And it's lonely here without you."

"You miss me, huh?"

"Bad." His tone conveyed his need. "It's no fun without you here, Munch."

A smile tugged at her lips. Marshall had started calling her the unusual pet name after she'd demolished a plate of fried catfish, and though Sage didn't like him teasing her, she'd grown to love it.

"What do you miss?" Sage pressed the phone against her ear, ensuring she wouldn't miss a single naughty word.

"Everything. Your gorgeous smile, your sexy laugh and the way you walk. But you know what I miss the most?"

Sage licked her lips. Nothing like a little phone sex to keep things spicy. Feeling exhilarated and aroused by the sudden huskiness of his voice, she pushed away her food and closed her eyes, blocking out the sounds of the office. "No, what?"

"Watching you drool in your sleep!"

Sage laughed so loud her coworkers Adam Morton and Ella Vaughn stood up and peeked into her cubicle. They exchanged quizzical looks before returning to their seats. "Ha-ha, very funny," she quipped sarcastically. "I've got my very own comedian."

"No, you got a man who misses you like crazy and who loves you very much. So tell those Las Vegas brothers to step off, because you're taken."

Pride welled in her heart. "I'll do that."

Sage heard Leo's voice and stuck her head out into the hall. He was talking to Cashmere, gesturing wildly with his hands, his stringy hair resembling a bird's nest. Something was up and she had a feeling it wasn't good. "Marshall, I gotta go. My boss is lurking around, and if he catches me on a personal call, he'll have my head."

"All right, but I just have one more thing to say." Heartened by their earnest talk, he cleared his throat and poured out what was in his heart. "Baby, I want to build a life with you. I know we just got back together, but my feelings for you are real, and growing stronger by the second. You're my destiny, Sage, and I love you."

Sage didn't realize the receiver had slipped from her hand until she heard it clang against her desk.

Chapter 20

"**I**'m getting married in Maui!"

French onion soup spewed out of Sage's mouth. The liquid dribbled down her chin, staining her clingy, flame-red dress. They were seated in the Olive Grove, an expensive, celebrity hot spot, and thanks to Tangela, Sage had food all over her face. Her gaze circled the room as she cleaned her mouth. A teen pop star had entered the restaurant, causing a stir and stealing the attention of the diners.

Sage blew her bangs out of her face. She'd been back in town for five days, and it seemed to be one problem after another. Leo was on her case, and her newest client had checked himself into rehab just that morning. "Tell me you're joking," she said, resisting the urge to grab Tangela by the shoulders and shake some sense into her.

"Why would I joke about something as important as that?"

"Because you guys have been at each other's throats for months."

Her eyebrows shot up to her forehead. "Lots of couples go through rough times. It doesn't mean they're not right for each other. It just means they need to work on their relationship." Tangela produced her left hand. A stunning pink diamond twinkled on her fourth finger. "We picked it out last night. Isn't it beautiful?"

"Gorgeous," Sage agreed, inspecting the ring. Tangela said it was from Harry Winston. A flawless, contemporary diamond, worth tens of thousands of dollars. Sage wanted to ask Tangela what had happened to her other engagement ring, but decided against it. It wasn't important. Her best friend was talking crazy again, and she had to set her straight. "Are you sure Warrick's on board this time? He's not just marrying you because he's scared of losing you, right?"

Tangela snatched her hand away. "Of course not. He loves me."

"No one's disputing that, but he's always been reluctant to tie the knot."

"Don't worry about Warrick. He's fine. We had a long talk over the weekend, and now he wants to get married as much as I do. He's a *hundred* percent on board."

Sage grunted. Her best friend wasn't fooling anybody, especially not her. Tangela had given Warrick another ultimatum and he had caved—again. Sage actually felt sorry for him. He loved Tangela; he just wasn't ready to get married, and there was nothing wrong with that. Few guys his age were ready to settle down. Twenty-eight-year-olds liked to hit the strip clubs and party with their friends, not sit on the couch, perusing bridal magazines and watching *The Wedding Story*. "Take your time, girl. You guys have had a rough few months. Warrick's expanding his company and his dad has had some health issues. The smart thing to do would be to wait until—"

Tangela interrupted. "Don't," she warned, her voice sharper than a piece of jagged glass. "I know what I'm doing, and I don't need you telling me what to do. You have no idea what it takes to make a relationship work, especially *my* relationship."

Sage felt her face warm. Annoyed that her best friend had snapped at her and had the nerve to do it in front of the waitress who had returned with their entrées, she tasted her wine. The veiled reference to her mistakes hurt her feelings, and her first inclination was to lash back. But Marshall's words came back to her. "Next time you feel yourself losing control, count to ten, collect your thoughts and respond in understanding, not anger." Sage took his advice. It didn't work.

"What are you getting at?" The greasy-haired man at the next table glanced at her, and she lowered her voice. "Just because I don't go gaga over wedding dresses and haven't been planning my wedding day since I was nine doesn't mean I don't want to get married. It just means that I'm not ready yet. And I hate to be the one to burst your bubble, but neither is Warrick."

Sage didn't miss the look of panic that flashed across Tangela's face.

"I'm not sixteen anymore, Sage. You don't have to look out for me." Admiring her engagement ring, she smoothed her thumb over the diamond, her eyes twinkling under the restaurant lights. "Save the lecture, okay? I'm a big girl and I know what I'm doing. I'm marrying Warrick and no one's going to stop me. I know you were hurting with all the Marshall drama, but all I want is for you to be happy for me. Just like I'd be for you."

Sage took a deep breath and exhaled. "What the bride-to-be wants, the bride-to-be gets." Sage picked up her fork. "So, when's the big day?"

"April 28."

Sage's spoon slipped from her hand and crashed in her bowl. French onion soup splattered on her cheeks. Annoyed, she grabbed Tangela's napkin and cleaned her face. "I'll be in L.A. for work, remember?"

"Cancel. It's not every day that your best friend gets married," she said matter-of-factly. "Since wedding season is well underway, we've decided to forego tradition and get married on the beach!"

"But you've talked about getting married in a Catholic church for as long as I can remember. It's your childhood dream."

Staring down into her bowl, she circled her spoon in the broth. A pensive expression marred her delicate features. "It's no big deal. I want to become Mrs. Warrick Carver, and that's all that matters." Her voice perked up, full of its usual shine and luster. "Warrick's covering the travel expenses for the bridal party and he's even going to hire a twelve-piece orchestra for the reception."

"How many people are you inviting?"

Her smile dimmed. "Warrick wants to keep it small. Three hundred people, max."

"That's small?"

"For me it is. If it was up to me, I'd invite everyone I know!" Her eyes showed brimming joy. "I can't believe it's finally happening! I'm so fired up, I can't sleep!"

Sage laughed. Tangela was over the moon, and it was good to see her so happy.

Disappointed that her weekend was in jeopardy, but wanting to be supportive, Sage pushed aside her reservations about the impromptu wedding and listened to Tangela chatter about the intimate and private island where her nuptials would take place.

The friends laughed and joked all afternoon and capped off the day with a trip to Tangela's favorite store, Belle Bridal. The posh, by-appointment-only boutique had the most extensive collection of designer gowns in the state. It carried top-of-the line jewelry, and they served everything from red wine to green tea to its selective clientele.

When Sage strolled into the boutique and saw Rachel, Warrick's younger sister, she knew she'd been had. Tangela had planned this informal dress fitting without telling her, and she was now smiling at her like a damn leprechaun. Within minutes, her arms were weighed down with bridesmaid dresses and Tangela was shoving her into a fitting room.

Ten minutes, and plenty of wiggles, twists and turns later, Sage was cursing herself for her lack of self-control. Every dress felt like a five-thousand-dollar strait jacket. Sage struggled for several minutes with the zipper of the strapless gown and sighed in relief when the hook snapped in place. Squaring her shoulders, she sucked in her abdomen and shuffled out of the fitting room.

"Can you stand on the platform?" the plump-faced seamstress asked, unaware of her discomfort. "I need to check the length."

God, I hope I don't split this dress before I pay for it, she thought, shuffling over. But with the help of the seamstress, and pure strength of mind, Sage hopped up onto the platform and took her place in front of the elongated, three-way mirror. She inhaled sharply, then assessed her look. The gold, double-faced Lazario gown was spectacular. The beaded trim and embroidered neckline of the taffeta gown highlighted her collarbone and the sleek, trumpet-line skirt accentuated her slim hips. Sage had never considered a man's opinion before, but she knew Marshall would love this dress. Classy, sophisticated and chic, the designer gown underscored her beauty in a simple, elegant way. Grinning back at her reflection, she swept her hair off her shoulders and struck a model-worthy pose. *Now, if I could only master sitting down.*

"Someone's put on weight," Tangela teased, an eyebrow raised in surprise. "Your hips are spreading faster than the Red Sea."

"Marshall wasn't complainin'," Sage shot back, a triumphant look on her face. "He likes me just the way I am. Big butt and all."

"Don't mind Bridezilla," Rachel said wryly as she emerged from her fitting room in an identical gown. "Besides, you could stand to put on a few pounds, Sage. Men like to have something to hold on to. You know, a woman with some meat on her bones. Some junk in her trunk." She grinned cheekily. "Like me."

All three women laughed.

Just shy of six feet, Rachel had a healthy appetite and figure, for a woman of her stature. A perfect size twelve, she was fortunate enough to eat whatever she wanted without the fear of gaining weight. And after having three babies within five years, she still managed to sustain her eye-catching figure and bright disposition.

"Oh, brother," Sage groaned, massaging her temples. *I think this dress is cutting off my circulation!* Her head was throbbing and it felt like the room was spinning around her. She parted her lips to ask the seamstress if they could take a break, but the middle-aged woman scooted down the platform and shifted her attention to Rachel.

"We're done. You can go change now," the seamstress told her. "Hang the dress outside your fitting room door and I'll collect it when I'm finished up here."

Thank you, Jesus! Sage practically knocked Tangela down trying to get back to her changing room. Unzipped, back to breathing, and feeling a hundred times better, she put her clothes back on and returned to the showroom.

"How's my kid brother doing?" Rachel asked, staring at Tangela through the three-way mirror. "Does he have any pre-wedding jitters yet?"

There was a trace of irritation in Tangela's voice when she answered. "Why does everyone keep asking me that? Warrick's too busy counting down the days to be nervous. He's absolutely thrilled!"

Sage rolled her eyes. After being in more than a dozen weddings, she knew what was *really* going on behind the scenes, and her best friend couldn't tell her otherwise. It was only natural for the groom to be nervous; men often had very real fears about settling down. Women spent their whole lives planning their big day, while men avoided the altar at all costs. But Sage wasn't about to tell Tangela that. Her friend often took up residence in never-never land, and Sage didn't have the time or the energy to go there with her today.

Deciding she'd had enough wedding talk, Sage gave Tangela a hug and promised to call her later. "Bye, girl," she said, strolling toward the front of the store before her best friend could protest. As she passed the cash registers, a pair of ankle-tie pumps with leopard trim drew her attention. After the week she'd had, she deserved a pick-me-up, and nothing bolstered her spirits like a pair of sexy shoes.

A size-eight pair in her hands, she lowered herself onto a cushion, kicked off her shoes and slipped her feet into the heels. They were perfect. Sleek, chic and trendy. A fitted dress and some gold accessories, and she'd be ready for a night out on the town.

Hands on her hips, she turned from right to left, smiling. If Marshall was here, she'd ask him to take her to the House of Blues tonight. Under soft lights and soul music, they'd kiss and dance, stealing the spotlight from the house band and creating a romantic mood all their own. An idea formed in her mind as she remembered the last conversation they'd had. Marshall could be her date for Tangela's wedding! What was more romantic than spending a week together in hot, beautiful Maui? They could talk about their plans for the future and enjoy long, passionate nights making love. Feeling better, she perused the clothing racks, determined to find a dress that would knock his socks off. Something short and slinky, that showed off her legs and made him drool.

At the register, she chatted for a few minutes with the well-dressed cashier about the new spring stock. "Your total is $939."

Sage ran her tongue over her teeth. Two months ago she would have slapped down her American Express card without a second thought. But ever since Marshall helped her create a monthly budget, she was more conscious about her spending. She had to make her money work for her in the long run, not the here and now. *Damn! I'm starting to sound like Marshall!* she thought, opening her purse and extracting her wallet.

Sage could hear Marshall's voice in her ear, and it quickly grew louder than the voices in her head. A thousand dollars was a lot of money to spend on a dress and a pair of sandals. And if she was serious about wanting to buy a house next year, she had to start spending less and saving more. Tapping her credit card on the glass counter, her gaze circling the boutique, she racked her mind for a plan. Not only were there a handful of other customers behind her, Tangela was only a few feet away. Sage didn't know the storekeeper, but she didn't want the woman to think she was cheap. Or worse, broke. "How much did you say it was again?"

The clerk repeated the amount. "Is there a problem, Ms.?"

"Is that all?" Sage said, affecting surprise. "I still have some more money to spend." Pointing to the far wall, she glanced over her shoulder at the clerk. "I've been dying to try on one of those pink halter dresses. I hope that's not a problem."

The clerk's face lit up, dollar signs twinkling in her eyes. "Of course not. Take as much time as you need. I'll check on you as soon as I ring up these customers."

Sage turned away, a satisfied look on her face. She disappeared through the clothing racks, slipped on her sunglasses and ducked out one of the side doors.

Chapter 21

"It's showtime!" Marshall threw open the back door of the rental car and handed Khari a lavish fruit basket. "Do you remember what to say?"

Shielding his eyes from the blinding sunshine, he said, "We practiced all the way over from the airport. Don't worry, Dad. I'm not going to mess up. I got it."

"I know. I just want everything to be perfect."

"But what if she's not here?"

Marshall glanced around the parking lot. His eyes rested on the sleek black SUV with gleaming twenty-four-inch rims. He knew Sage drove a Lexus sedan, and he'd bet his life savings, the car bearing the word *DramaQn* on its personalized license plate belonged to her. "She's here, all right," he answered, grabbing the gift bag. "Besides, I just called and the receptionist said she was with clients."

Father and son stood in front of the Japanese restaurant, surveying the celebrity traffic flowing in and out of Sapphire Entertainment. Renegade, an East Coast rapper, swaggered toward the parking lot surrounded by a squad of dark, burly men who looked like a broke-down SWAT team. Their eyes anxiously circled the lot, as if they were expecting to be ambushed at any second.

"Renegade, you're the man!" Khari shouted, stepping forward. "You're the best rapper in the game!"

The rapper turned and favored Khari with a gold-tooth grin. "You spittin' the truth, son. Keep buying those CDs and supporting *real* music."

Marshall gripped his son's forearm, preventing him from approaching the group.

"Dad, it's Renegade!" Fumbling with his cell phone, he snapped pictures until the stretch limo cruised out of the parking lot and faded into traffic. "Wow! Wait until I tell the guys I met Renegade! I wonder if Sage can hook me up with an autograph or something. That would be…"

Marshall tuned out. He had more important things on his mind than Khari meeting some washed-up rapper. Staring down at his recently purchased leather shoes, he took a deep breath, second thoughts looming in his mind like ominous storm clouds. Sage wasn't kidding when she said Las Vegas was an attractive city. Everything from the pristine, tree-lined streets, to the majestic hotels and office buildings, to the healthy, vibrant-looking people made Marshall feel out of place. Brushing off his doubts, he told himself Sage would welcome him with open arms. And she'd love his look too. After all, she'd picked out the linen button-down shirt and slacks during one of their many shopping excursions.

As Marshall strolled toward Sapphire Entertainment, he felt a sudden and intense bout of fear. He was on her turf now, and they hadn't spoken since the day he'd declared his love for her. He knew his confession had shocked her, but why hadn't she returned any of his calls last week? Marshall took a deep breath, restoring his self-confidence. He had something in his favor: Khari. Sage might be angry at him for showing up unexpectedly at her office, but she wouldn't disrespect him in front of his son. That he was sure of.

Inside, a slim woman with outrageously long hair extensions greeted them. "Welcome to Sapphire Entertainment. May I help you?"

"We have a delivery for Sage Collins." Marshall slipped off his sunglasses.

"She's tied up at the moment," she explained, motioning to the table to her right. "Leave them there and I'll see to it that she gets it."

His mind raced. Surprising Sage at work had seemed like a romantic and caring gesture, but he'd never anticipated this fork in the road. He tightened his grip on the bouquet. "We'll wait."

Khari spoke up. "We're from out of town, but we're *really* good friends of Sage. We'd really appreciate if you could help us, Miss"

Her face brightened. "Oh, I just love surprises!" She hopped out of the seat and came around the desk. "Give me five minutes and I'll see what I can do!"

"Damn!" shot out of Sage's mouth when she opened her e-mail. Renegade had only left her office twenty minutes ago, but in that time he'd managed to send her ten lengthy messages, all pertaining to his birthday bash. Sage read the revised guest list and when she saw the last name on the page, the frown slid off her face. Will Smith was Marshall's favorite actor. Maybe she'd introduce them. That was sure to impress him, and after all the drama she'd put him through in the past, he could probably use a good laugh.

After an hour-long meeting with Renegade and his dimwitted entourage, she'd booked the caterer, mailed out invitations and arranged to have his beachfront home cleaned from top to bottom.

Planning a birthday party for Renegade had taken over her life, but the more time Sage spent time with the rapper, the more she liked him. Beneath the chains, tattoos and baggy jeans was a street-savvy guy who was destined to top the Forbes 100 List. After the disastrous *Source* magazine interview, Sage had called him and put him on notice. "Embarrass me like that again and you're on your own," she warned. He'd been an angel with gold teeth ever since.

Sage only wished her coworkers weren't such a pain. Thanks to Nadine, everyone knew she'd met and fallen for a guy in Indianapolis, and they teased her relentlessly. Then yesterday, Leo ruined her day with a surprise announcement. She'd be teaming up with Brian to sign DeeLuv, the newest teen R & B sensation. Sage would rather shave off her hair than work with the obnoxious jerk, but she had no choice. Brian loved to hear himself talk, and had to have the last word, and everytime they met, Sage gave more thought to opening up her own agency.

Sage forwarded Renegade's messages to the party planner, left a brief message with his publicist and ordered ten more cases of Cristal champagne. Yawning, she stretched her hands high above her head. Exhaustion clung to her limbs and her eyes were heavy with sleep. She was due in Brian's office at one o'clock, and if she was going to make it through their meeting without strangling him, she had to have a clear mind. A catnap would perk her up. Twenty minutes was all she needed. Then she'd be ready to take Brian on. Folding her arms in front of her, she lowered her head on the desk.

"Her office is at the end of the hall," Cashmere whispered, indicating with a flick of her hand. "Go on and I'll give Khari the rest of the tour."

Nodding, Marshall watched his son leave with the bubbly receptionist. *So much for backup,* he thought, contemplating his impending fate.

Stopping outside of her cubicle, he pressed his ear to the wall and listened intently. The chug of the air conditioner, the whirl of female laughter and a hundred different voices fluttered across the room. Marshall cleared his throat and his thoughts. He had nothing to worry about. Women loved surprises and elaborate gestures. And a man in the doghouse could never go wrong with a fine piece of jewelry. He had all the bases covered, so why were his palms slick and his heart thumping?

Marshall knocked on the side of the cubicle.

Seconds passed. "Sage, are you in there? It's me, Marshall." When she didn't answer, he stuck his head inside the door. Face the picture of calm, Sage slept soundly at her desk. In that moment, Marshall understood why he hadn't slept all week, why food tasted like cardboard and why every song on the radio reminded him of Sage. He loved her. He hadn't set out to find his soul mate, hadn't expected to fall in love so hard and so fast. He'd protected his heart, but Sage, with her playful nature, tell-it-like-it-is approach and lively personality, had penetrated his shield and captured his heart.

Marshall planned to play it cool. No pleading, no begging and no matter how bad he wanted to, no touching. He'd hang back and take his cues from her. But when he saw her looking soft and pretty and vulnerable, he couldn't help himself. He cared about her, what she was doing, what she was going through, how she felt. The scent of her floral perfume assailed his nostrils, stifling him, cutting off his air supply, leaving him helpless. A deep, primitive hunger, one he had never experienced before, pulsed through his blood and settled in his groin with a thump. He ached to feel her, kiss her and smooth the dark circles under her eyes.

Love propelled him across the room. Resting the pink, heart-shaped gift bag on her desk, he crouched down in front of her and took her in his arms. God, she was beautiful. In a white blouse and slim black skirt, she struck the perfect balance between sexy and sophisticated. Hair swept over in a side ponytail, diamond jewelry and full makeup, she deserved a place on the runway.

Marshall kissed her forehead. Satisfaction didn't come, wouldn't come, until they were alone; but holding her and inhaling her sweet, familiar scent allayed his doubts. He wasn't going down without a fight. He'd always had a feeling for people, and he'd known from the moment he saw Sage that she was somebody special. "I've missed you," he whispered, burying his face in her hair. "And I'm sorry. Again."

"Marshall?"

He held her at arms length. "You're awake." Searching her face for clues, he stared down at her. It was difficult to gauge her mood at the best of times, so he didn't even try to guess what she was thinking now. "This is a long way from home," she said, freeing herself from his grasp. "Marshall, what are you doing here?"

"Surprising you. You haven't returned any of my calls and I got worried."

"I'm sorry. Tangela's getting married in Maui and I've been helping her make the arrangements."

"Maui, huh? Can I be your date, or have you already asked someone else?"

Her eyes filled with shock and she tripped over her words. "Y-you'd come with me to Hawaii?"

"Of course," he told her, pulling her back to him. "I can't

have those buff Polynesian brothers pushing up on my girl, now, can I?"

Unraveling at his touch, she braced herself against the wall. Marshall, *her* Marshall, was standing in her office, smelling divine and grinning like a rock star. He had pulled off the mother of all surprises. If that wasn't love, she didn't know what was. He had character flaws, but so did she. In the pursuit of power and success, she'd lied and schemed her way into his life, never once considering his feelings. Marshall had found it in his heart to forgive her. Couldn't she do the same? "I'm glad you're here," she confessed.

"Me too."

Sage smoothed a hand over his crisp, sea-blue shirt. "And I'm especially glad you didn't come up here in one of those funky plaid vests, because I would have bolted out the back door!"

Their laughter filled the office.

Tilting his head to the right, he cupped a handful of her hair and lowered his mouth for a kiss. There was a time when kissing her wasn't enough, but after a three-week drought, it was heaven. His desire mounted when she threw her arms around his neck, stroking his chest and her hips against his inflamed body. Delirious with need, he ran his hands down her waist and up her skirt. His muscles weren't the only thing that was rock hard, and he was rapidly reaching the end of his willpower. Marshall heard his son's voice in the distance, but didn't pull away.

"Looks like someone's happy to see me," she teased, her gaze sliding south.

Groaning audibly, he rubbed his chin against her ear, inciting a purr. "I never thought these words would come out of my mouth, but I wish Khari was at Oakley's!"

"Why? So you could take me right here?"

"Ah, Sage. Ever the romantic."

"I'm a straight shooter. I tell it like it is!"

"I know. That's what I love most about you."

Grinning, she slanted her head to the right, and stared up at him. "Do tell, Mr. Grant. What else do you love?"

Chapter 22

In between meetings with university officials and touring dormitories, Marshall, Sage and Khari took in the Motor Speedway, the Stratosphere Tower and after cruising down the Sunset Strip, played ten rounds of miniature golf in the punishing midday heat.

By the time the trio arrived in Los Angeles, they were pooped. Intent on giving Marshall and Khari star treatment, Sage had booked them into the world-renowned Bentley Beach Hotel. A twenty-four-hour-on-call staff, full-service spa and heated out door pools lured guests from all over the word. Infamous for celebrity sightings and surprise weddings, the resort-style hotel's *whenever, whatever* policy arranged deep-tissue massages at 3:00 a.m. and gourmet meals served by the live-in chef.

Anxious to check out the expansive grounds, Khari chucked his bag in a corner and dashed out the open door. "See ya!"

"Don't forget, we're going downtown this afternoon!" Sage called, trailing him out into the hall. "Be back by two!"

At the same time the elevator doors slid closed, Sage felt strong, powerful arms surround her. "Are you going to stand in the hall hollering like a madwoman, or come in here and spend some quality time with your man?"

Sage twisted around to look at Marshall, loving his little-boy smile and wondering what she'd done to deserve him. "I have to take a shower first. I stink."

Lips puckered like he'd swallowed a lemon, he waved a hand in front of his face. "You're right, girl, you smell ripe!"

"Jerk!"

Marshall chuckled when she pushed him away. In hopes of making amends, he reached for her, but she swatted his hands as if he was a pesky bumblebee.

"Don't even think of it, buster! And just for that, I'm not going to invite you to join me in the shower."

"We'll see about that!" Marshall yanked Sage back into his suite and slammed the door with his foot. "You're not going anywhere. You can use our bathroom."

"But my bags are in my suite," she protested.

"I still don't understand why you booked separate rooms." His mouth swooped down on her. Parting his lips, he lowered his head and sprinkled kisses along her neck. "Money wasted, if you ask me. We both know where you'll be sleeping tonight."

Her eyebrows arched. "I remember a certain someone kicking me out of his house when I got carried away. You practically threw me out on my ass!"

"I did no such thing."

"You did. Playing hard to get and whatnot."

His laughter echoed around the suite. "I wasn't trying to play hard to get. Girl, I'm easy. I was just trying to set a good example for my son."

"And now?" she asked, high on life and love.

"I'm trying to romance my lady."

"Having separate suites is a good idea. You can slip into my room and get back in the morning while Khari's still sleeping."

"I like how you think."

Sage fed him a saucy smile. "I thought you would."

"So, what's the plan for the rest of the week, Madame Tour Guide?"

"Khari's dying to go to Universal Studios, so I figured we'd do that this afternoon. Tomorrow, it's off to California State University."

Marshall massaged her shoulders, awed at how beautiful she

looked in a simple tropical-print dress and sling-back heels. Floor-to-ceiling windows provided a stunning, unparallel view of the Los Angeles skyline and bathed the room with a wealth of sunlight, but Marshall only had eyes for Sage.

"Are you getting all this?" she asked when his hands careened down her back. His chin grazed her cheek and a soft gasp escaped her lips. She couldn't squash her desire and didn't even try to put up a fight. When it came to Marshall, her body had a mind of its own. "Try to focus, okay?"

Nodding, an impish grin on his lips, he said, "Tell me more."

"Friday we're at Strayer University. In the afternoon we have a brief meeting with the dean and academic advisor over at Pepperdine. If we have enough time, I thought we could go to Spago for dinner before we head to Renegade's party."

His eyebrows spiked. "You're going to a party?"

"No," she corrected, motioning with her hands to him, then herself. "*We're going to a party.* All of us."

"I can't. I made plans to hang out with some old army buddies. Guys I roomed with in Kuwait. I'm supposed to call them later to confirm the time and place."

Sage didn't want to go to Renegade's party alone. How would that look? Like she was desperate, that's what. Shopping by herself was one thing, but going to a celebrity party solo was another. "Can't you hang out with them another time?"

"Friday's the only night Travis and Bo are free."

"Let's make a deal," she proposed, leaning in and brushing her lips against the hollow of his throat. "You come with me to Renegade's party and I'll go with you to the Civil War Museum on Saturday. I'll even spring for lunch at the Ivy."

"I've got an even better idea. You go to the party and we'll meet back at your room for a nightcap." He ran his finger along her cheek. "How does that sound?"

Sage folded her arms under her chest, a pout fixed to her lips. She didn't want to compromise. She wanted Marshall with her on Friday night, not out with his stupid military friends, doing God knows what.

"You're not mad at me, are you, Munch?"

"No, that's fine," she conceded, screening her disappointment behind a tight smile. "I guess it'll just be me and Khari then."

"No, Khari's staying here. He has to finish reading *The Autobiography of an Ex-Colored Man* and…"

Sage rolled her eyes. In the dictionary, beside the word *intransigent* was a full-length photo of Marshall. "Nobody does homework while they're on vacation, not even honor students!"

"Renegade's nothing but a glorified gangster, and I don't want my son around him." Her gaze tore into him and he cleared the malice from his voice. "I know he's one of your favorite clients, but the guy's trouble."

"You can't expect Khari to stay in the hotel by himself. He'll be fine. We'll eat, take some pictures with Will and Jada and come home."

"Will Smith is going to be at the party?"

"The one and only." Sage patted his chest. "It's too bad you have other plans, huh? I would have introduced you."

"Why didn't you tell me you knew Will Smith?"

"Oh, we go way back," she lied. The truth was she had only met the Oscar nominee once and would be hard-pressed to remember where.

"Could you get his autograph for me? He was incredible in *Ali*."

"You're not going to cancel your plans?"

"I'll make it up to you. Okay?"

Instead of sulking or demanding that he cancel his plans, which she knew he wouldn't, she relented. Narrowing her eyes, she cupped his chin with superhuman strength. "No strippers, no clubs and no titty bars."

Marshall shook his head, an amused expression clouding his face.

"And don't be late," she warned, her voice stern. "If you're not here by midnight, I'm starting without you!"

His shoulders rocked with laughter.

"Now, where were we?" she asked, grinding her hips against his growing erection. "Baby, you have no idea how much I want you right now."

Marshall stared back at her, a look of contentment reflected in his deep brown eyes. "What would I do without you?"

"Let's hope you never have to find out."

Nibbling on his earlobe, she tugged off his jacket and let it fall to the floor. Weak-kneed, he sank down on the couch, pulling her on top of him. Grabbing a fistful of her hair, he kissed her with such a savage intensity, she felt dizzy. He licked, sucked and rubbed her all over. His erection, long, wide and thick, pressed against her inner thigh. Had she ever wanted anyone as much as she wanted this man? *No!* resounded in her ears at a deafening pitch. Marshall tweaked her nipples and a delicious warmth spread from her breasts to her core. Her heart rate quickened and a sharp, tingly sensation pulsed between her legs. "We…we better stop. What if Khari—"

"Don't worry about Khari," he told her. Any fight in her died when he took her earlobe into his mouth. "I gave him twenty bucks and told him to get lost."

Sage laughed. "You cheap bastard. Did you forget you were in L.A.? Twenty bucks doesn't go far in this town."

Marshall slapped her butt, then laughed out loud when she told him to do it again. "Hey, you can't fault me for trying. I just wanted to make love to my woman."

"All right then…" Grabbing his wrist, she tapped the face of his watch with her forefinger. "We only have thirty-six minutes left. So quit talking and kiss me!"

He did—slowly, tenderly, completely. Ignited by his kiss, she leaned into him, gently stroking his face. Every nerve in her body screamed out for his touch. Kissing her with more passion than any of Hollywood's leading men, he caressed the length of her arms, the slope of her hips, and the tender spot between her thighs. Marshall touched her wetness and a moan ripped from her mouth.

A kaleidoscope of color swirled in her mind, snatching her thoughts and leaving her breathless. Pleasure cascaded down her back like a ninety-foot waterfall. Inhaling his scent, a mixture of aftershave, soap and cologne, she tried to remember a time when she was this happy. Nothing came to mind.

The backseat of her car was roomier than the couch, but Sage wouldn't have moved if the fire alarm went off. Grinding herself against him, she leaned forward, rotating her hips as if she were spinning a hula hoop around her waist. Nothing made her feel sexier than taking control and showing Marshall how it should be done, so she whipped off her bra, and guided his hands to her breasts. He cupped them, mashed them, kneaded them, driving her over the edge with the sensuous, erotic assault.

Her brain shut down, blocking out everything but his touch, his caress, his love. Holding his gaze, she took in his shallow breathing and the ravaged look in his eyes. Anticipation was a bitch. It was killing him and Sage loved seeing Marshall come undone. Gone was the control, the take-charge attitude. Under his strong, silent exterior was a loyal, generous man who just wanted to be loved. And love him she would.

When he cupped her breasts, they swelled like balloons. Lost in the fantasy, the moment, the emotions and feelings flowing through her, Sage kissed him with everything that she had. And when he tore off her thong and rubbed his thumb across her core, devastating words slipped from her mouth. "I love you, Marshall. More than I've ever loved anyone."

"I know." He licked the side of her neck and she struggled to remain upright. Easing off the couch, a lazy grin working its way onto her lips, she pushed his shirt over his head. Self-control took a backseat to desire and she yanked off his belt like a lion tamer cracking a whip. His erection was long, powerful, thick. Inclining her head to the right, she trailed the length of his penis with her tongue.

Eyes focused on his face, she slid him in and out of her mouth, creating a mind-numbing rhythm. Perspiration clung to his skin and every muscle in his body cried out for release. Groaning in sweet agony, his eyes rolled to the back of his head as if he were about to lose consciousness. Curses, grunts and growls ripped from Marshall's mouth. Gripping his shaft, she swallowed him whole. He dug his hands into her hair and swept her wavy locks off of her pretty face. Sage took her time, loving him, teasing him, tasting him. And when she returned to his lap and eased down on top of his erection, he was promising her everything from a Tiffany necklace to Manolo Blahnik stilettos.

Marshall stirred himself inside her and she answered the call by moving her butt in slow, tight circles. Her breasts jiggled in perfect rhythm with the thunderous beat of his heart. Feeling restricted and eager to love her without restraints, he lifted her up off the couch. He stumbled on one of her sandals, but didn't fall. "Carefully, Marshall," she cautioned, her eyes alight with laughter. "I'm too young to die!"

Legs entwined around his waist, hands linked around his neck, she kissed him. They staggered through the open partition and tumbled onto the bed. She climbed on top of him like she was scaling a tree. Leaning over him, a smile at her lips, she placed her hands on the wall. Her breasts hung over his face like melons on a vine and he plopped a nipple into his mouth.

Wanting to see every inch of her, he moved over to the middle of the bed and positioned her in front of the mirror. Then he spooned her onto her back, plunging into her—far, deep and wide. He felt every contour, every slope, every curve. Her ultra-tight viselike grip increased his pleasure and he released a deep, savage groan. When she cupped his butt, driving him deeper inside, he cooed like a pigeon. Sage knew what to say and do to make him feel like a stud, and her no-holds-barred loving drove him to delirium every time.

Four-letter words shot out of her mouth.

"Now, is that any way for a lady to talk?"

"Who said I was a lady?" She circled her tongue around his left nipple. "I'm a bad girl and you love it!"

Nothing about their lovemaking was soft or sweet, but he couldn't resist reaching and stroking the apples of her cheeks. Sunlight crashed through the window, filling the room with its splendor and illuminating the sparkle in her eye. Staring down at her, transfixed by her beauty, Marshall decided she'd never looked more gorgeous.

"That's it baby," she purred, planting her feet on the bed and thrusting her hips forward. "Don't stop…please, don't stop!"

Aroused by her pleas, he hiked her legs up in the air and plunged into her with renewed energy. Marshall felt like a swimmer catapulting off a diving board. The missionary position had never felt so good. His head was spinning faster than a propeller, but he couldn't let the moment pass without telling her what was in his heart. Through meeting Sage, he'd discovered a renewed sense of love. She'd opened his eyes to true love and proved to him there was such a thing as soul mates. "You're the only woman I want. The only woman I'll *ever* want. We…" His orgasm stole his words. Floods of passion erupted. Unforgettable pleasure coursed down his back like molten-hot lava. Head back, shoulders arched, he pressed his eyes shut and rode out the wave.

Sage sucked air into her lungs. Filled with an amazing sense of completeness, she snuggled close to him and laid her head on his chest. It was the middle of the afternoon, but the warm afterglow of exquisite lovemaking made her eyes heavy with sleep. Several deep breaths later, her mind cleared and she regained use of her tongue. "Wow!"

"You could say that again." Kissing her softly, he brushed delicate wisps of hair out of her face. "That was incredible, Munch."

"And the award for the Best Lover goes to…"

"Flattery will get you everywhere," he said with a laugh. "One of these days…" He stopped midword. Bolting upright, he peered down the narrow hall. He couldn't see Khari, but he could hear him. He must have been on his cell phone, because he was telling someone about his infamous meeting with Renegade.

"Shit!" Marshall sprang from the bed. How the hell was he going to explain this? He'd carelessly tossed the condom wrapper on the living-room floor, and if that wasn't bad enough, the heady, unmistakable scent of sex suffused the air.

"Aren't you going to get dressed?" he asked, tugging on his jeans. Sprawled out on the bed, her hair a tangled mess and her eyes glistening brighter than hubcaps, Sage looked like she was ready for her close-up.

"I would," she began, a laugh tickling the back of her throat, "but my clothes are in the living room."

Marshall cursed again. He watched the bedroom door, half-expecting his son to burst in quoting the Ten Commandments. "What are we going to do now?"

"That's what you get for being cheap," she scoffed, reaching over and smacking him playfully on the butt. "The next time you want to get some, give the kid a hundred bucks!"

Chapter 23

Renegade swaggered into the living room of his beachfront home flanked by two *Maxim* magazine cover models in yellow bikinis. The theme music of *Shaft* blared from waist-high speakers and a spotlight trailed him to a gold, thronelike chair. He sat down with the flourish of a king, a trophy girl on each side, a smug, arrogant grin on his lips. And when he blew out the candles on the enormous cake, bearing the word *PIMP,* guests broke out in wild, hysterical cheers.

Sage took a swig of her wine to keep from laughing out loud. Renegade was thirty-three. And he looked like a pimp in that ridiculous getup. Loud, flashy suit. Flowing silk cape. White top hat. Sage had tried to talk Renegade out of having a seventies-theme birthday party, but backed off when he got upset. What the client wants, the client gets. No matter how tacky it was. Everything, from the disco ball to the patchouli incense and multihued decorations, was a throwback to the year Renegade was born. Sage stood beside the punch bowl, bored out of her mind, but if the celebrity guests, empty Cristal champagne bottles and packed dance floor was any indication, the party was a hit.

Growing tired of KC & The Sunshine Band, the giggly, half-naked women bopping around the room and the hopeless fools who kept hitting on her, Sage searched the room for Khari. He'd been standing beside her a minute ago, then promptly pulled a David Blaine.

Convinced Khari was outside, she refilled her wineglass and sailed through the French doors. Spotting Khari near the hot tub, she weaved her way around the roller rink, narrowly avoiding a drunk female guest. Donning a pissed off, don't-mess-with-me look, she ignored the posse of black men beside the gazebo, shot past a former client doing tequila shots, and flew across the lawn without being accosted by any pimp wannabes.

"Where have you been?" she asked, tapping Khari on the shoulder. "I've been looking all over for you."

Khari turned and the grin on his face slipped. "Ah, hey, Sage."

Noticing the curvy teenage girl behind him, she drew back her hand and apologized for interrupting. "Do you mind if I steal my little brother away for a minute?"

Linking arms with Khari, Sage led him over to one of the food tables. Bay oysters. Crab cakes. Smoked salmon. *For a kid who grew up in Harlem, Renegade sure has expensive tastes,* she thought, admiring the lavish spread. "I'm ready to go. Let's leave now before Renegade notices that we're gone."

"Why don't you go on?" he suggested, plucking a shrimp off one of the silver trays. "I'm not ready to bounce just yet. I'll catch a cab back to the hotel later."

"No way. We came together, we leave together. Sorry, it's a party rule."

"I'm a big boy. I don't need you babysitting me."

"And what do I tell your father?"

"Nothing." He shrugged. "As far as he knows, I'm in my room sleeping, right?"

"Khari, I don't know," she began, her eyes circling the back-yard and resting on a well-known TV actor squirting whip cream on a redhead's cleavage and licking it off with his ruler-long tongue. "This isn't Indianapolis, Khari. It's Hollywood. Crazy things happen at celebrity parties."

"I can handle it," he assured her, draping an arm around her shoulders. "You and Dad can kick it without me getting in the way. Doesn't that sound nice?"

It did. Three days had passed since Khari had busted them

making love, and Marshall had been acting like a Boy Scout ever since. Aside from a few chaste kisses, he didn't touch her, and it was driving Sage crazy. She loved Khari and enjoyed having him around, but she wanted to spend some quiet time alone with Marshall too. "All right, we'll stay. One more hour and then we're—"

Khari cut in. "What happened to my cool, easygoing friend who encouraged me to assert my independence?" He wagged a finger in her face. "See, you've been hanging out with Dad too much. His controlling ways are starting to rub off on you."

Sage laughed. She didn't know all about that, but there was no harm in letting Khari stay. This wasn't a beer and weed party at a Newark housing project. Bodyguards built like WWE wrestlers kept watch, poised to pounce at the first whiff of trouble.

"Go," he ordered, gripping her shoulders and steering her in the direction of the house. "I'll be back in a few hours and Pops'll never know."

"I'll arrange with Renegade to have his driver drop you back at the hotel."

"Thanks, Sage." He pecked her on the cheek. "I'll see you tomorrow."

Marshall banged on Sage's hotel room door. He thought of going back to his room, but decided against it. They had agreed to meet at midnight, and though he was late, he had a feeling she was nearby.

Flipping open his cell phone, he scrolled through his missed calls and listened to her message again. His face broke out into a grin. The sound of her light, breezy voice brought him back to Wednesday afternoon. They'd gone at it full-throttle, and when he woke up the next morning, he'd felt the aftereffects in his bones. Nothing like good loving to make a man feel alive.

After Roxanne had left, he'd drifted from one meaningless relationship to the next, hoping sex would heal the emptiness in his heart. It wasn't until meeting Sage that Marshall realized what had been missing. Fun, passion, joy. Raising Khari, working sixteen-hour days and volunteering in the community had consumed his life for years and he'd forgotten how good it felt to have a woman in his life.

Shaking his head ruefully, he fished his wallet out of his back pocket. He'd forgotten that Sage had given him the extra key card earlier in the day. Marshall slid the card into the lock and pushed open the door. "What the…" His words died on his lips, as he entered the suite. Dozens of candles made a vertical path through the living room, their light giving off a soft, romantic glow. Will Downing purred with seductive soulfulness and the room smelled like a florist shop.

Marshall followed the candle trail down the short hall to the bathroom. The tub was overrun with bubbles, and hundreds of rose petals were sprinkled on top. Plump, juicy strawberries floated in flutes filled with champagne, and a bowl topped with chocolate syrup sat on a gold tray.

"Welcome home," Sage greeted, sneaking up behind him. "I've been waiting."

Marshall glanced over his shoulder. "Hey, hon. What's with all the candles?"

"Just trying to set the mood."

"I told you before, I'm easy. *Real* easy. You didn't have to go to all this trouble."

"I know, but I wanted to." Pressing kisses along the side of his neck, she tugged off his sports jacket. "You take such good care of me. It's time I pamper you."

"How was the party?"

"Boring as hell, but Khari had a good time."

Marshall chuckled. "I bet, he's probably calling everyone he knows to brag about all the celebrities he met."

"And what's wrong with that?"

"The hotel's expensive enough with Khari running up our bill. I have half a mind to go over there and—"

She put a finger to his lips. "You're not going anywhere. You're mine tonight. Now kick off your shoes and get in the tub."

"I don't take baths."

"Why not?"

"I'm just not a bath and bubbles kind of guy."

"That's too bad, 'cause I'm a bath and bubbles kind of girl," she joked, undoing the top button of his shirt. Not a woman to give up easily, she rubbed her chest against him, purring softly in his ear. "Honey, relax and let me take care of you."

"I've never done this kind of thing before. It feels…weird, that's all."

"Don't worry. I'll make it worth your while," she promised. "Now, strip!"

As she crossed her legs, her robe fell open, revealing a snatch of her lacy, low-cut panties. Perspiration clinging to his skin, Marshall rubbed a hand over the back of his neck. Her hot little number was making *him* hot under the collar. The sight of her sleek, brown flesh made every nerve in his body stand at attention. Her hair, a thick bundle of curls, tumbled around her face, softening her sexy, drool-worthy look. A red, high-heeled shoe dangled from her foot and her legs seemed to go on for miles. She dipped a finger into the bowl and licked the chocolate clean off of her fingers. He imagined how her tongue, so wet and moist, would feel around his shaft. The thought made his heart gallop and his mouth dry. Like a motorist who'd slowed down to catch a glimpse of the scene of a head-on collision, he couldn't tear his eyes away. It was hard not to stare at her. She was a centerfold. Tall, sleek and ridiculously sexy.

Her robe shifted. A diamond belly ring peeked out of the opening and drew his gaze south. Marshall felt like he was sneaking a forbidden peak, and enjoyed the unexpected thrill. Like a tidal wave engulfing a helpless surfer, the rush of making love overcame him. His body was on fire. Scalding hot. He had a deep emotional craving for her, and the more time they spent together, the stronger his need. Flowers, lingerie and music didn't mean anything to him, but that didn't give him license to criticize. "You're beautiful, Sage. And this is perfect. You're perfect."

"I am, aren't I?" she said, flashing him a cheeky smile. A perfect blend of beauty and brains, she teased him mercilessly, laughed her ass off at his corny jokes and inspired him to be a better man. And the sex was amazing. He'd never had such a powerful, immediate connection with someone, and when she touched him, his body became a raging inferno.

Marshall moved closer. He couldn't resist her and he didn't

want to. Kicking off his shoes, he shed the rest of his clothes, tossing them aside. Insane with desire, he reached hungrily for her, his fingers stroking the delicate curve of her hips. Her skin was soft to the touch. Heart beating a thousand beats per second, he pulled Sage to her feet and kissed her so hard that she staggered backward. Pinning her hands behind her, he licked the tender spot behind her ears and laughed when she playfully bit his shoulder. Pushing aside her panties, he slipped his thumb between her legs and stroked her until she screamed out.

Body tingling with need, her nipples straining against her push-up bra, she emitted a low, hollow moan. Panting, a glass-shattering scream in the back of her throat, she pressed a hand against the wall to steady her balance. Marshall brought out the animal in her, and the more he stroked her, the louder she groaned.

Marshall's cell phone rang. He glanced down at his clothes, lying in a heap in the middle of the bathroom floor.

"Don't even think of answering it," she warned, wishing she could toss the stupid thing out the window. "You and I have some unfinished business to take care of."

"I wouldn't dream of it," he said with a laugh.

Giggling, she noted the wild, predatory look in his eyes and his staggered breathing. She didn't think it was possible, but Marshall wanted her just as much as she wanted him. He felt so nice. His hands were in her hair, on her breasts, her stomach, inside her. His mouth blazed a trail from her ear to her breasts, and just when Sage thought she'd die of pleasure, he scooped her up, stepped into the tub and buried himself between her legs. Twining her arms around his waist, she gripped his butt and pulled him deeper inside her. Marshall knew her intimately, privately, completely. She had never felt more connected to anyone. He took his time loving her, slowly and carefully, with the patience and skill of an artist. It was the sweetest, most delicious sex she'd ever had, and she loved him for making her feel like a jewel.

The shadows of the night fell away, allowing the light of the sunrise to welcome them into Saturday morning. And when an orgasm tore through her with the ferocity of a category-eight hurricane, her wild, frenzied screams could be heard down the hall.

Chapter 24

Opening one eye, Marshall lifted his head gingerly off the pillow. He was in a dreamlike state, and it took him a moment to remember where he was. His eyes hurt and it felt like someone was standing beside him, whacking a pot with a sledge hammer. But that's what he got for polishing off a bottle of vodka and making love like a Kama Sutra junkie.

Outside, cooing doves perched on tree branches and the sounds of the busy street below filtered through the balcony windows. The bedroom was redolent of roses and chocolate, but it was the scent of bacon that made his stomach roar in hunger. "Ouch," he rasped, struggling to sit up.

Spotting a bottle of aspirin and a glass of water beside the bed, he wondered where Sage was hiding. Aware that he had overindulged himself last night, she had found pain relievers and had them waiting for him when he woke up. His girlfriend was an expert when it came to taking control of a situation, and he admired that about her.

He was guzzling the glass of water when he heard his cell phone ringing. Even if he knew where it was, which he didn't, he didn't have the energy to get out of bed. Just as he was about to roll over and go back to sleep, Sage entered the bedroom, carrying a tray topped with waffles, bacon, fruit and two coffee mugs. "Rise and shine, sleepyhead. We have a full day ahead of us and not a moment to spare!"

Marshall groaned, drawing a chuckle from Sage.

"Breakfast is served," she announced, positioning the tray in front of him. "Did you sleep well, baby?"

"You know I did." He grabbed her arm and pulled her to him for a kiss. Stunning in a red silk robe and dangerously high heels, he slipped a hand inside her covering and stroked her delicate skin. "Very, very nice, Ms. Collins. Are you coming back to bed?"

"Eat first and I'll think about giving you a taste."

Relinquishing his hold, he smacked her playfully on the butt as she sashayed out of the room. "What are we doing today?" he asked, adding cream to his coffee. "I thought we were going to hang out around the resort."

"Not today we're not. You guys have an appointment with Dean Rafferty at noon, and I have some business to take care of in Santa Monica."

From his position on the bed, he could see clear into the bathroom, and he grew aroused as he watched her lotion her legs. "Sage, come here. It's no fun eating alone."

She exited the bathroom. Holding out his cell phone, she said, "I took the liberty of fishing this out of the garbage can."

He frowned. "How did it end up there?"

"I didn't want you to be distracted from your assignment, so I put it in there for safekeeping."

"My assignment, huh? What's my grade?"

She leaned in. "An A plus, plus."

"Is that so?"

Nodding, she picked up his fork and fed him a piece of sausage. "I can't wait until we finally get to Maui. You're going to love the—"

Marshall's cell phone rang and Sage rolled her eyes. "Tell Denzel I'm going to kick his ass. Just because he's having problems at home, doesn't give him the right to call every five minutes."

"Go easy on the guy. Heather's making his life miserable." Putting the phone to his ear, he popped a strawberry into his mouth. "Hey, D. What's up?"

Sage threw open the closet, selected a multicolored dress and laid it on the bed.

"This is Marshall Grant."

Whipping around, she examined her boyfriend's face. Sage knew Marshall well enough to recognize alarm in his voice and the troubled look in his eyes. "Babe, what's the matter?" she whispered, moving closer to the bed. "Is everything okay?"

"But that's impossible." He pressed the phone to his ear. "My son's here, at the Bentley Beach Hotel. He's been here since eleven-thirty last night."

Sage felt a pain in her chest. Fear pelted her stomach and her throat was so thick she could barely swallow.

"Are you sure?" Marshall flung off the blanket, sending the breakfast tray crashing to the floor.

Frozen in place, she watched helplessly as Marshall struggled to his feet and threw on his clothes. He had a wild, crazed look in his eyes and the muscles in his jaw were pulled tight. "What is it?" she asked, gripping his forearm and forcing him to look at her. "Is Khari all right?"

"Cedars-Sinai. First floor. Room seventy-one," he repeated. "I'm on my way."

Forty-five minutes later, Marshall burst through the emergency room doors at Los Angeles's largest hospital, his face awash with fear, concern and confusion. Sage had to run to keep up with him, and by the time she reached the nurses' station, sweat was gushing down her face and legs.

"I'll page the on-call doctor. Please have a seat." Marshall started to move toward the row of blue plastic chairs, but Sage stepped forward, surprising the plump, blue-eyed nurse. "We're here on a family vacation, so I'm sure you can understand our anxiety. It would help if we could see Khari while we wait for the doctor to arrive."

The nurse looked from Sage to Marshall, then nodded. "He's just around the corner. I'll show you." As she moved briskly down the hall, she read the scribbled notes off the metal clipboard. "Your son was lucky. If he hadn't of been wearing his seat belt, he wouldn't have survived the crash. He has a dislocated shoulder, a broken leg and severe whiplash." She stopped in front of a partially opened door. "I should warn you," she began, lowering her voice in a soothing whisper. "He's pretty banged up, but don't be alarmed. The cuts and bruises will heal in no time and he'll be back to his usual self."

Sage sighed in relief, but when the nurse pulled back the curtain enclosing the bed, she stifled a gasp. Her worst fear had come true. Khari lay lifeless, his face black-and-blue, wires and tubes stuck to his hands, all because she'd been too wrapped up in herself to think things through. Anxious to get back to the hotel, she'd allowed him to talk her into something she knew Marshall would disapprove of.

Sage stretched her hands toward the bed, but didn't touch him. His big, beautiful brown eyes were swollen shut, he had a large welt on the right side of his face and his busted lip looked like it had a hundred stitches. "He's unconscious, but that doesn't mean he can't hear you." The nurse smiled kindly. "I'll be at the front desk if you need anything, and I'll notify Dr. Van Der Meer that you're here."

Marshall took Khari's hand, his eyes filled with a father's love. Emotion threatened to overtake her, but Sage ordered herself not to cry. She had to be strong. Marshall needed her. At a loss for what to do, she stood off to the side, a thousand thoughts—each one crazier than the last—running through her mind. Guilt rained down on her like torrential rains, blurring her vision and deepening her fears. How could she have been so stupid? So careless?

"I've always tried to lead by example."

The sound of Marshall's voice, so soft and gentle, made her eyes fill with water. "I pushed you too hard, but my dad raised me with an iron fist, and that's the only way I know." His voice cracked. "I've made a lot of mistakes, but from this day forward, I promise to not only be your father, but your friend."

Sage lost it. Tears came fast and steady and her throat burned with emotion. This wasn't the time or the place to tell Marshall the truth, but she couldn't listen to him blame himself for what happened. He hadn't failed Khari, she had. Telling the truth wouldn't be easy, but it was the right thing to do. Wiping her face with her sleeve, she stepped forward, clasping his forearm. "Marshall, there's something I have to tell you." She took lengthy pauses between her words, gathering her strength and shunning her fears. "It's about last night."

The door creaked open and heavy footsteps filled the room. Staring down at the bottom of the curtain, she wondered when this nightmare would end. But when she saw the starched polyester pants and the thick black boots, she knew it was just beginning.

"Mr. Grant?" a raspy masculine voice said. "I'm Detective Alvarez, and I'd like to have a word with you outside, if it's not too much trouble."

Taking a seat on the couch in the main floor family lounge, Sage sipped her coffee and waited anxiously for the detective to finish questioning Marshall. The young, baby-faced cop couldn't have been over thirty, but he had the hard, angry eyes of a man who'd seen the worst the world had to offer.

"I was the first officer on the scene, and although the weather was a factor, I have reason to believe drugs and alcohol were to blame."

Marshall dragged a hand over his face. He'd aged years since arriving at the hospital, and Sage wondered how much more he could take. "What happened?"

"According to eyewitnesses, the Lincoln Navigator truck your son and his friends were driving in sped through the intersection as the light turned red and T-boned a city bus."

His shoulders sagged. "This is like a bad dream," he confessed, shaking his head despondently. "None of this makes sense. We've only been in L.A. for a couple days. Who could he have snuck out to see?"

"Maybe it will help if we start at the beginning. Let's go over the events of the last week, starting with your arrival in Las Vegas. Go slow and try to remember as much as you can."

Sage listened patiently, waiting for an opportunity to inject the truth. Her moment came when the detective asked where Khari went last night. "He was with me. We went to a birthday party in Beverly Hills." Carefully not to mention Renegade's name, she answered his questions truthfully and honestly.

"Where was the party?"

Sage coughed. "At Renegade's house. I'm his manager."

"Were there drugs and alcohol?"

"Alcohol, yes. Champagne, wine, the usual party stuff. I didn't see anyone doing drugs, but it's possible."

He surprised her by saying, "If the party was at Renegade's house, there were definitely drugs. *Lots* of drugs."

"Are you sure?" Marshall asked, his eyes wide with terror.

"Do NBA players like blonds?" His sneer revealed yellow, stained teeth, and when he shifted in his seat, his stomach jiggled. "A couple of guys from my squad pulled the rapper's limo over last summer," he explained. "Not only did they find a thousand dollars in cash and an unregistered gun, they found dime bags of weed in the glove box."

Sage swallowed. It felt like there was a watermelon lodged in her throat. She remembered the incident all too well. The local news had covered the story, and every paper in the country had splashed Renegade's wild-eyed mug shot across their covers.

"When did you guys leave the party?"

"I, ah, left around eleven." Sage didn't dare look at Marshall. The heat of his gaze was burning a hole in her cheek. "Khari wanted to stay, so I arranged with Renegade to have him dropped back at the hotel when he was ready."

"You did *what?*"

Sage chanced a look at Marshall. His eyes were red and narrowed.

"You left my son at a party with a bunch of gangbangers?"

"It wasn't like that," she protested weakly, shifting in her seat. "I thought—"

"Are you insane?" He surged to his feet. "You don't know Renegade any more than I do. You see him, what? Once a month, or whenever he's in trouble? For all you know, he could be selling dope from out of his house!"

Sensing the impending blowout and not wanting to be caught in the eye of the storm, Detective Alvarez closed his notebook and stood. "I'll leave the two of you alone." On his way out of the lounge, he shut the door behind him.

"I didn't mean for any of this to happen." Sage reached for Marshall, but he ripped his arm away. Pacing the length of the room, his eyes blazing with fury, he grilled her for what seemed like hours. How many people were at the party? What did Khari eat? Who did he talk to? The questions came fast and furious, but she answered them all.

"Did Khari have alcohol? I want the truth. Enough lies."

Sage pried the words from her mouth. "He had a beer. One beer. That's it."

He struck his fist on the table. Khari was unconscious, and the only reason he was alive was because of the quick response of the paramedics. The driver had a shattered collarbone and an unidentified man was still in surgery.

"Marshall, I'm sorry. I'm *truly* sorry. It was a horrible error of judgment on my part. I wasn't thinking."

"I don't know why I'm surprised. This is just another kick in the groin, huh, Sage?" His anger had cooled, but there was something chilling in his tone. "You don't care who you hurt, as long as you get what you want. You took Khari to that party for one reason and one reason only. To persuade him to turn pro. That's what this whole trip has been about. Wooing him with expensive gifts and stupid parties. That's what this is all about. Money." His eyes were filled with hatred and matched the venom in his voice. "You've been trying to brainwash Khari since day one."

"That's not true. I've been encouraging him to get his degree."

"Right. And running into me at Champions Sports Bar was a coincidence."

Once they had laughed about the lengths she had gone to meet him and now he was throwing it back in her face.

"Do me a favor, will you?"

A glimmer of hope coursed through her. "Anything."

"Get the hell out and don't come back!"

"Marshall, you don't mean that. It's been a—"

"I do." He pulled back his lips, baring his teeth. "You're a liar, and I don't respect you. You lied about who you were, lied your way into my home and lied to my face about where my son was last night."

"It's not like that. I know in the beginning I—"

"You haven't changed, and it was stupid on my part to think you would. You'll always be a scheming, conniving…"

Hurt gave way to anger. She wasn't going to just stand there while he shouted at her and hurled groundless accusations. "And you're perfect, right, Marshall? You've never screwed up or made a mistake?"

"Leave." His tone was ice.

"I made a mistake. I've made a lot of mistakes. I can own up to that. But you're so blinded by your anger and resentment toward Roxanne, you can't even see the truth. You have to control everything, and you're not happy unless things are done your way."

"And you're a master at weaving tales! Is that something to be proud of?" His voice was full of disgust. A dark shadow fell over his face as his eyes swept down her body. "You're a manipulator. I can only imagine how many men you've screwed to get what you want. I'm sure there's a long list of us."

Her eyes swam with fresh tears, but Sage fortified herself against her emotions. She didn't cry when she'd spent that first night at the halfway house, and she wouldn't cry now. "I might be a lot of things, Marshall, but I'm no coward. And I'd never do anything to hurt someone I love. Can you say the same thing?"

Sage held in her tears. Her knees shook and her legs felt like rubber. Though she wanted to be there when Khari came to, she didn't want to fight with Marshall anymore. For a brief moment, she considered reaching out to him again, but drove out the thought. They were finished. And if she was smart, she'd leave before he lashed out at her again. Without another word, she picked up her purse, wiped the tears spilling down her cheeks and fled the hospital waiting room.

Chapter 25

The second she stepped into Sage's car, Tangela knew that her best friend had a serious case of the blues. The gut-wrenching classic "Hard Times Blues" played on the stereo, and the sad, pitiful lyrics sucked the life out of her. It was enough to make Tangela fling open the passenger door and hurl herself into oncoming traffic.

"Do we have to listen to this?" Tangela asked, clicking on her seat belt. They were going to Belle Bridal for another dress fitting, and she didn't want this slow, gloomy melody playing in her head for the rest of the afternoon. "No offense, Sage, but this song is really depressing."

"Well, that's the blues is," she explained with a shrug. "It's about a good woman feeling bad, and I couldn't feel any worse than I do right now. In an odd way, the song is starting to bring me out of my funk."

They drove in silence for several minutes. When they reached the next intersection, Sage slid open her cell phone and scrolled through the phone book.

"Who are you calling?"

"The hospital. I want to make sure Khari got the package I sent."

Tangela swallowed an objection. Sage called the hospital every hour, on the hour and had spent hundreds of dollars on flowers, balloons, candy and care packages stuffed with video games, T-shirts and sports magazines.

Turning down the music, she leaned back in her seat, and studied her girlfriend's profile. Hair pulled back into a sleek ponytail, her face flawlessly made-up, and clad in a lightweight plum-colored dress, it was hard to believe she'd once worked three minimum wage jobs just to make ends meet. Now look at her. She could afford to dine in class, was financially stable and had a successful career. All she needed now was the right man to complete the picture. Tangela stared down at her engagement ring, doubts about her future consuming her thoughts. Her relationship with Warrick was in trouble, but now was not the time to discuss it. She needed to be there for her best friend.

"How's Khari doing?" she asked when Sage ended her call.

"Much better." She released a deep sigh. "I feel like a weight has been lifted off my chest. It's such a relief, knowing Khari's walking around and joking with the hospital staff. I've been worried sick about him."

"And I'm worried about you. How are *you* holding up?"

"I'm not the one laid up in Cedars-Sinai." Her tone had a bitter, ugly edge to it. "The most important thing is that Khari gets better so he can go home."

"How do you feel about them leaving?"

Sage was on autopilot. She didn't know what to feel or think anymore, but she said, "I'm happy."

"Have you given any more thought to going by for a visit?"

"Marshall doesn't want me there, and I have to respect his wishes. That's the least I can do. It's my fault Khari's in the hospital in the first place."

"No, it's not. It's that idiot driver. Sage, this isn't healthy. You have to stop blaming yourself. You had Khari upgraded to a private room *and* paid for their hotel suite. I think you've done more than enough."

"Well, I don't."

"You should go see them."

She tightened her grip on the steering wheel. "It's not going to happen."

"I'm surprised at you, Sage. I never imagined you'd give up so easily."

Her eyes watered. What Tangela didn't know was that she *had* tried reaching out to Marshall. In the last week, she must have called his cell phone fifty times. In a moment of weakness, she had even called Mr. and Mrs. Grant and asked them to speak to him on her behalf. Four days later, and still no word.

Fingering the pendant around her neck, she allowed her mind to replay the night Marshall had surprised her with it. It was a Wednesday night, and they'd spent the evening making home-made pizza and watching TV. Sage didn't know what had brought out the beast in him, but they'd braved rug burn and made love on the living-room floor. Afterward they'd returned to the bedroom and spent the rest of the night talking about everything and nothing: their all-time favorite songs, extreme sports they were anxious to try and most importantly, how committed they were to making their relationship work. And just when Sage didn't think she could possibly love him more, he'd slipped a hand under her pillow and handed her a tiny, blue jewelry box. Inside was a diamond chain, the heart-shaped pendant twinkling brilliantly in the moonlight.

"I wanted to buy you that purse, you know the black one with the shiny buckles, but I couldn't find it at—"

Sage cut him off. "I love it, Marshall. It's gorgeous," she gushed, fixing the clasp around her neck. "I'm never, *ever* taking it off!"

As she clutched the pendant now, she was struck by how sad she felt. It was in that moment that the reality of the situation finally hit her. They were over. Marshall was gone. Out of her life forever. There were a million and one reasons why they were better off going their separate ways, but she didn't consider any of them.

"I met the most charming woman on my flight from London last week," Tangela said, turning to look at Sage. "She's Portuguese, and her English wasn't very good, but she told me an incredibly touching story about her youngest daughter, Francesca. Five years ago, Francesca, met a struggling artist from Greece while traveling through the Netherlands. They had a passionate six-week affair and, on a whim, decided to get married. But Yanni doesn't show up at the appointed time. Francesca waits for hours and hours, but no Yanni."

"Is this story going somewhere, or are you just exercising your lungs again?" Sage asked, rolling her eyes behind the safety of her Jackie O–inspired sunglasses.

"I'm getting to it." Her voice was rife with annoyance, but took on a sweet, melodious tone when she continued. "Francesca returns to New York heartbroken, but determined to move on with her life and find love again. Two years later, she's at Grand Central Station, having lunch with her boyfriend at a ritzy Italian café, and in walks Yanni. Their eyes meet across the crowded room and all those hidden feelings rise to the surface. Francesca realizes that she still loves him. That she's always loved him."

Sage held her breath. Tangela had sucked her in, and now she was anxious to hear the rest of the story. "Well, what happened? Did she talk to him?"

Tangela shook her head sadly.

"That's it? That's how the story ends?"

"Uh-huh."

"You said it was a touching story. It's not. Francesca doesn't know why he stood her up, and even worse, she'll never know what could have…" Sage trailed off. That could be her. She could be Francesca. Wondering, pondering, lamenting over what could have been. There was only one thing to do: clear her name. If Marshall didn't want her, fine, but he had to know the truth. And it had to come from her.

Sage stared out of the windshield, her mind racing from one thought to the next. Five years from now, she would be a lonely, bitter woman, still carrying a torch for Marshall. Wasn't their relationship worth fighting for? Didn't she deserve to be happy?

She was perfectly fine by herself and didn't need a man to validate her, but she loved Marshall with all her heart. Being in a relationship backed by love and support made her feel like she could do anything. Her eyes pooled with water, but she blinked her tears away. This was crazy! Crying because she missed someone, a man no less. Insane!

Never had she imagined loving someone this much. Or knowing someone so intimately, so deeply. Images of him—cooking, rock-climbing, skiing—turned over in her head like the pages of a scrapbook. Overcome by unfading memories, she realized that dating him had been the best thing to ever happen to her. Four months ago, she was a single, carefree girl, just trying to get a promotion, and now she had a family. Marshall and Khari spoiled her, indulged her and treated her with the utmost respect. And she couldn't live without them.

Excitement flashed in her eyes. This wasn't over. Marshall had fallen in love with her, then bailed. His decision to call it quits was impetuous. Rash. Foolish. They were good together. Hell, he'd said so himself. So they'd hit a rough patch. It didn't mean they should throw away a perfectly good relationship.

An electric current zipped up her spine at the thought of seeing him again. Marshall was no ordinary guy. He listened to her, gave thoughtful answers to her questions, and she loved every delectable thing about him: his strong, assertive nature, the way his eyes crinkled when he laughed and the deep, guttural moans that spilled from his mouth when she touched him *there*. Marshall Grant was her soul mate, her one and only, and she wasn't going down without a fight. Things could blow up in her face, but it was a chance she was willing to take.

"Hold on!" she hollered, bolting upright. Gripping the steering wheel, she did a U-turn at the intersection and stepped hard on the gas.

"What are you doing?" Tangela was clutching her seat belt, a horrified expression on her face. "This is not the way to Belle Bridal!"

Sage wore a cheeky smile. "I'm going to get my man!"

Chapter 26

"**I**'m disappointed in you, son."

Marshall choked down the rest of his coffee. He didn't want to have this conversation with his dad, not today, not at a crummy diner two blocks over from the hospital, not when he was carrying the weight of the world on his shoulders. He wanted to talk about the weather or the World Series. Anything but his defunct relationship.

"Dad, she lied."

"And?"

He saw the challenge in his father's eyes, but refused to pick up the gauntlet. The minute he called and told his parents about the accident, they'd hopped a plane to L.A. and set up camp in Khari's hospital room. They'd stayed at their grandson's side for nine hours straight, and Marshall could still see the effects of the sleepless nights on his father's face. "Sage should never have left Khari at Renegade's house. None of this would have happened if he had stayed at the hotel where he belonged."

"Son, I'm not saying what she did was right. It wasn't. She should have told you were Khari was, instead of keeping it from you." He sliced his pancake in half and stuck a piece in his mouth. "But you have to look at her intentions. Do you really think she was trying to hurt you? Or Khari?"

"No," he conceded, "but truth is the foundation of every good relationship. If I can't trust her, then how are we going to have a future together?"

The waitress trudged over, refilled their coffee mugs and shuffled off.

"We're talking apples and oranges, son. I'm not telling you to propose." He added, "Although, I wouldn't be against it if you did. I think she'd make a great daughter-in-law. And like Grandma Vera says, the two of you would make us some pretty grandbabies!"

Marshall pushed his scrambled eggs around his plate with his fork. "Sorry to disappoint you, but it's not going to happen."

Undeterred, his father continued. "I like Sage. She's got spunk and charisma and she thinks for herself."

"Dad, you're overlooking what she did. She lied to me, about really important things—her identity and my son." He held up three fingers. "Not once, not twice—hell, I don't even know what the truth is anymore. Her real name might not even be Sage!"

"You've been watching too much A & E." Mr. Grant chuckled. "I'm not overlooking anything, son. I've measured both sides of the fence and they're not equal. She's made some mistakes, but I can see how much she loves you and Khari. Look at all the things she's done. She helped Khari improve his grades, arranged meetings with all those illustrious university officials and put you up in that fancy hotel."

"Well…yeah. But…" Words didn't come. His father was right. Sage wasn't perfect, but she had always been good to him. Spoiled him, even. Comfortable in her own skin and at ease with herself, she'd given him the space he needed to hang out with his friends, had renewed his faith in true love and valued his opinion, even if she didn't agree with him. They'd come a long way since he'd caught her thrashing that machine, and even though it was over between them, he'd always love her.

"Take it from a man who's been around the block a few times, a good woman is hard to find. A sexy body and a beautiful smile is just the bait. Her nature, her aura, her spirit, that's where the substance is. That means something. It's those inner qualities that keep a relationship strong and intact, no matter what life throws your way."

"Thanks, Dad. I'll keep that in mind. So, when are you and Mom leaving?"

Mr. Grant stayed the course. "Call her. If you don't, you might live to regret it. She apologized and you should forgive her."

"I can't."

"Marshall, you haven't done everything right in life, have you? I remember a particular someone stealing my car keys and going joyriding with his friends back in the day." He smiled. "And how about the time you cut class to go see *Rambo?*"

"Dad, I was fifteen!" Despite himself, he chuckled.

Two days after the accident, Khari had come around, groaning in pain, and to everyone's surprise, asking for Sage. Later that day, he told his family what had happened at Renegade's party and accepted full responsibility for ditching the taxi and riding with the rapper's crew. Sage hadn't abandoned him as Marshall originally thought. She'd stayed by his side, making sure he didn't drink or disappear into one of the back rooms. And when Khari extracted a crumpled *Ali* poster from his jacket pocket, signed by Will Smith, Marshall's heart deflated. Not only had he shouted at Sage and ordered her to leave the hospital, he'd made her cry. The image of her pretty face wet with tears was burned into his memory, and no matter what he did, he couldn't erase it.

Wild with rage, he'd lashed out at her, pushing her away when he needed her support and love the most. Turning toward the dirty, streaky window, he studied his reflection. A haggard-looking man with a stubby chin, and flat, lifeless eyes stared back at him. Marshall felt like he'd aged twenty years in the last ten days. And he had.

"We've all done things were not proud of, son. Are you forgetting that I played thirteen seasons in the major leagues? If your mother had left me every time I screwed up, *you* wouldn't be here."

Releasing a deep sigh, he rubbed a hand over his chin. The last time his father had given him advice about women he hadn't listened, and Roxanne had ended up pregnant. But it didn't mean he was going to work things out with Sage. It was over, and nothing his dad said would change his mind. "This nightmare will all be over in a few hours."

"That's it?" His father wiped his mouth and threw down his napkin.

"What more is there?"

"Khari misses Sage, and so do you."

"There's nothing I can do about that."

"I'm not telling you what to do, Marshall. You're a grown man, free to make your own decisions. I just hate to see you all broken up over this."

"No one's broken up over anything, Dad." He shook his head. "You make me sound like a punk or something."

"Is that what you think? Admitting you were wrong doesn't make you any less of a man." Mr. Grant chuckled. "Quit listening to Denzel and Roderick. Sage was right, their bad habits are rubbing off on you!"

Marshall concealed a smile.

"The choice is yours to make, and no matter what you decide to do, we're behind you one hundred percent."

"Khari, Al's Diner didn't have any turkey burgers, so I got you a—" The words died on Marshall's lips when he saw the empty bed. Assuming his son was in the bathroom, he plopped the paper bag down on the table and turned toward the couch. He almost tripped over his feet. Sage was standing beside the window, looking every bit as gorgeous as he remembered. He felt like he was going to melt and implode at the same time. His heart pounding, he swallowed the lump in his throat and tried to look as normal as possible. Marshall didn't know why he was surprised to see her. Sage didn't scare easily, and he knew it was just a matter of time before she came by to see Khari.

"It's good to see you," he confessed, admiring the way her dress hugged her bountiful curves. Her slightly tousled hair and red, pouty lips made him want to crush her to his chest and ravish her with his hands and mouth.

His gaze pierced her, but she didn't look away. Sage didn't think it was possible, but her love for him had grown, and she ached to touch him. Fourteen days was a long time to live without him. She policed her thoughts as sexual nostalgia washed over her. No sense getting carried away. She was here to apologize, not examine how sexy he looked in his blue polo shirt and jean shorts. "Khari and your mom went to the gift shop."

"Renegade came by yesterday," he said after a long, awkward silence. "I thought it was a publicity stunt or something, but there were no cameras or reporters. He visited with Khari for a while before going to see his friends."

Motioning for her to sit down, he sat beside her on the couch. A week ago, he'd complained about the cost of a private room, but now he was grateful he could talk to Sage in private without fear of being overheard. "How have you been?"

"All right, busy helping Tangela with the wedding."

"Everything okay at work?"

Her eyebrows spiked. "Yeah. Why do you ask?"

"Didn't your mother ever tell you not to answer a question with a question?"

Sage smiled.

"I phoned a couple hours ago and Cashmere said you hadn't been in all week."

"You called? What for?"

"I thought maybe we should talk." Marshall rubbed his palms over his jeans. The air was filled with tension and unanswered questions weighed on his heart and mind.

She had the sense that he was waiting for her to say something. Facing him, she spoke from the heart. "I've said it before, but I'll say it again. I'm sorry about what happened. Leaving Khari at Renegade's birthday party was irresponsible, risky and foolish, and I'm deeply sorry for all the pain and stress I've caused your family."

"Khari told me about Coach Conway and how you helped him apply to other colleges." He added, "He said you arranged a ride for him before you left the party."

"I should never have let him stay. I should have brought him back to the hotel with me. I was anxious to see you and wasn't thinking straight."

They sat in silence for a few minutes.

"You were right, Sage. All these years, I've been resentful and angry at Roxanne for leaving us. For leaving me."

"And how do you feel about her now?"

"I'm working on it. It's going to take some time, but reuniting her with Khari is a step in the right direction."

"Khari wanted to share his good news with you himself, but I don't think he'd mind if I told you." Marshall beamed with pride. "Khari's going to UCLA. Learning that Oakley's living off campus sealed the deal."

"But you want him to study medicine."

"My son's getting a degree and that's all that matters." He added, "And UCLA is a damn good school."

"You guys are really close. It's going to be hard being so far apart."

"We'll see how it goes. I might just pack up and move down here."

"Really?"

"Why not? I can open up my own soul food restaurant. I remember a certain person telling me that Las Vegas was a gold mine for businesspeople."

Sage held his gaze. She couldn't have wished for any more. Thoughts of him walking out on her had plagued her mind for the last hour. But he was here, with her, laughing like old times. Realizing she was getting way ahead of herself, she checked her excitement.

"I'm glad you're here," he confessed. "I got used to you being around, and when you left I felt lost, like a part of me had died or something."

It was the sweetest, kindest thing anyone had ever said to her.

The desire to kiss her was overwhelming, but Marshall didn't act on his impulse. This wasn't about sex. It was about being true to himself. He loved Sage and he was ready to commit to her. Not because she was beautiful or because they shared an intense physical attraction, but because she filled his days with love and laughter. Marshall couldn't remember what she'd worn on their first date or how she'd styled her hair, but he would never forget how good it felt holding her in his arms.

"What happens now?"

"Sage, I want to be with you, but if this is going to work between us, I have to be able to trust you. Completely," he stressed, taking her hands in his. "We have nothing if we don't have trust."

"I know. I get that now." She'd bottled up her feelings far too long, and Marshall deserved to know the truth. The whole truth. "I ran away when my foster mom got remarried. Her husband was…weird. He'd come into the bathroom while I was changing or brush up against me in the kitchen. When my foster mom started working nights, I knew I had to get out of there." Head down, she smoothed the invisible wrinkles on her dress. "I can't believe I'm telling you this. This is so embarrassing."

"There's nothing to be embarrassed about, Sage."

Marshall understood her. She had to believe that he wouldn't laugh at her, no matter what she said. "My looks and street smarts have gotten me where I am today. I know it's not right, but I've gotten used to doing whatever it takes to be on top."

"And you're okay with that?"

Sage lowered her head. "I'm not a bad person, Marshall."

"I never thought for a second that you were." He added with a smirk, "Not even when you swiped my wallet."

Opening her heart and her mind to what he had to say, she spoke freely, knowing he wouldn't judge her or hold her past against her. "I've always had to do for myself, and aside from Tangela, I've never really had anyone I could rely on. I don't have a huge network of family and friends like you do."

He cupped her chin affectionately, his eyes filled with love and his voice a gentle caress. "It's okay to depend on other people, Sage, and I want you to know you can count on me. But it starts with respect. And trust."

"That goes both ways."

He was surprised by the sudden edge in her voice. In the silence, he gave himself an honest assessment. Sage wasn't the only one who had some growing up to do. He couldn't expect her to open up to him if he blew up at her whenever they argued. Khari deserved the same courtesy too. It took almost losing his son and the woman he loved to realize the error of his ways, but he wouldn't make the same mistake twice. "I've been lied to and cheated on by women more times than I care to admit. If we're going to do this, I have to know that you're serious about us, Sage. That you want this just as much as I do."

His confession validated her own feelings and bolstered her spirits, but doubt remained. "Marshall, I'm scared. Everyone I've ever loved has eventually left me. What happens the next time I mess up or do something you don't like?"

"We'll deal with it *together*," he replied fervently. "Munch, I need to know that you care, that you're in this for the long haul and for all the right reasons."

She wasn't afraid to admit she didn't have all the answers, but she wanted Marshall to know she was willing to try. "It's going to take a while for me to get this honesty thing down." A sheepish expression clouded her face. "Just be patient with me, okay? I might fall off the wagon every now and then."

Smiling at her, his heart overflowing with love, he bent down and kissed her. "I thought I'd lost you."

"Boy, please! You have to do a lot more than yell to get rid of me."

Marshall wrapped his arms around her. He was ready to build a new life for himself, and he wanted Sage by his side. Gazing lovingly at her, he decided his girlfriend and future wife was the sexiest, most captivating woman he had ever met. "You're some kind of woman, Sage Collins."

"Did I ever tell you I was an amateur palm reader?" she asked, opening his right hand. Peering at the waves and creases, her face lined with concentration, she traced her index finger down the thinnest, darkest line. "I predict a significant change in your life this year, and afterward you'll be not just comfortable but well-off."

"Well, that settles it. I'm moving to Las Vegas!" Chuckling heartily, he leaned forward until their heads were touching. "What else do you see in there?"

"Success, a long life and all that good stuff." Sage giggled when he scooped her up in his arms and spun her around the room. "Marshall, you're going to rip my dress—and it's a Prada design!"

"Do you know what I see?" he asked, lowering her to the ground. "A life filled with lots and lots of *passion*."

Her eyes were full of love. "I love you, Marshall, and there's nowhere I'd rather be and no one I'd rather be with than you."

He tilted his head to the left and covered her with his mouth. Her lips parted, welcoming him and fueling her desire for more. A tantalizing mixture of kissing, licking and touching drove her over the edge. Pleasure flowed through her and she felt herself unraveling. The feel of his hot, wet mouth on her lips was too much for her to stand. Infused with lust, she clung to him, deepening the kiss. Sage had a hand inside Marshall's shirt when she heard someone clear their throat.

They reluctantly broke off the kiss and burst out laughing when they saw Khari. He had his hands over his eyes and was standing in the doorway, his wooden crutches propped against the wall. "Are you guys decent?" he asked, laughing. "I don't want to repeat what happened at the hotel!"

"Get in here, boy!" Sage waved him inside. It felt good seeing Khari smile again. He still had bruises on his hands and face, but he looked cuter than ever. With the aid of his crutches, he hopped slowly into the room and plunked down on the edge of the bed. "Let's blow this joint. I'm going to throw myself out of the window if I have to stay cooped up in here another second!"

"Khari, you're on the first floor," Marshall pointed out. "You're going to land in the bushes and tick off the groundskeepers. And you don't want to mess with anybody sentenced to do community service!"

The trio laughed.

"I brought you a cheese bagel from the cafeteria," Marshall said, motioning to the brown paper bag on the wooden tray. "And there's a chocolate bar in there too."

"No, I want to go to IHOP restaurant." Rubbing a hand over his stomach, he closed his eyes and licked his lips like he was eating an imaginary stack of buttermilk pancakes. "I need real food and I need it now. I'll die if I don't eat soon."

"Oh, brother." Sage stood and picked up Khari's duffel bag at the foot of the bed. "You're going to do well in this town. You've caught the acting bug already!"

As they strolled down the hall toward the elevators, Sage spotted the nurse she'd tangled with earlier. To gain access to Khari's room, she'd concocted an elaborate but convincing story.

She was Marshall Grant's long-lost sister who'd returned just yesterday from a six-month missionary trip to Kenya.

Eyes tapered, gaze piercing, the silver-haired black lady stood behind the desk, watching them, every vein in her forehead popping.

"I have to stop at the nurses' station to let them know we're leaving," Marshall explained, steering her to the right. "It won't take five minutes."

Sage tightened her grip around his waist. "About that honesty thing," she began, biting the inside of her cheek. "The head supervisor wouldn't let me into Khari's room, so I sort of told her you and I were…um, brother and sister."

Marshall exploded into laughter. Noticing the elderly woman eyeballing them, he stopped abruptly and yanked her hard to his chest. "All right, 'Sis.' Let's *really* give her something to talk about!" Curling his arms around her waist, he lowered his mouth and kissed her. And for the second time that day, Sage thought she'd die of pleasure.

REQUEST YOUR FREE BOOKS!

2 FREE NOVELS
PLUS 2 FREE GIFTS!

KIMANI ROMANCE

Love's ultimate destination!

HELP CELEBRATE
ARABESQUE'S
15TH ANNIVERSARY!

2009 marks Arabesque's 15th anniversary!

Help us celebrate by telling us about your most special memories and moments with Arabesque books. Entries will be judged by the Arabesque Anniversary Committee based on which are the most touching and well written. Fifteen lucky winners will receive as a prize a full-grain leather duffel bag with the Arabesque anniversary logo.

How to Enter: To enter, hand-print (or type) on an 8 ½" x 11" plain piece of paper your full name, mailing address, telephone number and a description of your most special memories and moments with Arabesque books (in two hundred [200] words or less) and send it to "Arabesque 15th Anniversary Contest 20901"—in the U.S.: Kimani Press, 233 Broadway, Suite 1001, New York, NY 10279, or in Canada: 225 Duncan Mill Road, Don Mills, ON M3B 3K9. No other method of entry will be accepted. The contest begins on July 1, 2009, and ends on December 31, 2009. Entries must be postmarked by December 31, 2009, and received by January 8, 2010. A copy of these Official Rules is available online at www.myspace.com/kimanipress, or to obtain a copy of these Official Rules (prior to November 30, 2009), send a self-addressed, stamped envelope (postage not required from residents of VT) to "Arabesque 15th Anniversary Contest 20901 Rules," 225 Duncan Mill Road, Don Mills, ON M3B 3K9. Limit one (1) entry per person. If more than one (1) entry is received from the same person, only the first eligible entry submitted will be considered. By entering the contest, entrants agree to be bound by these Official Rules and the decisions of Harlequin Enterprises Limited (the "Sponsor"), which are final and binding.

NO PURCHASE NECESSARY. Open to legal residents of U.S. and Canada (except Quebec) who have reached the age of majority at time of entry. Void where prohibited by law. Approximate retail value of each prize: $131.00 (USD).

VISIT **WWW.MYSPACE.COM/KIMANIPRESS**
FOR THE COMPLETE OFFICIAL RULES

KP15ARACONTEST